# Widow's Walk

## Kenneth Weene

WIDOW'S WALK

ISBN 13:  978-0-9840984-2-2
ISBN: 0-9840984-2-9

Library of Congress Control Number: 2009906325

Cover Design by All Things That Matter Press

Cover Photo by: Tyler McCollett

Printed in 2009 by All Things That Matter Press

# Chapter One

Mary Flanagan pushes her glasses back on her nose. Then, with well-practiced ease, she slips her hands under her graying brown hair where it covers her ears and fluffs it out. These are customary gestures when she is concerned, what gamblers might call her tell. "Christ hae mercy," she says. It is Mary's strongest oath, one that she has used only three times before. She can remember those times well.

"Christ hae mercy," she had said when she was told that her son, Sean Jr., would be returning from Vietnam a quadriplegic. His jeep had hit a mine and rolled over with him trapped beneath. His neck had been broken, leaving him with only a slight amount of movement in his right arm, barely enough to operate the electric wheelchair which the Veterans Administration provided and which is now sitting unused and uncharged in his bedroom. Now he sits, as he does most days, watching television. The wheelchair in which he is sitting is one that Mary had purchased because it would be lighter for her to push.

"Christ hae mercy," she had said when she was told her husband, Sean Sr., had died of a stroke while driving his M.T.A. bus down Massachusetts Avenue. The bus had careened off a telephone pole and crashed into two parked cars. One pedestrian had died. Some of the passengers had been injured, some severely and some less so. Sean had been dead on arrival at Cambridge City Hospital.

"Christ hae mercy," she had said when her daughter, Kathleen, told her that she had lost the baby that she had so longed for. The doctors told her there would never be another pregnancy, a pronouncement that both Kathleen and Mary had tried to take with practiced Catholic stoicism. John, the would-be father, had not been so stoical. He had left his wife and remarried outside the church – a secretary at his office, a woman desired by many who did not know her.

"Kathleen, you're still married in the eyes of God," Mary had counseled with fervor. Kathleen, having given up hope for husband and child, took a job practical-nursing at The Sisters of Mercy Home for the Incurable, a hospice with a dramatic and palatial presence near Boston College and a reputation for providing loving care for terminal patients – especially those with contagious diseases.

Now, for the fourth time, Mary Flanagan is taking the Lord's name in vain. At least that is her feeling about it. As the words pass her lips, she knows that tomorrow she will go to confession rather than wait until her usual Friday visit. She knows that Father Frank will, of course, laugh at her sense of sin. He more often than not does. "Mary," he will say. "It's hardly taking the Lord's name in vain to ask for mercy. It's part of the mass itself." "It isn't the words, Ferther, but the way I said them," Mary will respond with her Irish accent still intact after living most of her sixty-three years in Boston. "It was an oath, and that I swear to." This she will say and cross herself with solemnity.

Then, to appease her guilt, Father Frank will give her a penance, which he'll already know will be doubled or even tripled. "She suffers from such religious pride," the priest will reflect as Mary leaves the confessional, "but that is beyond her grasp." He'll think this and shrug his shoulders in resignation.

That comes tomorrow. Right now Mary is dealing with the news. Her friend and confidante of thirty some years is leaving Boston, going to Florida to live with her sister. "I can't take any more of the snow, Mary. It leaves my bones aching. My sister says it's almost never cold in Fort Lauderdale, and they have electric heat just in case. Imagine, never being cold." Lois pauses for a moment. "You know, Mary, you and Sean could move to Florida, too. It would be a lot easier for you, and Sean would be able to go out more."

This last comment was, they both knew, ridiculous since Sean never went out except for his medical appointments at the V.A. Hospital in Brookline. Then she would call an ambulette, which would take him to the hospital entrance and whisk him home again as if he were hermetically sealed off from the world of the able-bodied.

And, of course Mary takes him to church, to mass.

Mary, with diligent resistance, considers her friend's suggestion. "I cannot leave Sean's grave and go to Florida. I have my duty. And, there's Kathleen. Would you ask me to leave my daughter without a home?" It is true that Mary visits her husband's grave as often as she can, bringing with her a small bunch of flowers to leave by the headstone. It is not true that Kathleen considers this her home. In fact, she has not visited this immaculate house since her husband had left and Mary had made her pronouncement of required eternal marital fidelity. In that pronouncement the church had alienated mother and daughter in a way that neither of them could ever discuss. Mary knows this because every night she kneels on the small, worn blue rug by her bed, eyes fixed on the "Bleeding Heart" and speaks to God of her sorrow. She offers her pain up to Him and for the redemption of her lost husband's soul.

"No, Lois, I'll miss you awful. But this is my home. This is the house that Sean and I made ours, and I plan to die here."

"Momma." The young man's voice is soft and labored.

"Yes, Sean, my darling."

"I need to use the facilities." Mary gets to her feet slowly – with the weight of years and sorrows. Carefully, meditating every step, she pushes her son's chair into the kitchen with its time-scarred pine cabinets and faded furnishings, and across the off-green linoleum floor to the door that had once led to the garage and which now connects to his bedroom with its carefully designed bathroom.

Mary had had the garage converted into a bedroom and bathroom for Sean so that he could stay in the house. The rooms had been designed with space for his chair and hoists to help move him about. Without those mechanical devices, Mary could not have helped him. Her body no longer has the strength that had once allowed her to raise her children, do the housework, and take in laundry to add a few dollars to the family budget.

She slips a harness around her son's inert body, and an electric motor hoists him upright. She pulls down his pajama pants and then slowly lowers him, keeping him positioned with one hand, onto the toilet. When he has finished, she raises him again, cleans his behind carefully with pre-moistened wipes as if he were an infant, spreads a protective salve, pulls up his pajama bottoms, and then – ever so carefully lowers him into his chair.

Sitting in the blue club chair, her head resting on a painstakingly crocheted doily, Lois waits in silence. Her eyes rest on the red and white bisque plant, an anniversary gift of long ago. She doesn't bother to look about, for she knows the room and knows that it holds neither secrets nor excitements. She knows from experience that this bathroom routine will take at least twenty minutes. That is of no concern. She also knows that the embarrassment it costs the young man is beyond calculation. The pain that it causes her friend, Lois knows, is also beyond her understanding; but she knows that this pain, like all of Mary's others, will be offered up without complaint.

Lois wonders how it is possible in a world run by a just God that the active young man whom she had once watched climbing the neighborhood trees, playing stick ball in the streets, and skitching behind cars along icy streets has been reduced to this impotent mass. It is also a source of wonder for her that he continues to live now that he can do so little to help himself. It is, in Lois's mind, a cruel trick of God to have so burdened a saint such as Mary Flanagan. Then, Lois has never been that much a fan of God. Her own life has given no proof of divine love, only of life's pain.

Mary, Lois knows, is another story altogether – devout enough for all of Boston's Irish. If souls can be prayed from purgatory, then Mary has rescued untold numbers. But that is not what has made Lois her friend. Lois values Mary Flanagan because she is decent and kind. Behind the well-worn quality of Mary's life, Lois senses those qualities of propriety and care. But there are some things more, some things which Lois can not quite define. If forced she would mention courage, yes courage, and … and, yes, intelligence.

Lois sits patiently until Sean is once again in front of the television. He is watching reruns of "I Love Lucy." Over the years it has seemed to her that Sean has only liked reruns, reruns from his childhood. Often she has pondered the why of this. "Perhaps," she thinks, "in those shows he can lose himself, he can make believe that he is once again whole."

"I'll miss you something fierce," Mary comments after she has settled herself on the faded red sofa.

"I know that, dear."

"I'll miss you, too," Sean adds somewhat surprisingly. "You're our only visitor." That is true enough. Over the years Mary and Sean's friends and family have slowly disappeared from their lives. Now, only Lois comes to see them. Many days even the postman doesn't come. They receive almost no mail other than bills, Social Security and veterans' checks, and third class mail addressed to occupant.

* * *

Saint Margaret's is quiet this morning. It is cold. Mary holds her coat tight. Still, she feels comfort or at least the expectation of comfort to come. Mary has never understood why she is so often the only parishioner waiting for the confessional. She often wonders how so many can take The Host on Sunday without first cleansing their souls. She doesn't believe for a moment that she is the only sinner in the parish – certainly not when it is so terribly easy to sin. A slip of the tongue, a wrong thought: these are sins too easily committed.

She waits patiently. She sits carefully erect in the pew closest to the confessional. She waits for Father Frank to enter his side. Then kneeling to cross herself as she traverses the aisle of the church, Mary slides into the penitential seat. "Ferther, forgive me for I have sinned."

Father Frank, wanting to make the elderly woman content, prescribes two Our Fathers and Four Hail Marys. He knows that Mary will triple each of those requirements and perhaps add a few of her own. In her hard faith she knows that Father Frank is too tenderhearted, especially when the older women of the congregation, like herself, are involved. It would never do to take one's penance too lightly. Purgatory looms too close at hand.

For Mary Flanagan growing up in Dublin, the realities of Purgatory and Hell were far more real than that of Heaven. Heaven is reserved for saints! On that point Mary is completely sure. It is not a question of her avoiding Purgatory. No, it is a question of how many eternities she must spend there before she might see the face of God. In her heart she only hopes that she might see Him before He has called the angels down to end this earthly creation. In her devotion she believes that glimpse would be enough, just as her faith in its possibility is enough to carry her through the trials of life.

As a little girl Mary had been preoccupied with the hereafter. While other youngsters talked of this boy or that, Mary would sit by herself, her startlingly beautiful blue eyes half closed behind the thick lenses of her glasses, and say the Rosary, counting the beads with a feeling that none of the nuns who had taught her could ever match.

It had been assumed that Mary would enter the convent herself. Her friends were always teasing her and calling her Sister. But Mary had surprised them all.

It was not a lack of vocation that had lead to her boarding the boat for New York. She had wanted to be a nun—oh, yes, she had heard the call. But a letter of supplication had come to her parents from her uncle in Boston. Written in stiff square letters and offering no concern for their or her wellbeing, he had made his request.

He had need of help with his business. Without extra hands, which Mary could offer, he would soon be out on the street. It was a candy and soda shop offering sweets and a place to sit and read the papers. His wife's arthritis had gradually worsened. She could no longer wait on the customers or clean the counter and tables. Since they had no children, it was natural enough for him to ask his brother to send Mary, the oldest and most responsible of the girl children, to help.

Mary had gone, unhappily but willingly – not changing her love for God or her desire for the convent but accepting – ah yes, accepting – her lot in life as a sure sign of God's eternal will. If it was to America that God would lead her, then it was to America she would go – only stopping at Saint Timothy's long enough to light a candle and pray for Him to hold her in His hand on the long journey across the perilous seas.

Besides her faith, Mary had not taken much with her from Ireland. In truth, there was little else to take. The Rileys were not a wealthy family. Jack, her father, was one of its least successful members. Her uncle had sent the passage money – steerage of course – and a train ticket from New York to Boston. He had included but a few dollars for spending, far less than she would need. Her belongings fit into a small suitcase, found at a thrift and secured with rope. With all her worldly possessions so tied together and her faith firmly in her heart, young Mary Riley had set sail.

On the dock, while lost in the melee of travelers and well-wishers, Mary had the good fortune to meet a woman, Mrs. Schale, who was also traveling alone but with considerably greater material wealth. Mrs. Schale was a widow. She was also making the journey from obligation not desire. She, like Mary, was being compelled by family considerations. For Mrs. Schale those considerations were the deteriorating health of her bachelor brother, an attorney in Baltimore.

If Mary had little to bring on board, Mrs. Schale had far more than she could handle. Hat boxes and parcels seemed to overflow her arms and hands. Mary, without thinking, asked if she could help. The older woman, equally without thought, thrust all her packages into the younger woman's arms keeping only her purse in her own possession.

Based on her discomfort on the dock, Mrs. Schale had already decided that the services on board would be inadequate to her needs and expectations. She had planned to look among the lower decks for an assistant. Now, unencumbered with parcels, she took the measure of the younger woman and decided that Mary would be ideal for the task. There it was – Mrs. Schale had determined that she had found a perfect traveling companion.

Mary could hardly refuse the offer. Not only was she being offered the small fortune of twenty pounds for her help, but also it was help she would have felt called upon to give if only asked.

Mrs. Schale proved a strict and demanding taskmistress, but she was also fair. She gave Mary time for her prayers and even knelt with her on occasion. Particularly during one stormy evening in the North Atlantic, the two women had knelt praying for divine intervention. When the calm of morning came, Mary was convinced their prayers had had a significant effect, and Mrs. Schale was sure that the ship had proven itself seaworthy.

The bond that developed between the two women had come to an end in New York. Mrs. Schale was going south to Baltimore while Mary was turning northeast to Boston. They had exchanged addresses, but Mary had been sure there would be no further contact.

Mary had been wrong. Three weeks after starting her slavery in her uncle's store, where she had been given a small, unheated room in the basement with a small electric bulb as her only light and mealy gruel her only food, Mary had received a letter from Mrs. Schale.

The letter was not an offer of employment, which Mary would have dearly loved. She had quickly determined that family obligation was a one way street where her uncle was concerned. It was instead a letter of introduction and a photograph. A distant relative, Sean Flanagan, who worked for the Boston transit authority, was looking for a good and honest wife. This quest had been duly promulgated throughout the family. Mrs. Schale had responded by recommending her traveling companion, the most cooperative, congenial, and faithful Miss Riley.

Given that she was not going to return to Ireland and the convent of which she often dreamed, Mary thought about the letter and her current situation. She thought about alternatives such as they were and resolved that marriage to a good man of Irish Catholic stock was better than being known as a single woman and, therefore, a woman of questionable morality. It was certainly preferable to her uncle's selfish demands and his wife's new expectations that Mary add domestic duties to her work in the shop. It was clearly better to marry than to suffer in this avuncular hell. And, Sean Flanagan, employed and from decent family, filled her requirements. Besides which, judging from the photograph, he wasn't a bad looking fellow in the bargain.

She prayed for guidance and forgiveness. Then she wrote to her parents requesting their permission and saying nothing against her current situation – that she would never have done. Her uncle also wrote, trying to dissuade them and complaining of his great expense in bringing Mary across the ocean. In the end, they agreed that a marriage to such a fine sounding man related to a woman of some wealth would be a good idea as long as she repaid her uncle for his great expense.

Three months after her parents letter of permission had arrived, Mary took leave of her uncle's basement. It was on a Saturday morning, and the streets of South Boston sang with the voices of children free from school and spoiling for adventure.

With her possessions again tied in the old valise, Mary set out for Saint Margaret's, which was to remain her parish church and sanctuary over the years ahead, and for a life of marriage.

The priest who had married Sean and Mary has long since died. His successor, Father John, now a Bishop serving at The Holy See itself and unquestionably slated to wear the red hat, has been in turn replaced by Father Frank, who came to the parish ten years earlier and – given his unassuming ways – is likely to remain for many more. This modest priest has grown accustomed to Mary Flanagan, to her piety, and to her rigidity. No matter what changes have taken place in theological thinking, Mary is a woman who wears the hair shirt of the church as armor against the tribulations of life.

The priest knows that she needs penance so that she can hope to forgive herself. To argue with her that her sins are trivial or even nonexistent would have been to destroy the very fabric of her life, a fabric that holds her together, that holds her swaddled in faith-filled security.

The priest is particularly aware of Mary's needs on Sunday mornings when she arrives half an hour before the mass pushing her son's chair the three blocks from their home. Then she wheels Sean Jr. up the ramp in the back of the church. It had not been built for Sean, but Mary and her son are its most frequent users. Father Frank, alerted by a doorbell, personally holds the back door open while Mary wheels her son into the church school. Then they make their slow way through the corridors, across the church lobby, and into the sanctuary. Dipping her hand in the holy water, Mary genuflects, crosses herself, helps Sean to do the same, and thanks the priest. Then, while waiting for the mass to begin, mother and son light a candle.

To Mary the consecrated wafer is far more than the presence of Christ in this world; it is the promise by which she lives her life. She believes, in a way that few of her fellow parishioners could comprehend, that the Blessed Virgin is suffering right there beside her. On those mornings when she awakens stiff and cold and reaches beside her to feel her husband's warmth and finds nothing, the Virgin is there with her. When she hoists her only son like a limp sack into the shower to scrub his body, the Virgin is there holding Her crucified Son, too. Every day of Mary's loneliness and

9

sorrow is shared with Her. The wafer represents that bond, the bond of purity and suffering. In commemorating The Son's sacrifice, Mary also commemorates that bond.

For Sean the weekly trip to church is another matter all together. He knows that it is the wellspring of his mother's life and does not begrudge her the going. He does, however, begrudge the stares of the able-bodied – especially the young who can neither remember nor comprehend the carnage of the war years. To them he is a curio, a freak, and worse yet an object for pity. So, Sean goes to Saint Margaret's each week not to share the love of God nor to accept his consolation but merely to acknowledge the woman, who having birthed him, now on a daily basis gives him sustenance.

At the end of the service, Father Frank always brings a wafer to Sean, seated as he is to one side. Sean always refuses the host, "Thank you, Father; but I will only take communion when I can walk to the rail to receive it."

"Don't refuse God's love, Sean. He suffered, too. He suffered for all of us."

"When they pulled me from under that jeep, I wished I were dead. The pain was so great that I couldn't imagine living a moment longer. The chaplain came over and administered the Last Rites. Everyone thought I would die. But, I didn't. I don't thank God for that. I wish I had died. Many days I still wish I were dead. Then, at least, my mother could go on with her life."

The brief, well-practiced dialog ends. The priest nods, as he has so many Sundays before, and with tears in his eyes makes his way back to the altar where he kneels down and takes the wafer into his own mouth and prays for Sean's soul. He does not pray for Mary's – that Mary would enter The Kingdom seems a certainty. Rather, Father Frank envies the sureness of her faith and the strength of her character.

\* \* \*

Kathleen, too, does not accept communion. Neither does she go to Sunday mass. For her God had died in her uterus. She knows that her mother had also had problems with having children, but her father had stayed – at least until the stroke. She remembers him well – not always warmly but well.

Sean Flanagan, Senior, Sean and Kathleen's father, was born in Cambridge, at the Mount Auburn Hospital. His mother had gone into labor three weeks early. His father, a merchant sailor was passing through the Panama Canal at the time of his youngest son's birth.

It was with a light heart that Tom would make his way down to the boilers, which he helped to stoke. During The Great War he had never gone below decks without wondering if he would go down trapped there in the engine room. After the war he could again enjoy the trips. The cargo on that trip was bound for San Francisco and peacetime uses. There were no enemies about, only the swell of the ocean and the birds circling overhead.

Tom wondered if his newest child would be another boy. He already had two and one daughter. They were a fine brood even if he only saw them occasionally. Their mother kept a tight rein. They knew their prayers and behaved in school. When he would return from each voyage, Thomas Flanagan would insist on a complete reckoning of the family's affairs in his absence. Woes betide the child who had run afoul of the nuns or his wife.

Thomas Flanagan was a proud man. He took pride in his work, his family, his honesty, and his ability to drink any man under the table. In port he was known to one and all as a great drinker and a great fighter. On ship he felt it his obligation to never touch the whiskey that might be on board nor to raise his hands in anger. His code was as rigid for himself as it was for his family.

Looking back on him, his children never lost their awe of this powerful and forthright man. He kept his family together through The Depression. No job would be too menial or too difficult if it meant his meeting his responsibilities.

Unfortunately, he did not know much of love. The children were treated fairly but roughly when he was around. The steel toe of his boot often found its mark against their backsides. Although their mother was less stern and Thomas was often away, the Flanagan children lived a life centered on fear. All four left home as early as they could even in the hard times of The Depression.

When Sean left school to go to work for the transit authority he was only sixteen. As soon as he received his first pay packet, he found a room. It wasn't much – in the attic of an old house off Kendall Square. From there he started out each morning at five to get to work on time. Secretly, Thomas was proud of his youngest son's determination and self-control. Of course, he would never tell him so.

Thomas Flanagan was to die, as he had feared, trapped beneath decks, torpedoed during the Second War. His four children and his widow went to mass to pray for his soul. By then the children had all married except Thomas Junior, who had entered the priesthood, a fact which had given his mother great joy and his father some cause for thought.

Also, by then Sean had met and married Mary Riley. They were living in a small cold water flat near Saint Margaret's. When war broke out, Sean had volunteered. He was inducted into the Army Air Corps and taught to fix airplanes. Sent to England, he spent the war years patching bombers that had limped back from Germany.

Although he was highly prized as a maintenance worker, it always seemed to Sean that he had somehow let his father down by not seeing action. The closest he had come to injury was when an engine had unexpectedly exploded leaving three of his colleagues in the hospital. Sean had even missed that. He had been sent to the supply room for parts.

The fact that his older brother had died in the Pacific did not make his safety feel easier for Sean. While he didn't think of himself as a coward, he wondered if he would be brave under fire. His brother, Michael, had won the Silver Star. Sean wondered if he too would have also shown such courage. "I always measured myself against him," Sean had written to Mary. "Now he's gone, and I doubt that I shall ever measure up." It was the last time that he would mention his brother and idol to her.

Even his other brother, Thomas Jr., the priest, had seen combat. He had served with a Marine Corps aid station and had almost been taken prisoner. Sean knew that Thomas was not particularly brave. He remembered all too well how terrified his brother had been of their father. When the old man started wielding his boot, it was Thomas, Tommy, who first dove under the bed where they would all eventually lie cowering.

Usually those times had followed their father's drinking. He would return from a voyage and after a brief visit with their mother go out on the town. Returning home the next day, he would roar, "Now tell me what's been happening while I've been away." Invariably, no matter how their mother would attempt to color the stories, the drunken father would find some excuse for attacking. Then it was every child for him or her self. Sean could vaguely remember the first time he had been 'given the tip of the boot'. He had been four years old. The memory had always filled him with a strange sense – a mixture of fear and pride, pride that he could take it like a man.

When Sean Flanagan returned from the war, he was determined that no son of his would ever be a coward. If there were another war, his sons would acquit themselves bravely. That, in his mind, was the only way to eradicate the stain he felt.

As it was, Sean Flanagan was to have only the one son, conceived the week after his return from Europe. Sean saw in his son, Sean Junior, the qualities that he felt he had himself lacked. Seany, as he was called, was expected to play football and to fight and wrestle with the other boys. Academics were not so important to his father, and his mother asked only that he go to church with her each Sunday.

Kathleen had been born two years later. Hers had been a difficult delivery, and Mary was told to have no more children. Being a good Catholic, she forswore sex – abstinence was the only acceptable way to avoid pregnancy. Sean Senior never forgave his daughter for that inconvenience. He never complained to Mary, but she – lying in their double bed and in the dim light that slipped its way around the edges of the deep-green curtains watching his sleeping face – blamed herself for the grimaces that reflected, what she assumed to be, his unhappiness.

Sean was not a man to cheat on his wife. Indeed, the one possibility, a dalliance with a girl named Flo Eagerly in England, had ended in his storming off to get drunk rather than go to another woman's bed. Having been forbidden sex by his wife's religious health, he threw himself even more fully into his toddling-son's manly development.

Physical courage was this father's byword. He would urge Seany on to climb a tree or onto a roof and then tell him, "You got up there yourself. Now get down yourself!" Then he would walk away leaving the boy to shinny down as best he could, often enough at the price of a skinned knee or twisted ankle.

When bigger boys played on the street, Sean would urge his namesake into the melee. "Grab that ball," he would scream from the sidelines, all the time knowing that to do so would bring a horde of larger boys down on his son's head. "Don't you go crying," he would admonish each time Sean Junior pulled himself up from one of those human piles. "Don't you go crying. Men don't cry! That's for women like your sister and your mother."

It never occurred to Sean that his mother would in fact cry. He knew that she was tougher than anyone. When the nuns at school had unfairly accused him of stealing Cormic O'Brien's milk money, it had been his mother who had charged up to Saint Margaret's Parish School and demanded a thorough investigation. When it turned out that Mrs. O'Brien had left the money on the table and Cormic hadn't taken it, it was again Mary Flanagan who, son in tow, had hard-charged the frozen streets, stormed passed the janitor, who was barely finished locking the doors behind the entering children, pushed their way into the classroom and demanded a public apology for her son. "I won't leave this room until you clear his name," she had insisted.

"Very well," conceded Sister Agnes. As soon as the class had settled into place, she announced. "Class, yesterday I was incorrect in accusing Sean of taking Cormic's milk money. Sean I'm sorry." He had mumbled his embarrassed acceptance of her words, and his mother had left. Of course, he, like all the children in the class, had known that Sister Agnes would take revenge using some minor misdeed to justify an extra whack with her yardstick. But, Mary Flanagan had felt vindicated. Faithful though she was, her personal courage allowed her to confront any authority.

Sean grew to be a somewhat contrary child. If there was a way to not do what he was supposed to, he would find it – especially in school. Often this meant leaving schoolwork undone while busying himself with other "more important" tasks, such as helping the janitor or moving the new books into the storeroom at school. At home, his oppositional approach found expression in being late getting home. "We had to practice late," he would declare when in fact he had dawdled away at least an hour making the walk from schoolyard to home. He was also adept at getting things nearly done, nearly but not quite finished.

"Did you dust the parlor, Sean?"

"Everything but the windowsills, Momma."

"Sean, why is this wastebasket still full?"

"Gee, I must have missed that one."

Each little opposition was a victory in the garden of his rebellious mind. Sean had grown to distrust authority. It was no wonder that when he graduated from Saint Margaret's the nuns did not encourage him to go on to the diocesan high school. "Let's be happy that he knows his catechism," said Sister Agnes, who was not at all sure that Sean knew even that much.

Sister Earnest laughingly added, "But he is one of God's great scamps."

"I can remember the time he hid all the chalk."

"Was that Sean?"

"And here I'd always thought it was Ryan Doherty."

"That momma's boy. Why, Ryan would never have done anything that daring."

"That is one of Sean's good traits. He's a brave lad."

"Indeed." "Truly." There was a murmur of assents, a chorus of nodded wimple-draped heads.

If Sean Senior had been listening to the nuns that day, he would have glowed with pride even as he would have planned to beat his son for the miscreant he was.

Sean had been enrolled in a city high school. Mary considered it a breeding ground for lay-abouts and thieves. She worried that Sean would take up with one of those girls who everyone knew to be tramps or, worse yet, Jews and Protestants. For the three years Sean attended high school, Mary had given him a lecture each morning over his breakfast. Prefacing her remarks by pushing her glasses back on her nose and fluffing the hair that laid thickly over her ears, she would intone her warning with gravitas. "Beware of girls who will lead you astray, Sean. Your father and I have brought you up to fear God and to follow His rules. Don't you let some fast talking girl mislead you. Save yourself for the right woman. Save yourself until you're ready to settle down and have a family."

"Yes, momma," he would promise. Then off he would go to meet his friends – friends whom Mary did not know and of whom she would surely have disapproved – to talk about various girls and to share fantasies that – had she known – Mary would have declared "sure tickets on the trolley to Hell".

By the end of tenth grade Sean had discovered an unused closet near the gym where he and his friends went for cigarettes, shots of cheap liquor or cheaper wine, and sex – especially sex. Many of the girls were on the pill and sex was free for the asking, particularly for the reddish-blond haired, slightly freckled-faced, well-muscled boy with the soulful blue eyes and quick smile who was so daring on the football field. Sean was the darling of the school, and there was seldom a day he missed going to that empty closet.

One balmy day during the spring of his junior year, Sean Flanagan Junior was hard at it in that closet. His partner was Judy Rosen, a girl both sensual and accommodating. They were both naked below the waist, and the girl's blouse was open so that Sean could nuzzle at the well-formed breasts beneath her bra. Half leaning against the closet wall and groping with full concentration, neither of them heard the janitor open the door. The new brooms, mops, and pails, which the school board had just purchased, were to be stored until they were truly needed. The empty closet was finally to have an official use. It would provide a perfect storage space. But, it wasn't an empty closet. Sean and Judy's parents were summoned. Both offenders were expelled.

The Rosens invested in a small private school. Judy went on to graduate college, to take a job in the financial office of a hospital, and – to her parents' relief and delight – to marry a physician. Not that it mattered to him, but Sean would never see her again.

For his part, having outraged his parents, Sean felt it wise to join the army. "He'll learn some discipline," his father had said and signed the papers before Mary could think of a reason to object.

Sean had hoped to be stationed in Europe where he could have some adventures, burn off some of his adolescent energy, and perhaps get an equivalency diploma.

If Lyndon Johnson had been less intent on nailing the coonskin to the barn wall, less intent on proving that the United States was the unbeatable superpower, Sean would not have been one of the thousands of casualties from that hell called Vietnam. As it was, he had not only survived a few firefights but had also learned how to smoke reefer and snort coke.

Sean's oppositional ways fit right in. His best buddy had fragged the captain, but nobody much noticed. It was a war of meaninglessnesses. The closer somebody was to the front, the more meaningless it appeared.

Sean's role in Vietnam did not particularly require bravery, nor was it at all for the cowardly. He simply got into helicopters, rode to places that looked each like all the others, unloaded supplies for other men, men who were to slog around in the paddies, fight, and often die. Then – when the supplies were on the ground – with bullets screaming and engines whining, with bursts of death roaring from the machine gun he manned, Sean and his fellow crewmembers would return to safe hooches, where they could drink, womanize, and get high. Whatever glory his father had hoped to enjoy vicariously through his son was lost in the sham of the wrong war being fought in the wrong place by kids who had gotten lost on the way to adulthood. Driving his bus along Massachusetts Avenue was, in the long run, as meaningful as anything his son was doing in Vietnam.

The accident which had left Sean a quadriplegic took place not on the way to glorious battle – unless risking syphilis is glorious, but on the way to a neighborhood whore house. Sean had already proven that he was no altar boy. In Vietnam he was intent on proving that he was "the Devil's own," a phrase that he had included in one of his letters. When she had received that letter, Mary had walked slowly and full of sighs to Saint Margaret's. There she had lit several candles and said a prayer that God would teach Sean the error of his ways before it was too late.

In fact it had been her prayer that was too late. The accident had taken place the day before the letter was delivered, a day before Mary's heartfelt prayer had been offered. Sean and two buddies had been on their way from their base to town when their jeep hit a mine – as it turned out an American mine that some enterprising Viet Cong had risked his life to reposition so destructively. The other two men were thrown clear. One had a broken leg, the other minor abrasions. Pinned helpless and paralyzed beneath the overturned vehicle, Sean's days of being "The Devil's own" had been abruptly ended. Instead, he had in that sultry instant become the property of V.A. hospitals and physical therapists.

While no one could show a direct connection, Mary was to wonder if her husband's stroke wasn't in some way connected to Sean's injuries. The stroke had occurred while Sean was still in a hospital half the globe away. Sean Senior would never have to see his son the quadriplegic. He would never have to see the wasting of that fine, brave body. It had been Mary who had arranged for the garage to be converted, and it had been Mary who had insisted that Sean come home rather than live in some facility.

At the suggestion of a V.A. social worker, Mary had visited the public relations department at The Massachusetts Institute of Technology and asked for help. Two young graduate students interested in human engineering had agreed to design the hoists and motors necessary for Mary to service her son. Then, every six months one of them would – with the dedication of self-righteousness – visit to make sure the devices were working properly and to make adjustments for Sean's changing weight and Mary's declining strength.

Both had refused remuneration, but the college had found a small amount of money to give them a special humanitarian award at graduation. Mary, wearing one of Lois's dresses, one with a blue background and white floral prints, had been present for the ceremony. She had, for that one brief moment, felt important. To think that such a place would take the occasion to recognize her need and that two such intelligent young men would take the time to help.

As it is, Mary has seldom asked help of anyone. Even Lois, whose leaving for Florida had been so distressing, had been allowed to give only minimal assistance. If Mary were ill, Lois might have brought a meal or two; but she had never stayed with Sean or helped with his physical care. Only Jem has provided any real assistance.

* * *

Jemimah Harriet Morgan to her parents and before God, Jem to the rest of the world, is the home health aide provided by the Commonwealth of Massachusetts, a token of assistance to an injured soldier. One day each week, usually on Thursdays, Jem comes to the Flanagan house and offers as much help as she is allowed to give.

Jem spent the first fifteen years of her life in Monroe, Georgia. When her mother died of a fever, Jem's father scattered the five youngest of his children, including Jem, to live with relatives – relatives scattered from Georgia to Chicago, from Birmingham to Boston.

Jem had ended up in a black enclave in Dorchester, where she had been sandwiched into the family of a maternal aunt – a family of little means and less promise.

Most of the women in that enclave, including Jem's aunt, were in service work. They cleaned white houses and businesses, drove white cars, cooked white food. While Jem and her cousins went to a school with indoor plumbing and heat, it was one of tattered books and poor repair. The school authorities expected that most of the children would drop out and go work for whites as soon as they were old enough – an expectation that was seldom disappointed. Economics took precedence over education.

Despite her difficult beginnings and her status as a castoff, Jem had been a bright and motivated student. A strong sense of faith allowed her to rise above life's torments and to greet each challenge with a smile. Her teachers tried to keep her in school. They urged her to join the In School Neighborhood Youth Corps. In that well-intentioned program, part of Lyndon Johnson's Great Society, she was given encouragement, a part-time job experience, counseling, and a sense that there might be a career available for her. Of course, the career opportunities discussed were only slight improvements over the traditional Black jobs. No matter what the carefully collected government documentation might say, nobody expected a Black man or woman from Dorchester to get a real government job or even a good paying factory position.

Jem had a natural kindness, a quality which led her counselor to suggest training as a health aide. This was not quite the same as a Licensed Practical Nurse. It would mean bedpans and cleaning. But, it could lead to a regular paycheck, and Jem found it congenial. She worked hard and devoted many extra hours to helping at the nursing home where the Youth Corps had placed her.

With her high school diploma and her certificate from the Youth Corps, Jem had found work in a home for the elderly. For five years she changed bedding and wet clothes, cleaned bathrooms, spoon-fed mush, and tried to engage the senile in meaningful conversations.

When Jem married Charlie Christobal, a cook at a popular Italian restaurant, he urged her to look for a better job. "Girl, you come home smelling of White pee and Black sweat. Why don't you look for something else? I make enough. Fact is, why don't you go back to school? Become a real nurse."

Jem might have done so if she had not seen the advertisement for home health aides in The Globe. When she went for the interview and learned that most of the care would be for veterans, it seemed like a good thing. "Besides," she reminded Charlie, "It pays thirty dollars more than I've been making and pays my carfare to get to their homes."

Fortunately for him, Jem was assigned to Sean Flanagan.

At first, Mary Flanagan had been suspicious of Jem – Mary's only contact with Blacks, whom she and her neighbors called Niggers, had been in the media. Lois, who was slightly more worldly, had been waited on by Blacks in coffee shops. In bigoted ignorance she declared them to be "shiftless, dishonest, and God knows what else."

Nevertheless, Mary had to admit that her one day of help each week was God-sent. How else could she have hoped to go grocery shopping, have a few moments without responsibility, or even pay proper attention to the flower bed in the front of their little house? Most importantly, how else could she have made her weekly trip to the church and confession?

At first, Mary had cautioned Sean to keep an eye on this colored intruder, and she had carefully hidden any money and jewelry away. However, as the two women got to know a little of each other, a trust and warmth grew between them. Both recognized in the other strength in the face of adversity and a deep commitment to faith, even if their choice of churches differed.

Sean for his part looked forward to Jem's visits. When she arrived, he would ask Mary to turn off the television and he would get himself ready to talk. There was never anything to talk about with his mother unless rehashing of God's ultimate goodness was considered a conversation or whether to have hamburgers or hot-dogs. But, Jem was different. She was receptive to the world around her and alive with its vitality. She read the papers and discussed the news with him. She talked about his war experiences, and together they tried to make some sense out of that war, which was now ending

Most importantly, Jem kept questioning Sean: "Why ain't you doin' nothing for yourself?" She always spoke softly with a warmth in her voice that suggested gospel at its best.

At first, Sean had resented those questions. After all, he was a cripple – that should be obvious to anyone. Slowly, however, he did begin to question what he was, or more exactly was not doing with his life.

One particularly fine autumn day, Jem had commented, "Your mother loves you so much that she's killing you." The truth of the accusation stung like a whip. While Sean tried to think of a response, Jem asked him, "Don't you never want a woman?" That question struck an even deeper chord.

On another brisk Thursday, Mary had returned, arms full of groceries, from the Stop And Shop to find a note: "Sean and me went for a walk." The idea that Sean might enjoy such an excursion had never crossed his mother's mind. Indeed, it would never have crossed Mary's mind that she might enjoy an otherwise pointless walk herself.

At some level Mary had come to trust Jem more and more. She could find no complaint with the way the aide looked after Sean. Indeed, she had once commented to Lois that Sean usually looked a little perkier after Jem's visits.

What Mary had no way of knowing was that with Jem's help her son was planning to leave her. He was investigating care and rehabilitation facilities and had written a letter, again with Jem's assistance, to a place in Minnesota. They had written back offering to fly Sean out for an evaluation.

That letter arrives two days after Lois had left for Florida.

"Christ hae mercy," says Mary Flanagan for the fifth time in her life.

# Chapter Two

In all her years of faithful attendance, Mary has never before been in the rectory of Saint Margaret's. It isn't that she has never been invited. Indeed, Father Frank has often suggested that she stop by for a cup of tea. It has been, rather, an integral part of her self-negation. How could she possibly intrude on the fathers or even on Mrs. Walsh, their housekeeper?

Today, however, is different. As she had knelt in the confessional, Mary had fainted. Father Frank, hearing the soft thud of her body hitting the floor, had rushed from his compartment into the penitent's and gathered Mary in his arms. He had been surprised by her lightness as he hurriedly carried her across the courtyard and, kicking at the door to get Mrs. Walsh's attention, brought her into the parlor and laid her on the red-brocade couch.

Mary awakens. The priest and housekeeper are both hovering over her. A capsule of ammonia has been broken under her nose, and her eyes are tearing. She can feel the reflexive gagging and tries to control it.

"Get some tea, Mrs. Walsh," Father Frank commands.

"Yes, Father. Oh, Mrs. Flanagan, are you all right?"

"What? Yes. I don't know." The words stagger out.

"The tea, Mrs. Walsh." The anxiety in his mind mocks the command in his voice.

"Yes, Father." The housekeeper, all-aflutter and confusion, scurries from the room, trots into the kitchen, and sets the kettle on the stove. "Oh my," she mutters. "My, oh my." It is not the first time a parishioner has fainted, but each time Mrs. Walsh has been overwhelmed. She takes personal responsibility for the smooth running of the rectory, and any disturbance is more than she can accept – it is as if some evil force has dragged dirt and disarray into her carefully cleaned and ordered world.

That evening Mrs. Walsh will once again offer her resignation. She has done so whenever one of the priests has had to speak to her twice. Of course, the offer will be refused, and she will be reminded how valuable a member of the team she is. The priest will ask who else could make such delicious meals or keep the large, old rectory so spotless.

In her way Frannie Walsh relishes these periodic offers to resign. They reassure her of her great worth. But, when they are made, they are made in an earnest sense of her shortcomings. Although they barely know one another, Frannie Walsh and Mary Flanagan are sisters-under-the-skin – sisters in the harsh faith of their upbringing and sisters in their determination to maintain order and cleanliness in a world given to the terror of disarray.

Mary looks around at the ornate rectory parlor. It was furnished at the turn of the twentieth century, yet every item is still in perfect condition. The silver candlesticks on the mantle shine from Mrs. Walsh's almost daily polishing. The oriental carpet is a deep wine red with intricate designs in blues and gold. The couch on which she lies and the chairs in the room are all stiff and straight backed. She wonders if the priests sit at attention while saying their evening prayers.

"We don't use this parlor very much." It is as if Father Frank has read her mind. "There's a much more comfortable room where we can lounge and watch television."

That information at once reassures and frightens Mary. She wonders why she has been brought into this formal parlor. Surely she has broken a serious rule. She knows that she will have to say an extra penance for it. "How did I get here?"

"I carried you from the church. You're not very heavy." For the priest to have carried her – now that surely was a sin on her soul.

"Frannie," he calls in a voice that is not so loud as it is imposing, "Where's that tea?" Then more softly, "I think you'd better eat something and have a cup of tea before you try to get up. Would you like me to call the doctor?"

"No, no, I'm feeling fine now. I can't imagine what happened. I remember starting my confession, but I don't remember anything else."

"No, I don't imagine you do. You must have fallen forward in a dead faint. I heard you hit the floor and came in to find you crumpled up. Have you been ill?"

"Ill, no. It's only..." The enormity of her emotions suddenly breaks through. Mary starts to sob. She can barely breathe with the heaving of her breast and the tears clogging her nose and dripping down into her throat. She has never cried this way in her life. Never, not when she had learned of her parents' deaths, not when Sean had died at the wheel of his bus, not when Seany had come home more helpless than he had been born, not when her daughter had lost the baby and her womb, certainly not when Lois had announced her leaving. She has shed few tears since she had come to America. Her strength, rooted as it is in her deep faith, doesn't allow tears. Indeed, the few times that she has cried over the years have been confessed as times when she has doubted God's grace and Christ's love. Now, however, Mary Flanagan is sobbing with an intensity that makes the compassionate parish priest step back and clasp his hands in dismay.

It is at least fifteen minutes before Mary has stopped sobbing – before she has caught her breath and is able to eat a bit of carefully-buttered toast and drink some of Mrs. Walsh's strong tea laced with the fathers' best brandy. Her face is deep red, and her eyes are even redder. Her nose is still stuffy so the priest gets her a tissue, which, having used, she tucks neatly under the cuff of her blouse. The orderliness of her soul is beginning to reassert itself. She unconsciously fusses at the hair over her ears. "I'm so sorry, Father. I've been such a silly bother."

"Mary, you have a right. This is your parish. We're here for you. In all these years I've wondered how you've stayed so strong. You're entitled to cry. We all have bad times."

Mary cannot help but protest. "Not compared to the Holy Mother, not compared to Our Lord. We don't have..."

"Mary, we're human, not divine. We have human frailties. Don't you think God understands that? He created us. He cares about us. He suffered for us. Surely, He also understands us."

Mary Flanagan snuffles one last time. "Thank you, Father. You're right of course. It's just – it's my son. He's leaving me, and I don't know what to do. I know it's selfish, but I'll be all alone if he leaves." She pulls the letter to Sean from her pocketbook. "Father, what should I do?"

Father Frank reads the letter carefully and then again. "You must let him go," he says with as much concern and comfort as he can give. "If Sean can have a more normal life, if they can help him, you must let him go."

"I know that, but what should I do?" This time she stresses the "I", and the priest understands the total emptiness of Mary Flanagan's life.

"Without service, without responsibility: how can she go on?" he wonders. He knows many women like Mary, like Fannie Walsh, like most of his parishioners – women whose lives are all about duty never about self.

On one wall of the parlor there is a mahogany bookcase with glass doors. Decorating the doors are filigrees of mahogany. The shelves of the bookcase are filled with books bound in beautiful red leather with real gilded lettering on the covers. The books and bookcase are collectors' items. Nobody ever opens the doors or reads the books. Indeed, as most are written in Latin, younger priests would have a difficult time making much headway in them.

Father Frank looks at the bookcase with its precious yet in some way meaningless books. He thinks of the value men put on such external things never thinking about their inner value. "How strange," he thinks, "this woman has such great inner value and none on the surface and over there is so much external value and none within."

He offers the only help he can, the advice that Mary has come to hear. "Let us kneel down and pray to God for guidance."

The three of them kneel: Mary, the priest, the housekeeper. "God we ask your guidance for this woman. She has to find direction in her life. She has served you faithfully these years, and now she is as Jonah, tossed on the sea of life. Help her, we pray in Your Son's name."

The three kneel on the wine red oriental carpet in front of the stiff backed sofa and they pray. They pray silently for an hour. One thought runs through Mary's mind like the refrain of some long lost song, "Mother of God, I need to know. Mother of God, I need to know." She is not sure what it is that she needs to know nor how The Holy Virgin will answer her.

Suddenly, without understanding why, Mary changes the cadence of the words which have become a mantra. The emphasis changes from "Mother of God" to I. "I need to know," iterates Mary. "I need to know!"

It is then that Mary crosses herself and silently says, "Thank you, God." She quietly rises, puts the letter, which has been lying on the sofa, back into her handbag, and leaves. She walks out the front door of the rectory with her head held high, knowing that she had every right to have been there. She walks out of the rectory also aware that she has changed and that her life will be taking a new road.

When Mary gets home Sean says, "I was worried about you, momma. Where did you go?"

"To talk with God. Where else would I go?" Unconsciously, she reaches up, removes her glasses, cleans the lenses and pushes them back on her nose. Then she slips her hands under the feathers of her hair and fluffs it.

"I hope He heard you," says Jem, who has stayed with Sean while Mary has been out.

"So do I." Mary pauses. "No, I'm sure He and The Blessed Virgin both heard. They hear everything. I just don't know how They'll answer." She pauses again. "But answer They will – that I know."

Suddenly Mary reaches out to Jem and pulls her close. "Thank you," she murmurs "Thank you for helping Sean. Thank you for helping me."

The two women stand in silent embrace until Sean clears his throat to remind them that he is there.

"I hope we won't lose touch." Mary says as Jem readies herself to depart. "I mean after Sean...." Mary isn't quite sure how to continue.

"Even if we do, I'll pray for you both." The two women are again embracing. Jem takes Sean's hand into her own. "Now you remember, I don't want you comin' back needin' me."

He smiles. "Thanks..." He cannot think of any words to add.

She bends over and kisses him on the forehead, turns and walks out of the door.

\* \* \*

There is silence. Sean watches his mother as she packs his few clothes, personal articles, pajamas, and dressing gowns in the bright blue plastic suitcase set, which she had bought only two days before. It had been on sale at Filenes – marked down repeatedly but still unwanted.

There had been no need for suitcases in the Flanagan family – not since the old valise from Ireland had been donated to a church rummage sale, from which it had found its way to the basement of the rectory where it still sat gathering the dust of ages.

Mary knows the rehabilitation facility is sending an aide to escort Sean to Minnesota in two days time, but she wants to do the packing in advance. It is a way of hardening her heart to the inevitable. As she packs she whispers to herself, "God grant me the courage to change the things I can change, the serenity to accept the things I can't change, and the wisdom to know the difference." She knows that this is something she can not change. And, deep in her heart, Mary really doesn't want to change it.

Sean sits watching and occasionally making suggestions. For the most part, however, he simply watches – watches the nuances of his mother's face and her strong hands that have been so long dedicated to his care.

He wonders, as does his mother, whether he will ever return to this house, to his room, which now seems more of a prison for all of its conveniences and engineering aids. He stares out the window at the flowerbeds which his mother had tended with such care during his childhood and which now seem somewhat neglected. "There are limits to her strength," he thinks sadly. "When I was a child, there were no limits – not so long as she had God."

\* \* \*

Karen, the blond aide, who has come from Minnesota, is not only friendly and wholesome but also attractive. Sean, for all his trepidation, can not help liking her and wishing that they were meeting under different circumstances. Mary, for all her maternal love, can not help resenting her and wishing that they had never met at all.

Karen is the soul of discretion as she tries to come between the over-attentive mother and her soon to become independent son. As she listens to Mary's explanations and descriptions, carefully taking notes on a yellow pad, Karen is all too aware, as she has been in so many similar situations, that the patient has been made an invalid by his family's love.

Her five years at the rehabilitation center have taught Karen how much even somebody as severely handicapped as Sean can do for himself if only allowed. As Mary seems to whirl about in a frenzy trying to anticipate each need and to get each article, Karen wants to ask if the goal is to save the battery in Sean's obviously seldom-used, electric wheelchair. Instead she makes a more positive comment. "I hope the next time you see Sean he can do many of these things for himself." Her voice has a softness that belies the flatness of her midwestern accent.

"What things?" Mary asks.

"All the little things you do for him."

Mary looks up with a mother's fierce defensiveness in her eyes. "I do what has to be done."

"Momma, Karen isn't being critical. The whole idea is for me to learn how to do more for myself."

"Mrs. Flanagan, I didn't mean to imply anything. Sean's right. The Center's whole goal will be helping him learn ways of coping. You'll be amazed how many tricks we can teach him, tricks we've learned from years of working with people."

"So, he won't need me?" Mary tries to say it calmly. Still her voice trembles with uncertainty. Unconsciously, She pushes her glasses back on her nose and slides her hands between her ears and hair. Then she fluffs the feathers of her hair.

"Momma, I'll always need you. But, I'd like to need you in other ways. I'm kind of old to have my mother giving me a bath and taking me to the toilet." Sean has never before given expression to his embarrassment, but it has been a source of pain from the day he first came home from the V.A. hospital. Even if his sister had been there to do for him or Jem, that would have been better than having to depend on his mother like a baby.

He has often thought of the time he had fallen from a tree and broken his leg. Within hours he was hopping about on his crutches and playing with the other kids. Mary had tried to caution him, to remind him not to play so hard. His father had simply laughed.

The cast had to be replaced twice, but Sean had gone on playing. Jem and now Karen have lit a tiny flame of hope, hope that he will some day be able to play again.

"Mrs. Flanagan, the ambulette is due in half an hour. Is there anything else I should know?"

"That I love my son!"

"Of course you do. I hope after the trial period is over – assuming that Sean is up to sticking with us – I hope you'll come visit."

"We'll see, but I'll tell you one thing. Sean Flanagan, Junior is no quitter. He'll stick with anything you can throw at him."

Sean laughs. It is a bright bell of a laugh that takes Karen by surprise. "I never knew you liked that in me. I always thought you wanted me to give up on things."

"Like what?"

"Like when I tried to keep up with the bigger kids and they kept pushing me away. You'd say, 'Seany, play with the kids your size. Don't try to keep up with the big kids.' I remember your saying that dozens of times."

"I'd say it to you, but to your father I'd say, 'Sean is a real terrier. He won't give up for anything.' That's what I'd say to him and to anyone else who'd listen."

"Thanks." He pauses. "I've always known you loved me, but what you just said, that means more to me than anything." There are tears in his eyes. "Momma," Once again, he can't think of anything else to say. They sit watching through the lace curtains for his ride to come.

The last picture Mary has of her son is of the ambulette elevator slowly lifting him from the ground and him, using his breath to clumsily steer the electric wheelchair, the one which for years has sat unused, inside. The driver closes the back doors and she can just make out the back of her son's head. Calling out, "God protect you," she does not notice as the driver and Karen get into the front seat or as the van pulls away from the curb. It picks up speed as they head down the street. Mary focuses on the back of Sean's head until she can no longer see him.

She takes off her glasses and wipes them with her handkerchief. It is unnecessary. Like everything else about Mary, her glasses are always spotless. Even when she cooks, each spot and spatter is cleaned before it can come to rest on the stove or a countertop. Cleaning her glasses is something she has always done when she has felt alone. It is an act of grieving. At the same time it gives finality to a situation as if she is cleaning the picture of it from her head. Then, replacing them, she pushes them back on her nose and unconsciously fluffs the edges of her hair.

Mary goes upstairs to her bedroom. She has not changed it since her husband's death. His clothes have been given to charity. His few pieces of jewelry have been given to Sean and their daughter. His pocket watch is in Sean's pocket now, a talisman of family love. It is there even though May knows that there was no way he can use it. Over the years, she has carefully wound it for him each day. She wonders if she has mentioned that to Karen. She wonders if someone will wind the watch for him in Minnesota. She takes off her glasses and wipes them once again.

Carefully Mary folds back the spread on the double bed. It is light green with a red border. She has had it since her wedding. Her parents had sent it – a present they could barely afford – from Ireland. So careful has she been with it over the years that it looks almost new. It had been a bone of contention between her husband and herself. Sean liked to throw himself down on the bed when he returned from work, but he had given in to his wife's protests and had learned to be as careful as she.

She puts her glasses on the nightstand and lines her shoes under the edge of the bed. Then she lies down so gently that the springs make no sound. She pulls the second pillow, the one that had been her husband's, over her face. With the sound muffled to conceal it from the empty house she sobs as she had done at the rectory.

* * *

From the day Mary Riley had been told she was going to America to help her uncle until this moment her life has been one of service. It has at times been reasonably happy. Sean had been a good man – not given to drink nor anger – and a dependable provider. It has at times been tragic. Throughout – in good and bad – she has been enduring, for she has had her responsibilities, her faith, and the meaning which her faith gave to the pain. Now, for the first time, there is only herself. She has no idea how to give meaning to her life.

She remembers how as a child she had envied the nuns with their ordered, certain lives. They had known that they would go to

31

Heaven and be with Him. Mary had often wondered if she would be worthy, if she could be deserving. Each time she has given to the collection at mass she has wondered if it was enough in God's eyes. She thinks of the widow's mite, but still she questions. Each time she has helped a neighbor she has wondered if she should perhaps do more. She remembers the Samaritan, but still she questions. She has never been sure. And, now she no longer has a way to give. She wonders, "Does this mean He no longer wants me?" Somewhere deep within she feels that she is truly forsaken by God?

It is that thought, that fear, that terror, which cascades through her mind as her tears soak the pillow. She sobs until she can no longer breathe. Gasping for air in short convulsive bursts of hyperventilation, Mary pulls the pillow away from her mouth and nose, which only causes her terrified sense of suffocation to intensify. The panicked feelings she experiences as she tries to "catch her breath" remind her of her children's births. She had marveled at how simply the doctor had started them breathing as if his hands had been the hands of God.

The thought of those moments soothe her, and Mary's breathing becomes more regular and deep. But, the sense that she has been so very close to death does not leave her.

It has always seemed to Mary that dying would be easy and without fear, that she would welcome it as the angels welcomed her and enfolded her in their wings. When she had felt fear, it had not been about the dying process but the judgment to come after. Now, for the first time, Mary feels as if she has come close to death. And, she knows that she is in fact terrified. She has fought for each breath like a baby sucking in life.

When Mary had lain down and covered her head, it had half been with the unspoken hope that she could die without getting up. Now, she realizes that it is time to live. "For everything there is a season and a purpose unto Heaven," she recites. Mary Flanagan is not quite sure what this means nor what her goals will be, but she has found a new determination – a determination to experience life.

She goes down to the living room and sits – for the first time in her life – in her long dead husband's favorite chair. Since he died, the only persons who have been allowed to sit in the big, leather upholstered chair and put their feet on the matching ottoman have been the priests who have occasionally made visits – visits of tea and shortbread cookies of reassurances and prayer.

There is something vaguely uncomfortable about the chair. After a few moments, Mary realizes what it is. She rises and, using all the energy she can muster, turns the chair away from the television and drags it to the front window. It is a big, slightly bayed window that looks on the front yard.

The delicate lace curtains that her mother had sent from Ireland when she and Sean had bought the house have always covered the window. It has been through them that Mary has watched the world. It was through them that she had watched for the ambulette that had taken her son away some two hours earlier. The curtains had come down only briefly each spring when they had been hand washed and then carefully pulled tight on wooden stretchers to dry. During that yearly two-day period, Mary had always felt slightly uneasy, vulnerable, as if the gossamer lace could filter the evils of the world.

Now Mary pulls the curtains back and ties them with two pieces of ribbon from her sewing box. She pulls the chair to the center of the window, puts the ottoman in front of it, and – having filled a small glass with the whiskey, which she had always kept for company but never for herself – she sits down to watch the world and to enjoy the flowers which she has so faithfully tended over the years – over the years of joys and over the years of sorrows – the white and yellow daffodils, the variegated tulips, and the just blooming purple irises.

\* \* \*

The telephone rings. Mary stirs in the leather chair. She has fallen asleep, partly from exhaustion and partly from the unaccustomed whiskey. The spring afternoon has passed. It is growing dark when the phone sounds again. Mary has no idea how much time has passed. She is stiff as she crosses the room. The beginnings of age have come; arthritis has begun.

It is Sean. He has arrived and has already found the center an exciting if challenging place. He has a roommate who seems like a good fellow even though he is a Protestant. When he tells his mother about the roommate, Sean expects some admonition, some kind of caution. During his childhood, Mary had often warned him about "Protestants, Jews and other heathens." When he had left for the army, she had told him to seek out other Catholics for his friends. But this time Mary surprises him. "Take care of yourself and work hard," is all that she says.

The conversation is over. Sean turns to the aide who has shown him how to use the phone without help and observes, "There's something different about my mother."

"Well, she has to adjust, too."

"No, that's not it. She does, but there's more." He thinks for a moment, and it comes to him. "This is the first time she and I have ever ended a conversation without her mentioning God. No 'God Bless', no 'remember to say your prayers', nothing." If he could have done so, Sean would have scratched his head in amazement as he had done in school when the nuns would teach about miracles or algebra or any other idea too occult for comprehension.

"I'm sure she's praying for you." The aide tries to be helpful.

"Yes, I'm sure." Sean smiles. He knows that the conversation is as beyond the well-intentioned aide's understanding as equations had been beyond his. He starts his chair down the hallway and turns into his new room. "Hi, Joe," he says to his roommate. Then he adds, "My mother says 'hi', too."

Everything that afternoon has been new and difficult for Sean. At each step Karen and then other staff members have tried to teach him little bits of self-help. He realizes that this is going to be a far more grueling experience than basic training or Vietnam. He is filled with hope and fear. When he is finally in bed, he whispers, "Joe, does it get easier?"

"No, harder."

That is the last thing Sean hears before falling into a deep and exhausted sleep. They will let him sleep late the next morning, but that will be the only concession he will receive during the months ahead.

Karen has warned him how hard it will be. During that first night, Sean dreams about her. It is the first time in years that Sean has allowed himself the luxury of dreaming about a real life woman – a woman capable of arousing his desire.

In the morning, when he awakes to find another aide sitting in the room waiting for him, Sean is embarrassed. He has had a wet dream. The realization makes him wish he could squirm.

The aide notices his embarrassment. "Don't be ashamed of still being a man."

There is a moment of quiet. Tears come to Sean's eyes. "You know something?"

"What's that?"

"You're right. I am still a man. I think I forgot that."

The aide helps him to master some of the many devices in the bathroom. Sean is amazed and delighted to realize how much he can do for himself. "Where's Joe?"

"By now at physical therapy. We usually get started at six around here."

"What time is it now?" Then it dawns on Sean that he could look at the clock just as easily as the aide. "Eight-thirty. Hey, we better get going. I don't want to waste my time here."

"Amen," says the aide not realizing how appropriate a comment he is making.

As they make their way down the hallways to the dining room where a place setting has been left for Sean's late arrival, he anticipates a day of wonder and effort. He wonders if his mother will ever realize as he has this morning that the real prayer is life itself.

* * *

Sean needn't have worried. Mary is already hard at work re-creating her own life. The transformation begins when she visits a nearby real estate office. It is only the first day of Sean's absence, but she has already decided that the house has to be sold. She doesn't really understand why, but it feels like something that has to be done.

It certainly does not seem important to her when the agent tries to assure her that the market is excellent – that she will receive and excellent price. She knows it is not financial need that has motivated her. Without Sean's disability money it would be difficult to live comfortably in the house, but comfort has never been important to Mary. The mortgage insurance had left the house free and clear when her husband died, and the taxes are low. She could stay by herself; or if she became lonely, she could rent out a room. She chooses to sell.

It is not physical discomfort that makes her want to leave. The years of her living there have made the house more than comfortable. It fits Mary like a favorite pair of shoes – well broken in and easy to wear. She chooses to leave.

It certainly isn't to run away from Sean or Kathleen. She loves them both and would do anything she could for them. "Perhaps," she had thought that morning, "I did too much for Sean." But, it is not to escape them. She chooses to move on.

Reflecting as she walks back from the real estate office, Mary realizes that she has reflexively gone to the realtor because she had known, even before she had consciously realized, that it was time for a new life, a new purpose.

The curtains had remained tied back when she had gone upstairs to bed after Sean's call. When she had come downstairs she had instinctively gone to untie the ribbons and let the lace veil re-envelop the room. But, she had stopped herself. Now, having met with the realtor, she goes to her sewing box and takes out more pieces of gaily-colored ribbon. She goes around the first floor of the house, from room to room, tying back the other curtains. She remembers a snatch of song that Kathleen had sung years before: "Let the sunshine in, the sunshine in." She isn't sure of the title and doesn't remember any of the other words, but she keeps singing it over and over as she opens her house to the light.

# Chapter Three

The Realtor had been right. The market for real estate in Boston is excellent, and the house sells quickly. Mary is happily surprised that she feels neither guilt nor loss in the selling. The new owners are a schoolteacher and an accountant. A young Jewish couple, they plan to raise their children, the first of whom was in the offing, in a quiet residential area. That they will be the first non-Catholics on the block is not a matter of concern to them. For her part Mary finds that not only has she no problem with selling to them but also that they are a delightful young couple with whom she would have liked to have been friends when she and Sean were raising their family. "I never thought about it," she reflects, "but I've been living in a ghetto, an Irish Catholic ghetto. I wonder what's outside the walls."

Mary offers the furnishings to her daughter, and Kathleen takes a few things for remembrances. Most of the remainder is given to charity. The equipment from Sean's room is returned to the charity which had helped pay for it. It is promised that Sean can have similar equipment when and if he returns to Boston and needs it. Mary finds herself two rooms in a boarding house and furnishes them with the few belongings she has chosen to keep.

After putting away ten thousand dollars for each of the children, Mary asks the lawyer who had helped with the closing to advise her about the remainder of her money. He recommends a good mutual fund and a broker with whom he is friendly. He reassures Mary that he has himself invested in the fund and with the man.

Mary, having no idea what a broker or a mutual fund might be, goes to the library and tries to do some reading. It proves to be a long and frustrating afternoon.

* * *

Despite her visit to the library, Mary is finding her first visit to the broker somewhat intimidating. She sits waiting for him, and a good part of her wants to leave, to run out of the strangely intimidating, far too busy office. But, she has an appointment and feels it would be unacceptably rude to leave without speaking with him.

People are rushing about, and the moving display of symbols and numbers flashing across one side of the room gives her the feeling that everyone is speaking an indecipherable language – a code which she will never be able to break.

The lawyer has suggested his friend and broker, Paul Harp. Once she is past the receptionist, through the common area, and sitting in Mr. Harp's private cubicle, Mary finds herself somewhat more at ease. He is a soft-spoken man of about thirty who acts as if he, unlike the hive around him, is in no hurry. When the phone rings, as it does a number of times, he asks if he can call back. Only once does he take more than a moment in conversation. Mary rises to go outside and give him privacy; but the young man covers the mouthpiece and says, "Stay right here, Mrs. Flanagan. This will only take a minute."

Despite Mr. Harp's pleasant demeanor and her attempts at research, Mary still feels overwhelmed by the world of finances. She listens attentively to his explanations of various stocks, bonds, mutual funds, and other options. It is far too much for her to absorb. With a sense of relief she hears the stockbroker make a specific recommendation, a mutual fund that he feels will do well for her. She is surprised but not upset that it is not the one the lawyer had mentioned. She writes the name down on the back of Harp's card.

"How many shares should I buy for you?" He plays with his computer terminal for a moment. "At the current price, we could pick up fifteen thousand or so."

"Fifteen thousand what?" Mary asks. She is feeling bewildered – beset.

"Shares. That's what we've been talking about."

"Oh, yes. Of course. But..." She hesitates.

"Is there something wrong?"

"No. It's just so sudden. I mean I'm a bit overwhelmed." She takes off her glasses and carefully wipes them. Her eyes have widened in concern. "It is an awful lot of money. I don't suppose I'll ever have to make such a decision again."

"It is a lot of money, Mrs. Flanagan, but you can sell the shares whenever you want."

"Yes, but will they be worth the same?" She pauses not sure what more to ask.

"Or even more," he adds.

"I'd like to think on it a bit." She has calmed, now aware that Paul Harp, for all his seeming stature, is in the end a salesman – perhaps meaning well but clearly looking to sell and by selling to make money for himself.

"Of course you can take your time, but you know the price is going up every day. You don't want to miss out." His tone speaks of a pressure and an immediacy that belie his words. "I wouldn't want you to wait too long."

"A salesman, that's sure," Mary reminds herself.

In spite of the voices of her childhood, the ones that insist she be polite and compliant, Mary rises from the pine and black leatherette side chair and blurts out, "I need time – time fer thinking." Clutching her purse she almost runs from the room. Paul Harp calls after her. She turns back, her automatic pilot taking control for the moment. "Thank you, Mr. Harp. Thank you for your time." She whirls around again and starts for the door.

Mary isn't sure why, but she knows that she wants to talk to another broker. It will be the first time in her life that Mary Flanagan will have ever asked for a second opinion about anything. Priests, nuns, doctors, lawyers, teachers: these have all been treated as if they were speaking for God. Now, she is questioning. It is a scary feeling and a heady one.

Still, Mary isn't sure where to turn for advice. She doesn't know anyone with money who can advise her. Probably this broker is as good as any. She starts to turn back, to go back to Mr. Harp and tell him to buy the fifteen thousand shares, but something won't let her.

She finds herself walking aimlessly down Huntington Avenue. She has been walking for some time since she left the broker. On her left are the imposing buildings of a college. There is a sign: NORTHEASTERN UNIVERSITY. Students are milling about carrying books and interacting excitedly. They seem young and full of life – filled with possibilities.

"Can you tell me where I can find somebody to talk with?"

The man she has approached looks like he might be a teacher. "That depends on the subject."

"About this." She makes a gesture to take in the entire school. Then she adds, "about everything."

"There's an information office in that building." He points to a large, impersonal cement and steel structure. "Perhaps they can answer your questions."

Mary starts to laugh. It is not her typical, self-controlled laughter. It is a laughter that has been stored in her soul in Ireland – filled with the beauty of a misty Irish morning and the unconscious happiness of seeing a herd of cows making their contented way home after a day of green grazing, their stomachs filled, their udders waiting for relief. Her laughter peels across the open space and seem to echo off the buildings. It is an infectious laugh, and the man starts to laugh with her. Various students stop to watch them and then walk on – some smiling and others even chuckling.

"Why are we laughing?" he asks. He thinks to himself that he has never seen more beautiful eyes than those behind her thick glasses. "She has lovely hair, too," he considers. "If she wanted to, this woman could be something special."

Once Mary's hair had been the majestic red-brown of a fine hardwood, but age had grayed it enough to take away the magical edge of Irish defiance and turn it soft and inviting. Her body, too, is fine to see: shapely despite her years, well exercised by honest work, kept thin by her disinterest in corporal pleasures. Only her hands speak of something else. Their roughness tells of the years she has spent cleaning, cooking, taking care of others, and even, her one sometimes hobby, gardening. Those lovely flowerbeds seemed to always need tending, and Mary had spent so many hours of happy labor kneeling beside them.

"I just realized how silly it all seems." Her tone has a tinge of embarrassment.

He looks at her questioningly. She seems like a nice person and is certainly attractive, but she sounds slightly mad.

"There's an office that can answer my questions." Mary starts laughing again. How ridiculously simple that sounded – how ridiculously untrue.

That had been the problem all of her life. Mary Riley had been brought up to believe just that – that there was an office that could answer her questions. That had been the simple faith of her parents. She starts to laugh yet again. Unconsciously she pushes her glasses back on her nose and fluffs the sides of her hair.

"I'm afraid I don't understand. You did say you wanted someone to answer your questions about the school didn't you?"

"I suppose I did. It's just that I don't think anyone can answer the important ones. I used to think they could. It was easy then. Now, now I'm not so sure. Maybe I have to answer them myself. Or, maybe there just aren't any answers." Unaware of her actions, Mary takes off her glasses and wipes them. Again he is struck by the deep blue color of her eyes.

The man looks at her in a new way. This good-looking woman dressed in her plain blue dress with her hair tied back and her dark framed glasses had at first struck him as an anxious mother looking for a school for her child or perhaps someone looking for a job. He had stopped to be polite. Dr. Arnold Berger always tries to be polite: when he is teaching his Foundations of Education courses, when he is visiting with friends, when he is shopping in stores, when he is walking down the street – wherever he is in life. He had stopped to be polite, but now he is staying out of interest. This woman has real beauty – physical and more importantly emotional – and real questions – not the kind that his students sometimes try to ask to either impress or distract him, but questions that come from the depth of mind and soul.

"I don't know if I can help, but I'd be happy to try. There's a coffee shop over there, and we can talk a bit about what the questions are. I'm not great at answers, but I'm terrific at questions."

"That's very nice of you, but I don't even know you."

"You didn't know me when you asked me where you could find somebody to talk with. Now I guess you've found somebody, me, Arnie Berger. I teach in the Foundations of Education Department."

Mary certainly doesn't know what the foundations of education are, but it sounds impressive. "I'm Mary Flanagan. I have two grown children. My husband died years ago. I have to do something." The words come in blurted staccato sentences.

"Something?"

"With my life. I don't want to waste it."

He notices the slight hint of tears at the corners of those blue eyes. Mary notices it, too. She starts to reach up for her glasses, again to take them off and clean them. She stops herself. She does not want to clean away the feelings that she is experiencing at this moment. They confuse and excite her, frighten and exalt. Most importantly, they are real emotions and they seize her by the soul.

"Coffee?" he asks.

"Tea."

"Then tea it is." He feels an unusual urge and offers her his arm. They walk down the street. It is a beautiful spring afternoon.

* * *

The coffee shop is crowded with students. It is a college gathering spot filled with noisy discussion and good-natured banter. Some of the students are in Arnie Berger's courses or have been in the past. A few say hello, and Mary is impressed that he seems to know their names. When she had been a girl in Ireland, the nuns had known all the names. When Sean and Kathleen had been in school, she had noticed how few teachers had even seemed interested in learning students' names. It had felt to Mary that the schools were like factories spitting out children as if they were automobile parts – often parts which didn't quite work.

"Do you like teaching?"

"Is that the first question?" There was a moment of mutual laughter – partly over the little joke but primarily from embarrassment.

He takes a deep breath. "It isn't that easy. It depends on what teaching is. I like getting a student's mind going. When they start asking questions and not expecting me to answer them, then I know I love to teach. When I'm sitting there correcting papers that try to mimic back my words, then I hate it. The kids who relate, like the ones in here who said hello, like the girl in the black blouse, they can be exciting. She, Louise, was a great person to have in class. Someday, she'll be a great teacher. You see the boy over there in the red-checked shirt?" He waits for her to nod. "He was in one of my classes, too. He's a Pharmacy major. He wanted an easy class and figured that education courses would be the easiest. He'd come to class, sit in the back row, and do his chemistry homework. I hated having him in the room. When he got a D, he went to the dean and complained."

"The dean? What's a dean?"

"He's like my boss's boss. He runs the entire School of Education. I guess deans are like vice-presidents."

"What did the dean do?"

"He asked me why I gave the kid a D. I told him I didn't give it to him that he gave it to himself. So the dean asked me to write a memo about why the kid got a D. That's not teaching. If the kid had come in to discuss the memo – I'm sure he got a copy – then it might have been education. We could have talked about his attitude and why everything has value not just the things that will get you a job. We could have, but I guess he just hoped I'd be intimidated." He pauses for a moment and then adds, "At least I wasn't."

Mary laughs, but this is a different kind of laughter. It is the laughter of appreciation. She is enjoying talking with this stranger. More than that, she finds herself trusting him because even though he teaches in a big college he isn't so sure of the answers. "I'd better be careful," she says.

"Of what?"

"The questions I ask you. We might both end up too confused."

It is his turn to laugh. "I think I'd like that." He reaches over and gently squeezes her hand. Part of her wants to pull back, but she doesn't. She is feeling emotions that she has never allowed herself to feel before. They are simultaneously heady and scary.

"Mr. Berger, I think I'd like it, too."

"Arnie, please call me Arnie." Arnie Berger, too, is feeling emotional confusion. There is something wonderful going on inside him. He realizes that at any moment the bubble of this chance encounter might burst, and that is an uncomfortable thought. He feels compelled to tell Mary the one thing that he thinks might make their relationship impossible for her. "There's something I'd better tell you."

"What."

"I'm divorced."

"Oh. Does that matter?"

"It might to you."

"Do you have children."

"We did. He died in Vietnam."

"My son didn't die. He's a quadriplegic. Sometimes – especially the times when I've seen the lostness in his eyes – then I wished he had died. But then, I'd feel guilty and go to confession. The priests all told me it was normal, that I hadn't sinned. I didn't believe them. It's got to be a sin to wish your child dead. Later I was glad he was there. My husband had died, and Sean gave me something … something to do."

"Where is he now?"

"In a rehabilitation center in Minnesota. He left two months ago. He's learning to be independent. And, so am I."

"Mary?"

"What?"

"Do you have plans for this evening?"

She chuckles. "I never have plans for any evening."

"Unfortunately, I usually don't either unless you count teaching an evening course. Would you like to do something? Maybe take in a movie?"

Mary can't remember the last time she has gone to a movie. she knows that it has to have been years ago. "All right." The idea seems fraught with excitement.

"Where do you live?"

She starts to give him the house address and then realizes she has sold it. She laughs at herself.

"What's so funny?"

Mary tells him and then gives him the address and phone number of the boarding house explaining that he would have to ask for her.

Arnie has an apartment on Commonwealth Avenue, not to far from the school; he gives her that address and his phone number.

He picks up the check. Mary starts to open her purse. "Please," he says, "let me."

Mary smiles in response. "Thank you." She wants to say more but doesn't know what to say nor does she know how to say it. There is a sudden discomfort as she feels herself venturing onto new ground, exploring in new directions. In the back of her mind, a voice tells Mary that she is feeling like a teenager, like the teenager she had never been, had never been free to be, like her daughter,

Kathleen, had felt years before when she had first dated. It is a voice filled with concern and possibility.

They walk out onto Huntington Avenue and realize that most of the students who had been milling about when they had gone for coffee have long since departed. Arnie Berger looks at his watch. "I'll pick you up at seven. We'll see a movie and have a bite to eat."

"That will be grand." In every recess of her mind Mary knows that she truly means it.

* * *

Mary Flanagan has brought the big leather chair with her. It, the matching ottoman, and a small club chair almost fill the smaller of the two rooms that are her new home. The windows look out on a busy street. There is a trolley line running down the middle. Mary likes to keep the window open a little, even when it is cool. She likes to hear the buzzing of the city and to feel its pulse as the background to her life. It makes her feel as if she is a part of something. But, in fact, until this day, when, propelled by her frustrated sense that nothing had changed, that nothing was going to change, she had been as removed from the world as she had always been. Today she has found her way first to the stockbroker and then to tea with a college professor.

Often during the preceding days, she had sat in the chair and watched the people hurrying home for supper. She would pick one person from the many and follow that person with her eyes and wonder what that particular person's life might be. This had been one of her favorite ways to spend time – in fantasy she was living through these strangers. "What would it be like...?" she would ask herself over and over again.

But this night, now, this was a different experience. Sitting at the window, Mary is waiting for somebody in particular – for Professor Arnold Berger, teacher of Foundations of Education, and a man whom she has met in a way that fills her with both confidence and apprehension. She can only wonder at whatever power within herself that had impelled her towards this stranger, this stranger who had become so immediately a dear friend. She feels as if she has known him for years. Yet, she realizes that she really knows nothing about him. She wonders if it's proper to go out with somebody she has met so casually. For a moment she wants to go downstairs to the pay phone and call him, to tell him that she has changed her mind. The urge passes and is replaced by the urge to call him and ask him to come more quickly. Mary wonders if Kathleen had felt this way when she was in high school, and she knows that she had. There had been many evenings when Kathleen, waiting for a date, would pace back and forth across the living room until Sean Senior had commanded her to stop before she wore a path in the rug. Mary wonders if it would help to pace, but she realizes that there isn't enough room. So she sits, anticipates, and watches.

Arnie had told her that his car is a red Buick. Each time a red car comes down the street she feels what she would have described as a hummingbird beating its wings in her chest. Then she jumps up and goes into the other room where she has a mirror, checks herself quickly, runs a comb through her hair once again, and then goes as quickly as she can back to the window to see if the car has pulled to the curb.

At seven twenty-five, the red Buick does pull up, and Arnie gets out. Looking down, Mary realizes that he is balding. It is a detail that she hadn't noticed earlier. In fact, she realizes that she hadn't noticed much about his looks. She knows he wears glasses with thin wire frames and that behind them are soft brown eyes. And, she can picture his smile. She had loved his smile. When Arnie had smiled, it had been with his whole face – it had been as if every surface had broken into a separate laughing countenance.

"What was he wearing this afternoon?" she wonders. Now, as she can see from her perch, he is wearing a light blue and gray jacket and gray slacks. His clothes are obviously not expensive, but they are neat, conservative, and tasteful. She likes that. She likes that she will feel comfortable on his arm. She likes that she feels so wonderfully natural and so very safe.

Mary knows that he has rung the doorbell. She can vaguely hear the voice of her landlady, Mrs. Callaghan, asking what he wants. Despite her excitement, Mary holds back. She waits for Mrs. Callaghan to call up the stairs. "Mrs. Flanagan, you have a visitor." The landlady's voice is shrill and her words clipped.

"I'll be right down." She gives herself one more check-over in the mirror and one last lick with the comb before she leaves the bedroom.

As she closes the door of her tiny suite, Mary has an urge to run back inside. She isn't sure if it is to check her appearance once more or to climb under the covers and hide. She forces herself to walk down the stairs. The house is old and Victorian. The staircase is curved and elegant in an outdated way. The rundles are overly ornate. Mary holds the mahogany banister as she slowly walks down the stairs. She feels dizzy and disoriented. She wonders if she is going to fall.

"I hope I didn't rush you."

Arnie's tone surprises her. It is so calm. He seems so composed. She is afraid that her own voice might break, but it doesn't. "No, actually you're right on time."

They stand awkwardly wondering what to do next. The landlady starts to laugh. "You do know each other don't you?"

Her question breaks the clumsiness of the moment. "Of course, Mrs. Callaghan, this is Professor Berger."

Arnie reaches out to take Mrs. Callaghan's hand. There are the appropriate smiles and nods.

Again there is silence.

"What are you folks going to do tonight?" Mrs. Callaghan asks trying to be helpful. Mary wonders how many times she had asked the same thing as Kathleen went out the door, and she wonders how many other mothers had asked Sean the same question.

"We're going to take in a movie and perhaps get a bite." Arnie's voice holds a hint of relief, of awkwardness ended. He leads the way to the front door and holds it for her.

"I feel like a school girl," she comments in a soft voice.

"You look lovely."

From the tone of his voice, Mary can tell that Arnie's compliment is genuine. "Thank you." Mary opens her purse to make sure she has the key to the front door. "Good night, Mrs. Callaghan."

"Good night Mrs. Flanagan, Professor."

"Good night." Mary goes out of the front door. She feels as if she is an escapee – but from what she has no idea. Then she imagines herself as Cinderella at long last being allowed to go to the ball.

Arnie holds her arm as they walk down the steps of the front stoop and reaches in front of her to open the car door. As he opens the door, he starts to laugh. His laughter immediately puts Mary at ease. She, in a bond of embarrassment, joins in.

Sliding behind the wheel, Arnie comments, "I haven't felt that way in years. It was like being back in high school. I felt like she was giving me the parental evaluation: would I be good enough for her tenant?" He is still laughing.

"You felt that way, too? I couldn't help thinking about my daughter when she was in high school. Sean and I would always give the boys a looking over. I'm sure it scared them and made Kathleen furious."

"At least she didn't give you a curfew." They both laugh again. Arnie pulls away from the curb. Mary looks over at her date and smiles. Silently she mouths the words, "Christ hae mercy."

It is a Thursday, and Boston – not yet filled with the summer tourists and just beginning the exodus of college students to their homes – is quiet. Mary, not having the slightest idea of which movie is which, suggests that Arnie make a selection. He picks a film about emotions and relationships. They buy a small container of popcorn and share as if they have been doing so for years. During one scene, Mary begins to cry. Looking to her left, she sees Arnie dabbing at his eyes.

Mary wonders if she has ever seen a man show such sensitivity. Sean had liked to watch the Red Sox on television. His second favorite had been Jackie Gleason and before that Milton Berle. She had only seen him weep twice, when his mother had died and when they got the news about Sean. Both times the tears had lasted a few minutes and then had stopped. Each time he had said, "Well, we can't have any of that." It was as if he were quoting some Biblical injunction that had been passed on through the generations. When he had said it, Mary had tried to stem her own tears – at least those she would shed before him.

She thinks of the many times when, after he had gone to sleep, she had gone down to the parlor to weep silently over so many of the pains which life had brought. She particularly remembers when Kathleen had lost her child. Sean had been so stoical – so removed – that she had felt ashamed at her tears.

"Well, we can't have any of that." Mary remembers Sean saying that to their children, too. She wonders if Seany had been allowed to cry would his life have been different. Would he perhaps have stayed in school instead of going to Vietnam? On the other hand, perhaps that Flanagan stoicism had helped him to survive the pain and helplessness of his wounds.

"Well, we can't have any of that." Had that been her attitude when it came to Kathleen's failed marriage? Over the years she has been able to weep for characters on the screen. Yes, she could weep at their pain. She could weep for her children – never in front of them but often for them. But for her own life, for herself? "Well, we can't have any of that," at least not until that day when her son had decided to leave and not until that moment of loss when she had watched the ambulette taking her boy, her Seany to the airport.

Arnie, unaware of her musings, takes Mary's hand in his. Gently he rubs the back of her hand. She notices that his hand is smoother than her own. The years of washing and cleaning and caring have roughened her skin and made her fingers strong. Arnie has the soft hands of somebody who has made his living reading books. Mary wonders if the chalk dust from the classrooms helps to smooth his skin.

The movie ends. They don't speak. The theater has been only half filled so their exit is unimpeded. Arnie again holds the car door open for her. They still don't talk. It is only after they have left the parking lot that Arnie asks, "What did you think of it?"

"It was very smooth," responds Mary, who is far more aware of Arnie's hand than of the movie.

"The transitions worked well," Arnie agrees. He is actually thinking of how easily Mary had let him take her hand in his. "I liked the emotion. There were a lot of feelings."

"Yes." There was another period of quiet. "I'm glad you asked me. I'm really glad."

"So am I." He pats her left hand, which is resting on her leg. "I'm so incredibly comfortable with you. It's like we've known each other for ever."

"And, the best part is we still have so much to learn about each other."

Arnie responds, "That will come. It will take time, but it will come."

Mary realizes that Arnie is making a commitment. She blushes slightly from excitement mixed with a hint of embarrassment. The importance of his words seems strange. At the same time that she wants to hold them against her breasts and to never release them.

This was not feeling she had had with Sean, not ever. Sean had been a good man and a good way out of her uncle's grip, and she had never regretted their union. But Arnie is … She gropes for a word. Her thoughts whirl. "An adventure: yes that is the word, an adventure. And something more – definitely something more. An event, an event to be savored – savored forever."

Arnie's thoughts are more mundane. He is trying to think of the right place to go for a bite, someplace that Mary will find acceptable, not anything too fancy, expensive, or whatever – just someplace pleasant. He decides. "Will a Friendly's do?" He asks. "If not, we can go somewhere else. It's just that I have a special fondness for Friendly's."

"Why is that?"

"They hire the handicapped. Not many businesses do. That's one of the things I'm interested in – professionally that is." It seems to Arnie that he's stammering.

"That's a grand reason." To herself Mary adds, "That's good. He cares about other people, about what's right."

"So Friendly's is ok?"

"Certainly." It has been years since Mary had been to a restaurant. She has no idea what a Friendlys is, nor does she care. "A bite of something would be nice." In fact, the only thing she has eaten since they had left the coffee shop had been the popcorn they had shared. Food had not seemed to matter. Now Mary is aware of the lack of eating, but her hunger seems unimportant. Her anxiety is so intense that she doubts she will be able to swallow anything. She wonders why she's feeling so anxious now, after the movie has gone so well.

"What will I say to him?" is the thought that comes to her. "What can I possibly say that will make me seem worthwhile?"

Then, another doubt comes to her mind. "Maybe he thinks I'm handicapped. Is that why he's taking the trouble?"

"What will we talk about?" is the thought in Arnie's mind. It is as if, having become so wonderfully comfortable together, they now have way too much to risk.

A teenager with a quick smile that reveals her braces seats them. After they are alone – sitting side-by-side in a booth – both unwilling to be separated by the table, Arnie says, "I don't think I've ever felt this way."

"Oh!" Her heart beats a little faster. "Where do these little birds keep coming from?" she wonders. "What is it that keeps getting me so excited?"

"Usually I'm so good with words, but right now I don't know what to say. I'm nervous.... nervous about you. I don't know what to say," he repeats. His mouth is dry. Arnie picks up the water glass, which the waitress has just put in front of him. His hand shakes, and water splashes onto the table.

Mary's hand is quick to wipe up the spill. Arnie's, a bit slower, touches hers. They look into each others' eyes and smile.

Arnie takes a sip and starts over, "I just want to make the right impression. There's something special. I'm not sure. It feels like … It's like Kismet."

"Like what?"

"Kismet, fate: I feel as if I've waited all my life for this evening."

Mary wonders if she feels the same, or is it just that she had been lonely for so long. It is hard to know. She doesn't want to worry about it. She just wants to enjoy the moment. She picks up the menu and busies herself looking at it.

Realizing that Arnie is smiling at her, Mary looks up.

"Don't you think it would help if you turned the menu right side up?"

Mary laughs. What else is there for her to do? Her attempt at escape has been blocked.

"Kismet?" she asks.

"Right."

"Possibly so. God works in mysterious ways."

"His wonders to perform."

"His wonders to perform," she echos.

"Do you know what you want?" asks the waitress, whose name badge identifies her as Sue.

"Two cups of tea and two tunas on toast, tomato and no extra mayo." Arnie has taken charge. Mary isn't sure she wants a tuna fish sandwich, but she feels relief that he has ordered.

"What kind of bread?"

"Whole wheat."

"Chips ok with those?"

Arnie hesitates. "No, let's splurge. Fries. OK?"

"You've got it." Sue smiles and turns away.

"I hope you don't mind," he says after she has left.

"No, I'm glad. I was too flustered to order."

"So was I. Actually, I hate tuna fish. I just didn't want her standing there."

They laugh again. It seems to Mary that they are always laughing. She hopes the laughter will go on and on; she has missed it for so many years. She hadn't realized it, but she has missed it so.

*  *  *

It is almost midnight. The streets of Boston are quiet. The red Buick pulls up outside Mrs. Callaghan's boarding house. The landlady is lounging in her front parlor. She is trying to look as if her being there is accidental. It is partially that she likes her newest boarder, but it is also her love of gossip and snooping that has kept her awake. She is waiting for Mary's return.

Mary closes the door as quietly as she can. She does not want to disturb.

Mrs. Callaghan, faking a yawn, calls out in an equally faked sleepy voice, "Who's there?"

"It's Mary Flanagan. I hope I didn't wake you. I tried to be quiet." She peeks around the corner of the half-opened door.

"I'm glad you did. If I spent the night in this chair, my back would feel like a pretzel in the morning. Come in and chat a spell." Mary has been standing at the parlor door not wanting to intrude on her landlady's privacy yet dying to share her excitement with someone, anyone. She walks across the faded tan carpeting and sits on the couch, which is upholstered in well-worn gold fabric. The room speaks of genteel age and wear.

Mary begins talking at once. "I had the most wonderful time. He's a charmer. A gentleman. You don't find many gentlemen these days." Mary isn't sure if this last statement is true or only her distortions from watching too much television.

"Where did you meet him? What does he do? Where is he from?" Mrs. Callaghan has a list of questions at the ready.

"I met him at Northeastern University."

"What on earth were you doing there?" Mrs. Callaghan can't imagine her somewhat dowdy boarder having any business in a college.

"I was walking. I had a question. I asked him. He teaches there." Mary strung the answers together without breathing. "He teaches there – Foundations of Education. He was married, but divorced. I think he comes from Boston." She is forced to stop and take a deep gulp of air.

"Did he behave himself?" Mrs. Callaghan fancies herself a bastion of traditional manners and morality. The women – and it is only women, who board at her home – are expected to behave with gentility. Although, the truth is that Mrs. Callaghan takes much more pleasure when they don't and she has something to cluck over.

"He's a perfect gentleman," Mary gives a detailed description of Arnie's behavior. As she reviews the many little acts of courtesy and kindness, she is struck by what a delightful day she has had. "It really was wonderful," she summarizes her date.

"I'm happy for you, dear. So many of the women who have stayed here over the years have had such terrible experiences. Men often lie. I'm sure you know why. Some of the stories I could tell. I worry about all you ladies."

In reality the saddest of all the stories is Mrs. Callaghan's own. Hers had been a loveless and often abusive marriage that had ended when her husband had run off with a younger woman leaving her with only five hundred dollars and seven more years on the mortgage. She has survived on her own, but at no small cost. She is, by choice, a lonely woman who seldom leaves the house except to go shopping – living vicariously through the progression of boarders whose lives she has scrutinized from this very room. In her reclusive anger Mrs. Callaghan has never considered the possibility that her ex-husband had done her a favor – his subsequent wives might have enlightened her from their various hospital beds.

Mary cannot help wondering if Mrs. Callaghan had seen something about Arnie, something that she in her eagerness has missed. She wants to ask the landlady what it is that men were after. She especially wants to ask if she should she trust Arnie

Berger. To Mary it seems like this embittered woman has wisdom far beyond her own. Tired as she is, Mary would gladly stay and talk. But, having satisfied her curiosity and her spleen, Mrs. Callaghan is ready for bed. "Good night, Mrs. Flanagan," she says abruptly and rises from her chair.

Mary's questions go unasked. "Good night." She half climbs and half dances the stairs to her rooms. She sits in the big chair and watches the few lights still darting about the street. Finally, she falls asleep sitting there – never having changed her clothes.

In her sleep Mary Flanagan dreams of a window covered with Irish lace. She can see through the lace and out the window, but everything is hazy. Far in the distance she sees a hill. She can not see what is happening on the hill, only that people are gathered there. She wants to be with them but knows that she can not pass through the window. She wakes with a start. It is morning. She opens the window wider to let in the fresh late spring air and the clang and crash of traffic – the wonderful new sounds of life.

Mary kneels beside the chair, crosses herself, and prays. "Thank you God for Your creation, for Your Son, Jesus, and for the promise of eternal salvation." She has started her days in this manner since she was a little girl. Mary starts to rise. Then, sinking back to her knees, she adds, "And, thank you, thank you for the joy of last night!"

# Chapter Four

The days are passing in a wonderful dizzying confusion of activities and discussions. Mary Flanagan, who has lived so many years within a simple structured world, finds herself exploring what seems like a new, if somewhat scary, universe. Even when she and Arnie visit a place she has been before, his appreciation and their shared excitement make it a new and amazing experience. Arnie is well educated. He enjoys teaching Mary, who has a surprisingly quick if untrained mind. The quality of their discussions grows, and Mary begins to wonder what things there are to learn, what might be worth the knowing.

Of all their excursions, she enjoys the glass globe at The Christian Science Church the best. To stand on the glass bridge looking out at the surrounding world gives her a sense of solidity and peace. She looks at Ireland and then at Massachusetts, and for the moment they don't seem so far apart – certainly not as distant as her worlds before and after her son's leaving for Minnesota.

At Faneuil Hall and Bunker Hill they talk of American ideals. At Lexington they picnic and speak of the magical mists of Ireland. Mary had spent the previous day in the ever more friendly Amelia Callaghan's kitchen preparing the food – deviled eggs and carefully cut sandwiches, cupcakes and gingered fruit.

For Mary it is an idyll and a voyage of discovery.

On a few occasions, Mary attends Arnie's classes. She still isn't sure what the foundations of education are, but the discussions are lively and involving. Arnie teaches well, involving the students and challenging them with a quick but gentle wit.

At first Mary sits at the back of the room, and Arnie makes no mention of her. Although she is the oldest, there are enough adult students that no one notices Mary's presence. Over time, she gradually moves forward. One day, after Mary has clearly become comfortable in the setting, Arnie introduces her to the class. "This is Mrs. Flanagan, a very dear friend of mine. You may have noticed she sometimes comes to class to listen in. I'm sure you can appreciate what a pleasure it is for me when she comes."

Mary has never thought of herself as a pleasure. After the class, while they are walking arm-in-arm along the long hallways of the university, she asks Arnie if he had meant it. "Of course, I did. You don't realize how much you brighten my days."

Mary smiles broadly. Impulsively, she leans forward and kisses Arnie's cheek. It is the first kiss between them. A part of Arnie wants to throw his arms around her and gather her to him, but he knows that he mustn't. "Delicate flowers must be picked with care," he tells himself.

Summer has come to Boston with all its heat and humidity. Nevertheless, the two middle-aged companions walk miles chatting about everything and anything. Often they walk along the Charles River watching the sailboats and the rowers. At other times, they explore Newbury Street with its faded grandeur or go window-shopping at the department stores. From time to time one of them sees something in a store window, and they go inside to investigate. Neither of them particularly enjoys shopping. It is just another part of their shared entertainments. Nonetheless, without comment, Mary finds herself looking for clothes for Arnie. He can't help noticing outfits that he'd like to buy for her.

Sometimes, they sit at a particular outdoor cafe on Newbury Street. He drinks cappuccinos, and she nurses a pot of tea. Oblivious to both the people and the time passing, they share memories.

One evening, Arnie talks about his marriage and divorce. It has been nine years since the divorce. When their son, Robert, had died, his wife had left him. It was, she had said, the only way to deal with the pain. The last he had heard, she was living in Los Angeles with an unsuccessful film director whose estranged wife and daughters also lived in the house. Mary is scandalized by the living arrangements. Although she has become much freer over the weeks, Mary's basic moral judgment is unchanged.

Arnie seems to have neither anger nor remorse about his marriage. Susan and he had parted as friends. She had asked for nothing but her freedom, and he could not – would not – deny her. If he has any regrets, it is that they had not kept better contact. They had been married for twenty years. It seems, he says, that they should have had enough to keep them connected. However, their real connection and separation lay in a military cemetery.

* * *

Today, Mary wonders, as she has before, whether her husband's death had been his way of dealing with Sean's injury. For the first time, there is somebody with whom she can share such questions.

It is a beautiful day. The sky is soft and blue with cumulus clouds scattered like inviting pillows. It is the first time Mary has visited her husband's grave since she had sold their house. Somehow, her dedication to visiting the cemetery over the years now seems strange.

On the bus, on the way back from that visit, she thinks about all those trips. "Perhaps it was my way of staying married." This is an intimidating thought for Mary. Marriage is such a powerful idea. "I don't feel married." The words are aloud. Other riders turn to stare, but she is unaware. The words have battered her ears with a shock of recognition.

* * *

It is a Friday evening, two days after her cemetery visit. They are sitting in their favorite outdoor café. Suddenly, Mary's face turns solemn. She asks Arnie if he would go to church with her. "I'm not Catholic. You do know that don't you?"

The truth is that Mary has never let herself think about it. Her world has always been divided into Catholics and everyone else. Her parents had taught her that while she might have occasional dealings with others, it was only Catholics with whom she could have real relationships. It had been so hard for her to accept Jem and especially Jem's effect on Sean. Then she had sold the house, Sean and her house, to a Jewish couple. Now, Arnie, for whom she has so many feelings, is asking her to face this dreadful truth, a truth that she had been so assiduously avoiding.

"What are you?" she asks her voice quavering – fearful yet knowing that she must ask. "What do you believe?"

"I'm not sure."

"You're not an atheist are you?" Now her voice is less fearful than horrified.

"No, an agnostic, or maybe I just believe in everything."

"Everything?"

"I don't know what's true, but it seems like something from each religion has value. How can I know how many gods there are or where to find them? Maybe God is in everything."

His last sentence is the only thing Arnie has said with which Mary can agree. "Certainly He's everywhere and in everything."

"I hope so."

"I know it."

"How?"

Their voices have risen during this exchange. Although they are not angry, both Arnie and Mary feel threatened. They both know that this is the issue on which their relationship hinges. Some of the other people sipping coffee stop talking so they can overhear this disagreement. It seems at that moment for the two of them as if Boston has gone three hundred years back in time, to an age when disagreements about theology mattered more than any other issue.

"Because I have faith," is Mary's answer. "I have faith in God."

Arnie looks down at the croissant on his plate. "I wish I did," he replies. "I just don't know."

"Didn't your parents teach you?"

"Mary, Mary, my parents were non-believing Jews. They sent me to Hebrew school because everybody said they should, especially the Rabbi. I didn't believe then. But when I was in the army and I went to Germany and saw the camps. They were empty by then but they were so horribly real. And all those poor displaced people – people from everywhere – begging their way from town to town trying to find what had been their homes and families. When I saw that, it was so overwhelming – something beyond human. I actually started to think there might be a god or gods who ruled the earth. I just didn't know what kind of cosmic joke was being played. Some events are too overwhelming to ignore and too horrible to accept."

"God has His reasons."

"For those camps?"

"For everything."

"For my son's death?

"For everything."

"For your Sean's accident?"

"For everything."

"For my loving you?"

Mary does not respond. She cannot. "How," she wonders, "can he talk of love when such a gap exists between us? How can I love him if he doesn't believe?"

"For my loving you?" he repeats.

"For everything."

"For your loving me?"

Her face burns as she answers in a suddenly hushed voice. "Yes, for that, too."

Neither of them speaks. Arnie pays the bill. They walk hand in hand up Newbury Street toward the Public Gardens. Arnie stops and turns to face Mary. He places his hands on her shoulders and pulls her toward him.

It is a long, lingering kiss. Neither of them has ever kissed like this before. It is a kiss from storybooks. It is a kiss filled with love and gentleness. When at last they separate their lips: "If you want, I'll go with you," he tells her.

"Christ hae mercy on us both," thinks Mary Flanagan. "Christ hae mercy on us both."

* * *

Mary has continued to attend Saint Margaret's. Instead of a brisk walk, it now requires a trolley ride and then transferring to a bus. She has come once each Friday for confession and again for the early Mass on Sundays. Once, Father Frank had suggested that she try one of the churches closer to the boarding house. "No, this is my home," she had replied. The priest had bowed his head as if to the will of God and said no more.

Each Sunday, Mary nods to her fellow parishioners and kisses a few of the women on the cheek. When it is her turn to receive the wafer, Mary never takes it into her own hands – that she considers unholy as if it detracts from the Sacred Body. When Father Frank places the Host on her tongue, Mary crosses herself and prays earnestly for God's love, not simply for herself but for the entire world. Sometimes, she adds a special prayer for Kathleen, "Heal her heart and give her peace." And always for Sean, "Give him the strength to overcome the infirmities of his body." Lately, she has also added an occasional prayer for Arnie, "Let him see Your light."

This day Arnie is keeping his word. He has picked Mary up and they drive to Saint Margaret's.

Saint Margaret's has remained the special concern of Bishop John Powers. Even after his talents had found him a place at The Vatican, he continued to keep Saint Margaret's in his thoughts. It had been his first church and one in which he had served happily. The congregants, all working families, looked to him for guidance; and he had seldom met opposition. Moving to other parishes and up the church hierarchy had taught him to appreciate the luxury of such unquestioning obedience – based as it was on a quiet faith that had seen generations through turmoil, war, poverty, famine, and immigration to the shining shores of Boston.

The Bishop's concern has not reflected itself in church money for the parish. The building, which had been built by painful sacrifices of the faithful, has slowly come to show the effect of wear and years. Pews that had been scarred by boys carving their names during religious instruction have not been replaced. Indeed, had Mary wished to, she could have found her son's name carved into one of the kneelers to the rear of the nave. Some of the stained glass windows have cracked. On particularly blustery New England mornings the parishioners can feel the cold pulsing through the larger cracks. The royal red carpet runners, which had long ago been installed along the aisles, had become dangerous minefields of holes and ragged edges and had eventually been removed – the floors have been left bare. The paint on the walls has grown shabby and discolored over the years until a pervading sense of grime fills the air.

No, the Bishop's concerns have alleviated neither the years of use nor the ever-smaller collections of an ever-smaller congregation trying to keep this center of their world afloat. Moreover, he has personally interceded with the Cardinal so that Father Frank has been prohibited from selling the beautifully bound collection of Latin texts, which are of no earthly use to the parish, or any of the other valuables that furnish the rectory. To the Bishop, these material things are proof of the church triumphant.

Bishop Power's concern is, however, reflected in his occasional unannounced return to say mass. Whenever his work for The Vatican has brought him back to Boston, which is at least twice each year, Bishop Powers calls upon Father Frank to be kind enough to let him officiate at the ten o'clock mass. It is, as he has explained more than once, the only occasion at which he can deliver a homily and expect people to listen and to take to heart.

\* \* \*

It is by chance that Dr. Arnold Berger, professor of Foundations of Education at Northeastern University and professed agnostic, sits in Saint Margaret's Roman Catholic Church this sunny late-summer Sunday and listens to the preaching of Bishop John Powers, assistant to the secretary of His Holiness The Pontiff of Rome for American Affairs. It is Arnie's first time actually attending a mass. Up to that point, desirous as he has been to understand the Catholic Church's ideas on education and faith, Arnie has limited himself to reading and to watching masses on television. Even as he sits next to Mary with his attention focused on the brilliant red chasuble of the Bishop and that man's forceful voice, Arnie wonders if it is proper for him to be here. He feels himself the anthropologist observing, perhaps even taking some small part, but still removed and perhaps even judgmental.

Despite his questions about the propriety of his own attendance, Arnie is much taken by the Bishop's sheer force of personality. He realizes that there is no way that the man's charisma could have been transmitted through the media. The entire church seems filled with his presence.

Had the Bishop not been in Boston that Sunday, Arnie would have heard a very different sermon. The homily that Father Frank had written was about acceptance of the difficult demands of the Church.

Father Frank listens regularly, both in the confessional and in his office, to couples wrestling with birth control. At least once a month a young woman comes seeking his guidance about an unwanted pregnancy. Sometimes it is a pregnancy caused by rape or even incest. Then there are the other painful issues of life. He knows of one man, suffering from Alzheimer's, who, during his lucid moments, contemplates suicide. In his own soul Father Frank wonders if God would truly condemn the act.

"It is difficult," the priest would have sermonized, "to follow the teachings of the Church. We are all tempted, but Our Savior was also tempted. Sometimes we give in. Even Peter gave way to temptation and denied Our Lord. God can forgive our stumbling and fear. If we ask with a contrite heart, He will forgive us. We stumble and He lifts us up. It is our responsibility to avoid stumbling, but we rest – assured in the never-ending mercy and grace of Christ."

One of the qualities that Mary tends to dislike in her priest is this easygoing charitable approach to the rules of the Church. For herself, she has always made sure to keep the rules rigidly – even after the Church has relaxed them. She never eats meat on Fridays, goes to church on all the holy days of obligation, makes confession every week before receiving the Host. Hers has been a life of exemplary Catholic living, and she doesn't appreciate Father Frank's liberalism.

Bishop Powers is much more to Mary's taste. He is an old-time hardliner, a demander of obedience. Tall, thin, with thick glasses and aesthetic appearance, he often confounds first time hearers with his deep, booming voice. Up close his Bishop's ring and platinum pectoral cross seem too big for his slight frame, but from the middle of the nave at Saint Margaret's that Sunday, the jewelry merely adds to his imposing presence.

Since it is not his see, Bishop Powers does not wear his miter nor carry his staff. Only his ring, cross, and zucchetto mark his rank. But he still cuts a dramatic figure. The Bishop's white alb is secured by a cincture of bright red. His stole, too, is snowy white with gold crosses embroidered at each end and in the middle, where it rests on his neck. He wears a red chasuble with a large gold cross emblazoned on the back.

As is his want, the Bishop has requested that certain readings be used that Sunday. Father Frank, always aware of his guest's importance and of his own humility, has changed the order of service accordingly.

The senior deacon reads The Old Testament. The reading is from "Genesis 39", the story of Potiphar's wife. It is a story that Arnie recalls with difficulty.

Father Frank, dressed in an immaculate if slightly frayed white linen alb, reads from "Paul's Epistle to the Ephesians." Despite his readings in "The New Testament," Arnie feels somewhat uneasy as the pastor reads. The sincerity of the priest's belief permeates his voice. "Be very careful, then, how you live – not as unwise but as wise, making the most of every opportunity, because the days are evil," Father Frank reads. Arnie, listening intently, experiences the fear of evil as he never did when reading such words himself.

Slowly moving to the pulpit and removing his zucchetto, Bishop Powers prepares to read from "The Gospel of John 4," the story of the woman at the well.

He ends the reading with the words, "Then Jesus declared, 'I who speak to you am He.'"

The Bishop pauses for the words of his reading to sink in before offering the words of blessing to which the congregation respond.

The homily is directed to the women of the congregation. It is a stern and ringing denunciation of those who would give in to the temptations of sin, particularly the sins of sexuality. "Marriage is the only bed that is right for sexual pleasure, and procreation is its only righteous purpose," he declares.

"Yet," the Bishop promises, "There is hope for the sinners among you. If you thirst after righteousness and turn your need to Christ, you shall be given the water of redemption."

He finishes his remarks with a quotation from The Thirty-Second Psalm: "Then I acknowledged my sin to you and did not cover up my iniquity. I said, 'I will confess my transgressions to the Lord' - and You forgave the guilt of my sin."

Arnie looks at Mary's face and can see that she has taken the Bishop's words to heart. Looking around, he can see that many of the other women seem equally effected. Some have moved away from the men with whom they have been sitting. Others have a look stricken and embarrassed discomfort.

As Mary approaches the altar to receive communion, Arnie, remaining in the pew, wonders if they can bridge the gap between their religious views. He knows that he can accept her Catholicism if it doesn't impinge on their lives. "But," he wonders, "can Catholicism accept our lives?"

Once, when he had taken Mary to one of Boston's best steak houses on a Friday and she had ordered halibut, Arnie had joked, "And I thought keeping Kosher was tough." Then he had promised to keep her preference in mind.

Now, he is wondering, "What about birth control?" He isn't completely sure that Mary has passed menopause, but he is absolutely sure that he doesn't want another child. It is at this moment – sitting in Saint Margaret's and watching Mary take communion – it is at this moment that it suddenly dawns on Arnie that he is contemplating a life, a full and complete life with Mary. He realizes that she is more than a friend, that she has become his heart's desire.

When Arnie had asked Susan to marry him, it had been a carefully planned event. Their families had already met and liked each other. He and Susan had common values and interests. They had gone to the same college and had dated for three years. He would be leaving for graduate school in Oregon, and it had seemed like the obvious practical move. It had been a marriage of sensible and courteous people. Passion had not played a part, but neither had anger. The only time Susan had ever surprised him was when she had gone off to Los Angeles. He could never have imagined the Susan he knew, the one who carefully clipped coupons before going to the Star Market, sharing a house with her lover's ex-wife and children.

But then, he also could never have imagined feeling the same tenderness toward Susan that he is experiencing watching Mary receive communion. He realizes with a mix of sadness and joy that there had been more emotion between them the last Sunday when they were riding the Swan Boats in the Public Garden then there had ever been between Susan and himself when they had been between the sheets.

Robert had been carefully planned. Even though he and Susan had not previously been trying to have a child, she had insisted they use fertility awareness in order to time the pregnancy. She had wanted Robert to be born in May or June. "The summer is too hot for pregnancy, and the warm weather makes it easier to take a newborn outside," she had reasoned. Thinking back, Arnie wondered at the lack of emotions in their ever so carefully planned lives.

He knew that the pain of Robert's death and the unsettling reality of divorce had made him a better teacher – less didactic and more aware of his students' feelings. In his classes Arnie talked more about the need to reach children's feelings, not just their minds. Picking up on something a colleague had said, he read Patrick Dennis's "Auntie Mame" and often quoted his favorite line,

"Life is a banquet, and most poor suckers are starving to death." It always drew a laugh from the class, but Arnie realized that it was he who had been the poor sucker. Sometimes, during the years after the divorce, when alone at night, he has wept for the moments not spent with his son, for the mourning not shared with his wife, for the tenderness unexperienced, which he now realizes is one of the greatest rights of every person.

Arnie feels a wave of tenderness sweep through him as he watches Mary. Mary blesses herself and rises from the altar. As she walks towards him, Arnie quotes T.S. Elliot to himself, "We grow old. We grow old. We wear our pants' legs rolled. Do I dare to eat a peach?" "Do I dare?" he asks himself. "Do I dare?"

# Chapter Five

Mary knows that she has to tell Kathleen and Sean about Arnie. She realizes that neither of those conversations will be easy. Although – in the Church's eyes – Arnie's first marriage had no validity – it having been performed by a Justice of the Peace, she knows that her children, and especially Kathleen, will have difficulty accepting that technicality. Having insisted that Kathleen not consider remarrying because of her divorce, Mary wonders if she has the right to now be involved with a man who is legally – if not religiously – divorced. Also, Arnie isn't a Catholic, not even a Christian, in fact not even a believer in The All Mighty. Given Arnie's doubts, Mary is sure that The Church would consider him eternally damned. How can she ask her children to ignore the teachings that she has always tried to instill in them?

Then there is Sean. However upbeat his letters and phone calls seem, she knows that he can never hope for marriage. He has kept her up to date, telling her of the many daily tasks which he has learned to do for himself. He has also shared his hopes of mastering a computer well enough to get some form of a job. Doubtful as she might be, Mary prays that this optimism will bear fruit. But, none of that could involve sexuality. Does she have the right to consider eventually marrying when she is sure that her son can not? Can she allow herself to have love when she is sure that he has no such possibility?

Mary knows that her dead husband would never have approved. Sean had been a hard-nosed man. He seldom deviated from the rules – at least the ones in his own head, and one of his strongest rules had been marital fidelity. He had told Mary of his one moment of temptation during the war, "I'd never cheat on ya, and that's fer sure. Nor would ya ever be cheatin' on me. That's what marriage is about, isn't it now?"

She had agreed with him then, and she still agrees with him. "Is it cheating," she repeatedly asks herself, "to love another man after years of being a widow?" In her heart she recognizes that Sean would have considered it being unfaithful. That was simply the way he was.

So many times, sitting in the big leather chair absent-mindedly wiping her glasses and thinking about Arnie, Mary can not escape these questions.

Mary knows that she could always go to Father Frank with her questions, but she wonders if he could understand the growing turmoil of her competing feelings. On the one hand, she wonders if the priest can understand the depth of her faith – if he can understand that she needs to be in complete compliance with the will of God. On the other hand, she knows that he has never been married, never had children, and most importantly – at least in her assumptions – never been in love except with God. Love changes things. That is one thing Mary has truly learned. The love she feels for Arnie Berger has thrown her life into a happy chaos, and it has changed her from an unquestioning, submissive woman who accepts all the rules which she has inculcated over the years into someone who knows only how to question – to question authority and herself – but not, no never, to question the will of God.

Mary has never been a book reader. Her limited education makes reading difficult. Even when she reads the magazines next to the register lines at the supermarket, she has to use a dictionary. She wants to ask Arnie to recommend books for her, but she is afraid that she won't understand them and that he will be disappointed. She knows she could also ask Father Frank to suggest books, but she feels that he would only suggest books which support the Church's positions. She knows that if she is to really understand God she must go beyond the teachings of Rome.

Most importantly, Mary knows what she does not know and is determined to understand more of life and its purpose.

It is with this goal in mind that Mary has signed up for two adult education courses. The courses are "Great Literature" and "Philosophy for Life." The classes meet every other week at the neighborhood junior high school. One course is being taught by a retired college professor. The other is offered by a high school English teacher who is using the small paychecks to save for her first trip to Europe. The classes meet in old-fashioned classrooms with desks bolted in rows to the floor. The building itself smells of years of oil soaked into hardwood floors and of bathrooms with chipped fixtures, bathrooms that had probably never been cleaned properly since they were new.

Mary tells no one about her new venture until after the first class. "That's great," is Arnie's enthusiastic response to the news. She hears Sean take a deep breath over the phone before he too gives his somewhat less than wholehearted support.

It is Kathleen who seems the least positive. "Don't you think it's a bit late to rethink your ideas?" There is a bite to the last two words. She peers at Mary through her matching thick glasses. Mary has often thought it strange that Sean had inherited the beautiful blue of her eyes and Kathleen their terrible weakness.

Mary knows how much she has hurt her daughter. She hopes Kathleen also knows how much Mary hurts for her.

Mary can not explain her sudden interest in education. She still isn't ready to tell her children about Arnie. "I have to keep growing, or I'll wither away and die," is all that she feels ready to tell them.

"You could go to Florida and live with Lois and her sister. You wouldn't wither away there. I just don't see the point, not now, not so late in life."

Mary understands what Kathleen is really trying to say: "Don't you go changing your mind – not after I've given up life for so long."

Arnie often asks about Mary's children. He wants to meet Kathleen. He keeps suggesting that he fly with Mary to Minnesota. On both counts Mary put him off. "When the time is right," she says and takes off her glasses and carefully wipes them clean.

Then he hugs her to him and gently caresses her back and kisses her gently on the forehead. He wants to reassure her. He wants her to know that he is willing to wait.

"When the time is right," he echoes gently – the subject for now being pushed aside.

\* \* \*

Amelia Callaghan has become Mary's friend, not just her landlady. She and Mary often share a pot of Lipton's at the end of the evening. Then they sort through the day's events: usually what has taken place between Mary and Arnie. At other times they share the varied pains of their past lives.

Amelia's life has been anything but well ordered. The youngest of three girls, Amelia was only three when her parents had divorced.

Her mother had immediately disappeared. It was only years later that, when Amelia was in her twenties, she had learned her mother's whereabouts, the California State Prison for Women. The mother and her lover, the man with whom she had run off, had committed a series of daring bank robberies during the fifties. Although they proclaimed themselves revolutionaries, no known organization would claim responsibility for their actions, and they personally could offer no statement of doctrine to support them.

Before that life in crime they had habitually moved around. The last place in which they had briefly settled was a commune in New Mexico. There they had engaged in minor thefts until the entire community had demanded they leave. Having drifted and panhandled for a while, they had then taken up the life of desperados. Their last robbery had been in Orange County. It had ended in a hail of police bullets which left him bleeding to death on the sidewalk and her, Amelia's mother, with a piece of lead so close to her aorta that the doctors decided not to try to remove it.

At the time of the arrest, the story had made national news. To their embarrassment, an enterprising reporter had located Amelia and her two sisters. The reporter had learned nothing for her efforts; but Amelia, Sharon and Linda had been devastated. Their father had died only months before. An aneurysm had burst in his brain, and in seconds he was lying dead on the floor of Linda's kitchen.

Amelia had been unable to cope with the combined blows. She had become so depressed that her husband, a quiet man of half European and half Burmese stock with a violent temper, had hospitalized her.

Shock therapy combined with medications eventually lifted Amelia's depression – not, however, before her husband had left. They had had no children, and she had no income. He had left the house with its mortgage and five hundred dollars in their bank account. The lawyers told her that trying to chase him down to collect the alimony the courts might have awarded her would be a waste of time. So, Amelia had opened her home as a boarding house for women. She took in four boarders at a time to whom she offered breakfast, dinner and a change of linens and towels once a week. By means of careful management and occasional help from her sisters, she had made ends meet. With the mental scars to show for it, she had survived.

An outsider, untrusting, quick to smell deceit in any man's statements, Amelia Callaghan had made no friends over the years. But, in Mary Flanagan she had found warmth, openness, and caring that had disarmed her distrust. Their pots of shared tea had become precious to her. The friendship had become dear to them both.

When Amelia is finished sharing her mother's story, Mary asks, "Have you ever gone to California to see her?"

"No. Sharon did – she and her husband. Sharon's the oldest. She remembered our mother best. Sharon had always said we were better off without her, that she was selfish and uncaring. I guess our mother wasn't much of a housekeeper or a mother. In fact, I guess she spent most of her time drunk.

"But Sharon still went. She visited the prison once. That hadn't been her plan. She went thinking that they'd bond, spend time together. She was going to spend a week visiting every day, catching up, trying to understand. But once was enough. She, our mother, only wanted to know if Sharon could give her money, cigarettes, and stuff like that. She never even asked how Linda and I were. Sharon didn't bother to go back. Instead, she and Bill went to San Diego – sightseeing. When she came back, she said that the koalas were much warmer than our mother. I guess that summed it up.

"She did leave our addresses, but we never got a letter, not even a card." Amelia starts to weep. Mary, putting her arm around her friend, weeps, too. Helpless loneliness is a feeling that she has known well – far too well.

With the growing closeness between the two women, Amelia has changed her wary animosity toward Arnie to a far more positive attitude. She wants Mary to be happy so she tries to believe that Arnie is different. More importantly, she knows that he loves Mary and that Mary will flourish in the sunshine of that love. So she encourages Mary to see Arnie as much as possible. Her advice is straightforward and strong. "If he asks you, say 'yes.' Sean would understand. Your children will understand. Say, 'yes.'"

One night Mary asks her friend why she doesn't go out herself. Amelia answers that one desertion is enough for anyone – to be deserted by both ones mother and husband seems beyond comprehension or survival. So, Mary shares her stories of charming picnics and loving dates with Arnie, and Amelia lives them vicariously.

It is a measure of Arnie's sensitivity to her that Mary never feels the need to omit anything they have done. Arnie has never attempted to do more than kiss her or gently massage her hand or back. Mary is more circumspect when it comes to talking about Arnie's personal life, but the moments they have shared are nothing that would embarrass her even if Amelia had sat next to them and watched.

From time to time Amelia has wondered about Arnie. She wonders how he can go so slowly and carefully. She thinks that she knows men; and based on her own marriage, she can not imagine that Arnie or any man is really so patient.

Arnie, too, wonders at his patience. He is a normal man with great urges, and he's not getting any younger. His yearnings express themselves in fantasy and in the privacy of his bathroom. Even though he has his own apartment, even though he lives alone, Arnie Berger is too much the gentleman to masturbate in any other room.

Occasionally he hints at his frustration to Mary. "Someday, we'll be married. Then we'll be able to share our love."

Another time, "I wish we could be much closer."

On yet another occasion he asks, "Do you think we'll ever have more than this?"

Mary knows what he is asking, but she also knows that she can not reassure him. She just hopes that Arnie will continue to be patient.

"I love you so much," she invariably answers. Then she carefully cleans her glasses. The Lord has not yet revealed what actions He expects of her. How then can she assure Arnie or herself of what is to come?

* * *

In her philosophy class, the teacher passes out three by five file cards and asks everybody to write a question they would like to explore during the course. Mary writes, "How do you balance the commitments to God, to others, and to yourself?" She starts to pass the card forward and then pulls it back to add a second question, "How important is love?" She blushes as she writes and is tempted to put the card into her sensible black pocketbook, but she is also embarrassed to not take part in the exercise. She feels that every eye in the room is at the back of her neck. She adds her card to the trickle that moves toward the front of the room.

During the break, the teacher reads the cards. Later he shares a few with the class. "How do we know what is good?" was one question he reads. "That's really important," he comments.

"What are the moral implications of Einstein's Theory of Relativity?" He reads the question aloud and adds, "That's a real academic question. I'd wait for graduate school for that one." Some of the class laughs. Mary makes a mental note to ask Arnie what the question meant and why the teacher's comment was funny.

"How do you balance the commitments to God, to others, and to yourself?" The teacher pauses. "How important is love?" He pauses again for the questions to sink in. Mary, sure that he will make light of her questions, turns slightly red and starts to wipe her glasses. "Now, those are the questions of somebody trying to use philosophy in life. Whoever wrote this card, thank you."

Mary can not believe her ears. The slight red of embarrassment turns to a glow of satisfaction.

At least somebody appreciates the conflicts and questions within her.

\* \* \*

It is a long trip by public transportation to the cemetery where her Sean lays buried. Carrying a small bouquet of flowers, Mary once again makes her way to the outskirts of Newton, to the Cemetery of the Holy Presence. At one time she had made this visit almost weekly, but that is no longer the case.

This morning, almost a year after her Seany's leave-taking, she knows that she has to go and talk with her dead husband.

It seems a strange but a necessary mission. Mary knows that his soul is not there. It, she knows with sweet assurance, is surely in Heaven. "Perhaps," she thinks, "I should be talking to the Holy Virgin." Still she walks through the fine haze of spring pollen, through the rows of headstones, until she finds his. The inscription is simple: "Sean Flanagan" and underneath "Know God's Peace." She kneels facing it and carefully lays the flowers against it.

In a whisper Mary starts to speak. "Sean, I don't know what to do. It isn't that I don't still hold you in my heart. You were a good husband. I had no complaints. I know, too, that you had a right to some yourself. But a woman gets lonely, and I love him in a different way, Sean. Forgive me! I know you'll think I'm being unfaithful. I'm not sure about the right and wrong of it. I only know how much I need him. He's a good man, Sean, wise and caring. I'm so truly sorry, but sorry doesn't make it right. I can only ask: Forgive me!" She crosses herself, makes sure that the flowers are properly propped against the stone and rises – just a trifle arthritically – to her feet.

Turning with her back to the grave and without looking back, Mary Flanagan, her shoulders back and he head stiffly high, strides out of the cemetery – her decision made, her course set.

The ride back to Amelia's house seems much shorter than the trip to the cemetery. One of the greatest weights that has ever rested on her shoulders has been removed – left at her husband's grave.

There is a church around the corner from Amelia Callaghan's boarding house. It isn't a Roman Catholic Church. At this moment, that doesn't seem to matter. Her trip to talk with Sean completed, Mary now feels compelled to talk with God.

Hours later, when she comes to offer Vespers, the minister finds Mary still silently kneeling in the front pew.

Reverend Patricia Michaels comes to the church every afternoon to offer prayers, but she seldom finds anyone else there. As she approaches, she hears Mary's muted words. "God, please give me a sign. God, please tell me what I should do."

The minister slides into the pew. She kneels next to Mary and puts her hand on the work-worn hand of this middle-aged stranger "I'm sure He's listening to you."

Mary is startled. "Who...?"

"I'm the minister of this church. I came to say Vespers. Have you been here long?"

"I don't know. I came in to pray. I was at the cemetery ... my husband. I want him to understand."

"To understand what?"

"I've fallen in love. I want to remarry."

"How long has he been dead?"

"A year. Oh, no, that was when my son, a year ago. Sean died years ago, but still I feel that I'm married. Marriage should be for ever. I just know he wouldn't approve."

"Not while he was alive."

"What do you mean?"

"Do you believe your husband is with God?"

"Of course," Mary shrinks back. She can not imagine any alternative. "He was a good man. I'm sure he's with God."

"Don't you think God has opened his eyes and heart?"

Mary thinks for a few minutes. "Are you saying that God may have taught him something different about marriage?"

"I'm sure God has taught your husband ... What was his name?"

"Sean, Sean Flanagan"

"I'm sure God has taught Sean Flanagan to want true happiness for those he loves just as God loves us and truly wants us to be happy."

It has never occurred to Mary that God might want her to be happy. She has always believed that true happiness would come after death – after death and atonement in Purgatory – not on earth. The nuns had taught and re-taught that lesson when Mary had been a little girl. She can hardly bring herself to ask, "Do you really think God wants us to be happy on earth?"

"Aren't we a part of His wonderful creation? Doesn't he want us to make a joyful noise? Of course He wants us to be happy. Why else would He have sent us His good news?"

"I suppose that you're right. I never ..." Mary, in sudden confusion, takes off her glasses and wipes them. She puts them back, resting them gently on the bridge of her nose and then fitting the frame behind her ears and fluffing the wings of her hair.

"Thank you," she says and slides from the pew.

"Thank you," she says it again louder.

As she nears the door, she calls out one last time, "Thank you."

# Chapter Six

Arnie has avoided using the word "marriage." With his innate sense of Mary, he has avoided the twin subjects of marriage and sexuality. He knows that she will eventually give him the opening they will need. It is, however, difficult to restrain himself. During the years after Robert's death and his divorce, Arnie has buried himself in work. Sublimation was the word his friends in the Psychology Department used to describe it as if they were telling him something more than he already knew.

His loneliness had led friends and relatives to fix him up on a variety of dates. Most were one night and hardly worth that. Only one woman had been sufficiently interesting and interested to warrant more than a month's relationship. That had ended when she met another man, one whom she married half a year later. They had parted friends. She had even invited Arnie to the wedding. He had declined – sending the latest in automated coffee pots in his stead.

He has no rational explanation for Mary's effect on him. Arnie can only marvel at and enjoy it. But he is paying a price for that pleasure: his sexuality, which has been 'sublimated' into scholarly articles and beautifully prepared lectures, now tears at his mind almost every waking hour. He can think of little else. Arnie Berger wants desperately to get Mary into bed. Even more desperately he wants to get her before a priest, minister, rabbi, Justice of the Peace, or whomever he can find to make them one. To accomplish that he would even be willing to convert, but he doubts he could find a priest foolish enough to not recognize the unholy reason for his profession of faith.

As the fall colors brightened New England, Arnie and Mary are locked in a polite dance, a minuet, replete with implications but lacking in action. It seems to Arnie that he now has to relieve himself after every date. His physical cravings dominate his day-to-day life. Sitting in his office at the university, he often stares into space and wonders where Mary might be. In reality he usually knows exactly where she is, sitting in her rooms, with the Webster's

New Collegiate Dictionary, which he had given her, by her side. There she sits reading the books for her courses and the others that he has occasionally mentioned. There she is trying to make herself worthy – as if anyone but she cared which books she has read.

But, it is not Mary reading that Arnie fantasizes. He visualizes Mary walking throughout the city of Boston, and he wants to be beside her. He imagines her walking by Symphony Hall, in Coply Square, about The Fens, on Beacon Hill, through The Commons and The Public Gardens. He loves Boston and its history. In his mind it is the perfect backdrop for the ever-present picture of Mary Flanagan.

\* \* \*

If she would have permitted, Arnie would certainly have been with Mary at this moment, when she has eventually gone to talk with Kathleen. Arnie knows that Mary has wanted to tell her daughter about him – about them. Arnie has repeatedly offered to go with her. But, Mary has refused. That revelation would come at the right time, and there was no way that Arnie Berger could encourage the ponderous wheels of Mary's inner clock to move more quickly. Nor was there any way that she would bring him with her to that confrontation. It would be between her and Kathleen – for good or ill – between them alone.

It is six in the morning. The Sisters of Mercy are gathered in their chapel. Every morning on rising and every night before retiring, they assemble to submit their wills and to dedicate their bodies and souls.

While the lay staff are not required to attend these services, Kathleen Flanagan (she had – in a subtle defiance of the eternity of her failed marriage – returned to her maiden name) always does. It is neither an act of devotion nor of penance. Kathleen's strict religiosity has been in its way another act of defiance. It has been her way of telling God and her mother that she did not and does not deserve the curse they have placed on her. Divorced and childless, she has felt rejected by both the Church and her mother. Outwardly observing the rules of piety, Kathleen, within, takes no solace from religion. Nor does she accept communion. In her deepest heart, Kathleen feels that her sacrifice, her martyrdom, has been too great and that she needs not God's grace but rather his apology.

Angry as she is, Kathleen is also the soul of tenderness. Working with the terminally ill patients of the hospice, she has always been gentle and caring. The patients often ask for her. No matter what the hour, Kathleen willingly leaves the staff residence to tend to the needs of a terrified sufferer. So it has been that Kathleen has often been the person in attendance as a patient breathed the last breath of this world and entered the next. One of the nuns with a bent for classical learning had dubbed her Charon, and the name had spread throughout the hospice.

"Send Saint Charon to me," a patient, knowing she is about to die will ask. The nuns, in grateful respect for her devotion to the ill, send for Kathleen. "Now I can go in peace," the woman might say and draw her last breath. Kathleen then gently closes the corpse's eyes, folds her hands in repose, and pulls the sheet over. Then she goes into the hall and tells the waiting others, who, Kathleen knows, will cross themselves in piety while she walks away.

"Your mother is here," says Madeline Adams, the secretary, who has quietly entered the chapel and tapped Kathleen on the shoulder.

Kathleen has not seen Mary for weeks. While they have spoken occasionally on the phone, they have been separated by far more than the five miles between Mrs. Callaghan's boarding house and the hospice. Kathleen doesn't want to follow the stiff-backed older woman with her severely tied-back hair and sensible cardigan sweater. Nevertheless, reluctantly, taking a deep breath, Kathleen walks toward one of the visiting rooms, which are usually used for families visiting their dying loved ones. Indeed, as she walks toward those rooms, foreboding is deep upon her. Kathleen imagines that either Sean has died or that Mary, herself, is about to. Despite her apprehension, she follows dutifully – feeling perhaps like a child who has been summonsed to the principal's office.

The visiting rooms are furnished in cast-off Danish modern. It is all furniture that has gone out of vogue. A variety of insurance companies, stock brokers, and real estate agencies have taken tax advantages and donated mountains of it to the United Way, which has in turn distributed it to places like the Sisters of Mercy Home for the Incurable. The furnishings, like the patients and Kathleen herself, are not quite forgotten and not quite gone. They exist in a phantom world of beiges and grays – a parallel universe which is too unpleasant to visit and too frightening to completely ignore.

Entering the room, Kathleen is struck by the changes in her mother. Not only is Mary wearing a brightly colored skirt and a beautifully tailored blouse but also there is an obvious change in her physical presence. After a quick burst of irritation, the radiance that emanates from Mary brings joy even to Kathleen's hardened heart.

"There's something I have to tell you."

"Is Sean all right?" Kathleen knows that her mother is not there because of any problem with Sean – not beaming that way – she simply can't think of anything else to say or ask.

"He's fine. It's about me." Mary motions to a place beside her on the blue-green Naugahyde cushions. "Why don't you sit down?"

Kathleen crosses the room and sits in a separate, stiff-backed chair. She sits very straight and plants her feet firmly, a specter of a world long gone. She wishes herself back with one of the women who will soon die in her care. There at least she has a sense of purpose. Unmarriageable, childless, Kathleen feels that her life is long since over and that it is the woman sitting across from her and that woman's Blessed God who have condemned her. In no way does Kathleen want to hear about her mother's happiness no matter how much love she might still feel for her.

"I've met someone, a man." Mary waits for the tirade she has told herself to expect, but Kathleen sits mute – unable to comprehend this seemingly total improbability. "His name is Arnie Berger."

Kathleen still makes no response. Inside herself she can feel the muscles tightening – in surprise, outrage, pain.

Mary continues. "He teaches at Northeastern."

Kathleen stares at her mother. Her eyes are slits, but from them Mary can feel the beams of rage. Mary tries to hold back the pain and sense of rejection she is beginning to feel. "I must try to understand Kathleen's pain," she reminds herself. The guilt is overwhelming. The tears of helplessness are on the verge.

Finally, Kathleen manages a choking inquiry. "Why are you telling me?"

"Because you're my daughter, because I want you to know, because I love you, because I need your happiness for me." Mary's staccato list is accompanied by her tears finally welling and spilling over and down her cheeks. To herself she adds, "Because I need your forgiveness."

The rage Kathleen feels is visible on her face. "My life is over, and you want me to be glad for you that you're starting a new one? Why don't you ask your God for happiness? I can't give it." Kathleen rises and starts for the door.

Mary is now sobbing, but her tears have no effect on the young woman in hospital whites whose wounded heart holds neither compassion nor forgiveness.

"Please, Kathleen, I want you to meet him."

Kathleen is at the door, holding the knob. She turns her torso so that she can see her mother. "Why? So I can envy you? Hell, I envy Sean. At least he doesn't have to think about what could be, what could have been – only about what can't." She pauses, obviously searching for words. Then, in a less angry more pain-filled voice, she continues. "I even envy the people here. They're dying, not little by little for years, but now. They don't have to think about the death inside. Every day, that's all I think about, dying inside, inside me like my baby." Kathleen's body shakes, but she does not cry. Her tears have long ago been exhausted.

Although Mary has known that her daughter has been angry with her, she has never until this moment really understood what she and the Church have taken away from Kathleen. There is a small marker in the Flanagan plot, just below Sean Senior's. It marks the resting place of Kathleen's miscarried infant. Mary has always avoided seeing it when she has gone to visit her husband's grave. She has never placed flowers on it. She has never wanted to recognize that it marked the end of her daughter's greatest hopes and dreams.

As a little girl, Kathleen had played house by the hour. Her dolls had been cared for with the same strict concern that had marked Mary's care for Kathleen and Sean. Kathleen had insisted on learning how to sew, to cook, and even how to clean so that she could someday be a good wife and mother. She had made her mother an ideal to be followed, a goal to be aspired. All those hopes now lay marked and forlorn in The Cemetery of The Holy Presence.

Kathleen slams the door of the visiting room. Mary can hear the thud of her daughter's footsteps stomping in anger down the hallway and back to her world of dying patients. At that moment, Mary wishes that she too were dying – dying so her estranged daughter might in charity come back to her.

Mary is left to contemplate the chaos which following the rules has created for Kathleen. On the other hand, she thinks, there is Sean, Sean who had never followed the rules. His life, too, is in chaos. As has so often become the case these days, Mary can not make sense out of it all.

"Perhaps," she thinks, "Arnie understands." At some level that is her hope, that Arnie will be able to make the confusion of life as clear for her as the nuns had once done – so long ago and so far away. Life had been so simple then – no confusions only compliance – no questions only obedience.

Half blinded by her own tears and grief, Mary stumbles toward the front door of the hospice. "Was I wrong?" she asks herself. "Was the Church wrong? Kathleen is suffering. The only way she can face life is through death. Did I do that to her? Was that God's purpose? Is that Christ's love?"

Wrapped in her cloak of guilt, Mary wonders if she can ever think of marrying Arnie while Kathleen remains doomed to such despair.

\* \* \*

Each of the rooms of the hospice has been given the name of a saint rather than a number or letter. Some say it makes the hospice less impersonal. Others think that it makes the process of dying more sacred. For those who live and work there and for those who are in the process of perishing, the names of rooms are unimportant.

There is an old man dying in St. Michael's room. The old man believes that he knows a secret – that he alone among the patients and staff of The Sisters of Mercy Home for the Incurable knows God's plan for the world. The doctors have said the virus has invaded his nervous system and that he is psychotic. The sisters aren't sure. Perhaps the doctors are right, or perhaps he had been crazy even before contracting HIV. Max doesn't believe that he is crazy. He doesn't believe that he is delusional. Max believes that his prophecies are the words of God, that his secret is divine.

The nuns humor Max when they have to and then quietly ask the doctors to prescribe more and stronger drugs to control him. They do not know how cleverly he cheeks the pills only to spit them out after they have left the room. If they did know, it wouldn't matter; they don't listen to Max anyway.

Only Kathleen listens. Only Kathleen accepts the possibility that this strange man, ignored by the world as he slowly dies from this newest plague, might just be revealing something important. "Certainly," she thinks, "his lunacy can't be any more demented than all the rest of us."

"We are all alone," Max intones. "God ignores us. Don't look for Him anywhere. I looked, and what did I find? Gonorrhea. That's God's answer. You pray for something. What do you get? Syphilis. You live by all the rules and act the way you're supposed to. What is your reward? AIDS! It's all the same. It's all nothing. I know! God has a plan, He plans to make jokes. We're The Three Stooges, and He's laughing our heads off."

When Max yells too loudly, Sister Mark, the head nurse, gives him a shot of Valium, which he can't cheek. Then she sits in Max's – Saint Michael's – room praying over the stupefied and gratifyingly quieted man. But her prayers go unanswered. Each day Max awakens to continue preaching his blasphemous secret – usually quietly enough to escape the needles and loudly enough for Saint Charon to listen.

Max is an enigma. No one but Kathleen knows much about him. He had come to the hospice on his own. He claimed to have no family, and a check of the city's various hospitals' records only confirmed his diagnosis and homelessness. It is believed that he had been an intravenous drug user and had had unprotected sex for years. Given those assumptions, nobody is surprised that Max is dying. Certainly Max isn't. The lesions on his face and arms are a constant reminder to the staff that he is close to the end. And, the writhing pain of body and spirit is a constant reminder to Max.

"Max, Max, where did you come from?" Kathleen is half speaking and half crooning to the dying man.

She assumes that he has dropped into sleep, but she is wrong.

"From Scarborough Faire, for that is where, I met Kathleen with her fine brown hair," he croons in response. Painfully, he turns his head and smiles.

"You are a rogue, and you know it. Don't you?"

"Of course I do. Would you begrudge a dying man a little flirtation along with the pleasures of his sponge bath? Besides which, there's too little flirting and too much work in your life."

The feeble dying man is propped in his hospital bed. Kathleen is giving him the gentle yet thorough bath for which she has become famous throughout the hospice. Bathing dying and decaying bodies is an unpleasant task. It can be reasonably well done as an offering to God, but it is much better for the suffering recipient when it is done as an exercise in unconditional love.

Many of the patients try to ignore Kathleen while she is ministering to such private bodily functions as bathing and toileting, but Max has no embarrassment as she touches the various parts of his body. "If the body is the holy temple of the soul, I hope my soul has taken up residence somewhere else." He chuckles, and then adds, "There isn't anything left to be embarrassed about, nor proud. Now, once ... But that's a different story – one I'd just as soon forget."

"And, why is that, Max?" Kathleen asks.

"Now, how do you think I ended up here? The sins of the flesh will do you in quick as a wink." With that he winks at her. Kathleen winks back and smiles.

"You have a lovely smile, my dear. I wish you'd show it off outside these not-so-hallowed walls. You need to live, to have fun. You're too young to be living like a cloistered nun."

"Do you think I should give in to the sins of the flesh, too?"

"Sins, no! Pleasures, yes! It's all a joke anyway."

"What is?"

"Life. Life is the greatest joke of all."

"What about God's purpose?"

"God's purpose is simply to get a good laugh from our poor demented efforts to find meaning. I don't care about that impostor's purposes." In a softer voice he adds, "Once I did. Oh, yes, once I did."

"Tell me, please," Kathleen had pleaded.

Afterwards, Max won't be sure if he hadn't planned to tell her all along, if he had given in to a weak moment, or if the pleading tone of her voice had somehow reached him. But, Kathleen is the only member of the hospice staff to whom he will ever confess – if confess is the right word – the upheavals of his life.

"Like you, I was born into a very religious family," he begins.

"How did you know ...?" Kathleen starts to ask.

But Max waves his hand as if to say, "Don't bother me with silly questions. What's obvious is obvious."

"In my home," Max continues, "there were few choices that were acceptable. We could teach, become doctors, go into nursing, or become nuns and priests. I have a sister who's a nun and two who are nurses. My oldest brother became a doctor. The next brother – well, he was the scapegrace, the drunk. Then there was me, my mother's baby."

Kathleen waits, but Max does not offer. "So which did you become?" she asks at last.

"Why the priest, my dear, of course, the priest."

"You're a priest?" Disbelief permeates her words.

"Yes, a priest, or at least I was. That was a lifetime ago."

"What happened?"

"Let's say I fell from grace. I found that the pleasures of corruption were greater than the fears of Hell. But, that wasn't until I had made my mark. I became the senior priest at a large church. I won't tell you which. Then the Cardinal called me to serve on his staff. I was even elevated to Monsignor. There were some who said I might become a Bishop.

"But, that was before I met John, a young priest who was doing youth work in a struggling parish. John was dedication personified. If he wanted to have relations with some of the young men or the altar boys – and he did admit that was his fantasy, he had the strength and the grace to deny himself.

"I, on the other hand, could not deny myself the pleasure of being with him. He taught me how to love, how to be physical, how to be sensual.

"I know that I was only second best for him ..." Max's story has been interrupted by a bout of coughing.

The bouts of coughing have become more frequent. "It means that his lungs are going," the doctor had told Kathleen at a staff meeting. "He doesn't have too long in this world."

That day, after the meeting, Kathleen had gone to the chapel to cry. As the days have passed, the coughing bouts have become more regular and severe; and Kathleen has spent more time weeping.

The paroxysm has stopped. "Some water, please," Max asks. He takes a long draught and sighs. "How sad and how wonderfully comic that a simple drink, a sponge bath, a bowel movement without blood – that these have become the moments of happiness in my life. With John I knew the stars and heard the choirs of angels singing. Now I must settle for the nuns singing hymns as they go about their tasks. At least I know my passing will be marked with song. I laugh at them, and I must admit I envy them. Their piety is so ... so ... simple. I don't suppose there's a better word. For them everything is part of a plan.

"I chose. I had to choose between that piety and the wonders of the flesh. I know, you're thinking it was the Devil tempting me. Hogwash! God created us with urges and desires. He made man and woman to look at one another with lust. For some it is just a different desire.

"I looked at John – the first day we met. I looked and I chose. Or, perhaps, I didn't choose. Perhaps I really couldn't have done otherwise. I don't know. I only know that eventually we rented a small apartment and that we met there. At first once a week. Then twice, then three times. Passion burns with a consuming heat, and we were being burnt to a crisp.

"Then, fate intervened. A bus driver has a stroke. The bus goes out of control. And John, who is blithely shopping for a present – a present for me – is mowed down." Max weeps.

Kathleen is crying, too. Then she has a horrible thought and blanches. "How horrible," she thinks, "it might have been my father at the wheel of that bus. Oh, my God!"

Managing to hold back his tears, Max continues, "I haven't cried for him in a long time. I knew that day that he would never be replaced – not in my life. What farce. God has one weird sense of humor."

"There it is," he whispers with honest resignation.

"But how did you get sick?"

"You must have been very sheltered if you have to ask. When God's jokes have left you bereft, there's little to do except try to enjoy what's left. So, I did my best – to enjoy that is.

"At first I hid it from the Cardinal. Then I started to make jokes about being a party animal. Finally, well, he couldn't look the other way forever.

"He tried to be gentle when he confronted me. I really think he was a good man. Certainly he was a real believer. He wasn't like a lot of the politicians who make their way up the Church hierarchy. Some of them are the worst of sinners and have no repentance in them.

"He wasn't like that. He tried to remonstrate with me, and I told him that I had to leave the clergy. Oh, there was a period of counseling. He asked, and I agreed. It's no small thing to give up your vows to God – not even when He's given up His to you."

"It was no small thing…" Max's voice drifts off. Kathleen wonders if he is too tired to continue. She starts to back away from his bed.

"Where are you going?" he asks suddenly, sharply.

"I thought you were tired."

"Tired? Yes, I suppose I am. I think that I'll welcome that long nap." He strains to lift his head from the pillow – to look out the window.

"I suffered the guilt of leaving God, and that guilt led me to do so many stupid things. First I considered moving away, but there was no point. I was already on my own – living in my own world – in my own hell. Did you think I came from Boston?" He didn't wait for an answer. "I won't tell you where I'm from. Let's just say that I have no family, no roots.

"Here I was as free to indulge my appetites and my guilt as I would have been anywhere. They became one and the same."

Again, he is interrupted by the wracking cough. When it has subsided, he resumes. "Then this plague started. I was one of the first, at least that I know of. I'll be one of the first to go. I don't mind. Facing death has given me the perspective to face myself – and to face Him.

"It's all been so absurd. That's the wonder of it. God's plan ... God's plan is a farce – the best of all theater, the best of all comedies. The trick is to keep laughing."

"Eat, drink and be merry because tomorrow you may die?"

"No, eat drink and be merry because there's always the scam of believing in tomorrow." Max starts to close his eyes. "I think it's time I took a little nap."

Kathleen looks so worried that he feels compelled to reassure her. "Not the big nap, no, not yet. Just a little one."

Once again he closes his eyes. "Sleep well, Max," Kathleen says softly. She moves noiselessly away on her sensible crepe soled white shoes.

"Yes, just a little one," Max mumbles.

* * *

"Is there a Heaven?" Kathleen asks Max one day while she is bathing him. She has been tormented with the doubts that have been stirred once again by her mother's recent visit.

Kathleen, unlike the nuns, enjoys listening to Max's pronouncements on faith. To her, they seem like an antidote for the simpleminded homilies of the priests and of her mother. She hopes for a new, better perspective.

"Sure there is, girlie. God sits there judging us all and making up his damn tortures and jokes. The folks he likes get to stay around – to take part – to make up their own little torments for all us bit players down here. The others, they just disappear."

"Into Hell."

"There probably isn't any Hell. They just disappear. Didn't they get tormented enough down here? I guess they die when God gets bored with them. Yeah, He just gets bored – writes them out of the script."

"What about praying? Does God listen to prayers?" She isn't sure that she wants to hear his answer, but she asks anyway.

"You pray to God, and you know what you get? Tuberculosis. Goddamn T.B. Seriously, do you think a jokester like The Almighty wants to waste His time listening to a bunch of whining? No way!"

"Max, I need to know. Who gets into Heaven? Don't the faithful? I mean what about Jesus? What about the Sermon on the Mount?"

"Tell me something, my little saint. Do you buy into every advertising campaign? Some hype and a few phony claims and He sets up a business that's thrived for two thousand years. Madison Avenue could use him."

"So, who does get in? Who makes it to Heaven?"

"Me, Saint Charon, me. I get in. Know why?"

"Why, Max?"

He goes into one of those sudden painful spasms of coughing. He is so weak that each cough sounds like the rattling of his skeleton.

Propping his head, she holds a glass of water and slips a straw between his lips. He takes a sip and then coughs and spits the water out. Kathleen wipes his chin with a tissue and holds the glass so he can take another sip. As the coughing subsides, she asks again, "Why, Max, why do you get into Heaven?" There's a tone of desperation in her voice.

He takes another sip of the water and then slips backward. Kathleen lets him rest against the pillows. "Because I get the damn joke." He grimaces in pain, chuckles once and dies. He dies with Kathleen as his witness, the witness to his personal creed and to his private bitter laughter.

When the doctor comes to do the paper work, he comments to Sister Mark, "It looks like he died laughing."

Kathleen misses Max. The woman whom they move into Saint Michael's room had received a contaminated blood transfusion. Her family comes to visit her all the time. They sit around the woman's bed and say The Rosary. Kathleen knows that not all the Hail Marys and Our Fathers in the world will give her the solace of Max's appreciation of the cosmic joke.

She tries, but she cannot feel the same tenderness for this afflicted woman as she had for the fallen priest.

\* \* \*

"Is that it?" muses Kathleen. "Is it all a joke?"

The thought of her unbaptized child, the much prayed for little girl, languishing in Limbo, and the guilt she can not shake that somehow she had caused the miscarriage are as much a part of her as breathing. How else could God have allowed such a loss? It must have been something she had done. Why else would she be unable to conceive? John had left her. That, too, had to be part of her punishment – for what sin she did not know, but there must have been something.

As a child Kathleen had always tried to be good. Her father had called her his little angel. Perhaps that had been her sin - the pride she took in his praise. Her brother had been the wild one, playing rough games in the streets, getting into trouble in school; but she had tried so hard. She had been brought up to believe that God rewarded good and punished evil. "Whose good? Whose evil?" she now wonders.

She had cared for Max when no one else wanted to. He had been a difficult patient. Sometimes she wonders if her brother, Sean, is being equally difficult in Minnesota. Does he, like Max, find a different meaning in suffering?

With a smile of sarcasm, Kathleen wonders what her mother would have made of Max. How outraged would she have been? Was Mary's visit also part of the great joke, the game God played? Was ferrying the dying across the River Styx a job requiring somebody with a sense of humor? It had seemed so simple once upon a time. Now, Kathleen can only wonder.

The days pass, and so do the patients. The memorial services are an almost daily recognition of the growing power of the AIDS epidemic. There are places in Africa, Kathleen knows, where the infection rate is close to fifty percent and always soaring higher. There are children, she knows, born already dying and others who will face growing up without a culture – with only the dying remnants of a generation that has relished its sexuality without thought, to guide them. She wonders if, when they reach adolescence, those children will – like young elephants growing up without elders – become rampaging monsters. "Perhaps," she thinks, "that's what humans are anyway, chaotic demons wrecking havoc on themselves and the world around them."

Each morning at six, Kathleen joins the sisters at their prayers. She kneels and wonders. She wonders if Max is watching her. If he is, she knows that he is laughing. She can still hear the wryness of his chuckle, that chuckle that marked his way into death.

She can hear Max's laughter, but still, she can not forgive.

The woman who had followed Max into Saint Michael's room has taken a turn for the worse. Her family prays harder and longer each day. Occasionally one of the nuns joins them on their knees. They keep what Max would have called a farcical vigil. In the midst of it, Kathleen moves in and out of the room trying to focus on the tasks at hand. The woman is sinking ever faster, and she clings to her family in growing terror.

Kathleen, feeling her own sense of terror – the terror of a life without meaning – clings with equal fervor to those little tasks of kindness which have so endeared her to the community of the hospice. The antiseptic smells that permeate the old mansion with its ornate marble adornments and large fireplaces comfort Kathleen just as the rosary beads comfort the dying woman.

Underneath her endless efforts, Kathleen appreciates the irony: Max, a man who ultimately had rejected all virtue, had faced death with wisdom. This woman, who has lived what has apparently been an entirely religious life, is finding only fear in her own mortality.

When the woman finally dies, her entire family comes to the memorial service. The chapel is overflowing. The service runs long. Kathleen does not attend. She has volunteered to stay on duty.

When Max had died, the service had been brief and attended only by the priest who had officiated, the nuns who were required to attend, and by Kathleen – his sole mourner.

Now she can not help wondering which of the two souls, if either, at this moment resides in Heaven.

\* \* \*

Weeks have passed since Mary's visit. Kathleen has not spoken with her mother. The first snows have swirled their way through Boston's crooked streets and coated the world with the gray slush of urban life. Kathleen wonders if Mary is still seeing "that man." She floats through the world of the incurable-dying wrapped in the cocoon of self-absorption. Only ministering to the dying matters. That has become her truth and her way.

Kathleen often thinks of Max and she thinks about his secret.

"As you do unto the least of these my children, so also do you do unto me." The Biblical quotation seems somehow to have been written about her months of caring for Max – Max who had nothing of this world.

Thinking about Max, Kathleen finds solace. She can not help wondering what Max would have made of the whole thing – how he would have reacted to Mary's news.

Of course, Kathleen had not been there when Mary's philosophy teacher had told the class, "Appreciation of the absurd is the first requirement for survival." Max, however, had taught her the same lesson. The rage, which had been burning inside her, had cut her off from that truth. She knows that she has to come to terms with herself and with that rage or she will not survive, at least not as a full human being. She looks around her at the nuns going through their synchronized daily rituals of prayer and service and wonders how many of them have truly survived. "Are they dead inside?" she wonders. She thinks of some of the angry, scolding harridans of her school days. "Max for all his physical decay was alive – he survived." Kathleen says to herself. She weeps at his memory, and they are tears of closeness and caring.

Kathleen has never studied philosophy or metaphysics. Her training in theology had been limited to Catechism and Pre Cana classes. She feels lost puzzling at the questions and conflicts beating at the walls of her soul, so she decides to do something – something actual – something which will allow God to act within her life. Just as she has always found relief in the myriad of little tasks she has done each day at the hospice, she hopes to find answers in a new direction.

Autumn is almost at an end. The trees along the broad avenues are dropping brown leaves that crackle under her feet. Kathleen likes to walk in the evening, but that evening she has another activity on her mind. As she walks, Kathleen stops to look at pay phones along her route. She examines them carefully. She doesn't know which one she will use. She certainly can not say what it is for which she is so carefully looking. She cannot even say why she hasn't simply used one of the hospice phones.

Finally, guided by forces of which she is unaware, she comes to a booth from which she can look across the street and see the beautifully landscaped front of a church. That it is a Protestant church does not matter to her. It is a beautiful church – one that speaks of loving faith. She drops her coins into the slot, then realizes that she can not remember the number, takes a little spiral notebook from her purse, and hesitantly dials her mother. "I'd like to meet him," she announces without introduction.

"What?" Mary's response comes out automatically. She recognizes her daughter's voice and hears the words, but she can not connect to the meaning. She feels as if the wind had been knocked out of her.

"I'd like to meet him," Kathleen repeats. Her tone is flat. Her voice is uncompromising.

"Of course. I can't tell you how much this means ... Will you come for dinner?" Mary is flustered, excited, and scared.

"Where?"

"His, Arnie's, apartment. I can't really cook or entertain here. There isn't enough room. I don't have a kitchen. I'm so happy that you ..."

"If that's what you want?" Kathleen interrupts. There is a hint of hesitation in Kathleen's voice. Mary wonders if her daughter isn't sure of herself or if she isn't sure of the sincerity of Mary's excitement.

"I really do."

"Don't you need to talk with him first?"

Mary laughs. "I'm sure he'll be as happy as I am," she blurts out. He's been asking and wanting to meet you – you and Sean. I'm really glad you called," she says as if the excitement in her voice didn't already make that clear.

Mary gives Kathleen Arnie's address, and they agree on Saturday evening. She wants to offer that Arnie will pick Kathleen up, but she senses that this would not be welcomed by her daughter. They say goodbye. Then Mary, shaking with fear-filled anticipation, calls Arnie to give him the good news.

Arnie has been well aware of Mary's fears that Kathleen might never come around – that she would never be reconciled with her daughter. Mary had shared the details of her disastrous visit to the hospice and her realization of how terribly and deeply she has hurt Kathleen over the years. He is excited by this turn of events, but he is also worried – worried that another devastating interaction may lay ahead, one which he will not able to control and from which he will not be able to protect the woman whom he has come to love so deeply.

He says nothing of his trepidations. "Of course, that will be wonderful," is all that he does say. His concerns will keep him up that night, but he keeps them to himself.

Arnie keeps his qualms to himself during the days before Kathleen's visit. He and Mary clean his apartment. Mary tries to impose some order on his maze of books and journals but settles for stacking them on shelves. His apartment, like the man, is comfortable and lived in. Mary realizes that this is more than sufficient and that if there were more it would probably alienate Kathleen as showy and unnecessary. Still, a part of her worries that something will not be enough.

Mary wants to cook the meal, but Arnie is having none of that. He plans to do the cooking while Mary and Kathleen talk.

Saturday arrives. It is a cold, blustery day, the kind of day that tells people that autumn is coming to a close and that winter is fast approaching. The bone-chilling rawness of the wind coming off the harbor inspires Arnie to buy a PrestoFlame log for the fireplace in his apartment – a fireplace that is seldom lit. He moves the table in front of the fireplace, covers it with a linen cloth and matching napkins left over from his marriage, and sets it with his best china and stainless – neither of which are of particularly high quality having been purchased as a reflexive jab at having been left to fend for himself. He puts two bottles of white wine in the refrigerator. He can't afford great wine, but he is sure they will do.

Dinner is to be roasted chicken with wild rice stuffing, peas, tossed salad with a simple homemade vinaigrette, and fresh fruit for dessert. He doesn't want to seem to be trying to impress, yet he definitely wants Kathleen to be impressed. He feels as if he is once again a young man about to meet one of Mary's parents rather than her daughter. There is this lingering, nagging sense that he must obtain Kathleen's approval.

There was no need to have worried. They eat, but neither woman tastes the food. The emotions filling the room are far too powerful for the mere senses of taste and smell to interfere.

The dam has burst. Kathleen pours out her feelings of guilt, of God's and Mary's condemnation. Mary can only reach out and hug her daughter. There are no words strong enough to make sense of Kathleen's pain – none that can express the love of a mother who feels so much hurt for her child and so much blame for causing that child's pain. The ache of reconciliation is almost more than Mary can bear. Simultaneously, its sweet happiness sets her heart into a song of joy. It is a moment of catharsis. It is a moment of sublime gladness.

Over dinner Kathleen talks and talks. She talks about Max and about the woman who had followed him in Saint Michael's room. She tells of her own doubts about God and about the nature of Heaven.

After she has finished expressing her own troubled views, Kathleen turns to Arnie. "Do you think it's a cosmic joke?" she asks. The words come out in short staccato blasts – as if they are bullets coming from the muzzle of a rifle.

Arnie nearly chokes on a forkful of stuffing. "I hope not. I hope there's a reason."

Mary wants to reassure them all, especially herself. "Perhaps the reason is..." She doesn't know how to finish. The pregnancy of the silence mixed with the intensity of the issue sets the three of them to uncomfortable laughter. The laughter sweeps through the room like a cleansing breeze. It is followed by a long silence as the three slowly eat – chewing well on both their food and their thoughts.

Finally, Kathleen breaks the silence. "Sometimes I've wondered if you could understand the Hell you and the Church have condemned me to."

"I never meant to, Kathleen. The Church teaches us certain things. I didn't know a way around them. Either we're good Catholics or we're not. I never questioned."

"Well, I want to question. It isn't fair. It wasn't fair for me to lose my baby. It wasn't fair for John to walk out. And it certainly wasn't fair that I had no hope of remarrying or having children. I can care for the people who are dying. I cared for Max – he was special, and I learned from him – I learned how to see the joke in life. But, but caring for others, that just isn't enough. I hate the Church, and a part of me," Kathleen's voice which has been growing louder and more intense suddenly quavers, "hates you."

"There's a part of me that hates myself," Mary sobs. "I can't give you a reason, not for your losses, not for Sean's, not for anything."

"Maybe we're all Job," Arnie inserts. "Maybe we're all Job trying to play Auntie Mame."

Mary chuckles through her tears.

"Who's Auntie Mame?" asks Kathleen.

Arnie takes a well-worn copy of the book from his shelves. "Read this." He thinks for a moment. "Read it out loud so Max can hear. Wherever he is, I'm sure he'll appreciate it. His spirit, his soul – he'll appreciate it." He smiles, and Kathleen feels his warmth and reassurance.

Into the night they talk. Mary tells Kathleen that she loves Arnie. Arnie tells Kathleen that he loves Mary. Kathleen tells them both and herself that she wants to be free to love.

They talk about Sean. Then they talk about Sean Senior and Mary's conviction that he is in Heaven and now understands the importance of enjoying life. Kathleen asks about her unborn child and Mary answers, without hesitation, "She's in Heaven, too."

Hearing her mother say that reassures Kathleen. It has never occurred to her that Mary might not believe in the horribleness of that helpless soul's wandering aimlessly through the eternity of Limbo.

"Kathleen, why haven't you found somebody since your divorce?" Arnie knows the answer to his question, but he wants to play devil's advocate. More importantly, he wants to see Mary's reaction to his un-Catholic views.

"I'm still married in the eyes of the Church. You know that. I'm sure my mother's explained it to you." Kathleen speaks with the weight of two thousand years on her shoulders.

"I'm not sure that the Church really teaches that, but if that is your understanding, well – then leave the Church." As the words pass his tongue, Arnie knows that he has taken the responsibility and has said the inexpressible. He can hear the labored breathing as Mary tries to compose herself.

"Leave the Church?" Mary's voice seems higher pitched than usual. "Leave the Church?" Her face grows red, and her hands begin to tremble. Then Mary thinks of the minister who had comforted her. Her visage relaxes as if caressed by angels. "There are other churches, Kathleen. There are good people in them." Mary does not think about it, but in that moment she has denied a lifetime of belief and prejudice.

"In my Father's house there are many mansions," quotes Arnie.

Kathleen sits in wide-eyed horror and happiness as she realizes that her world has just been transformed – that change is possible.

* * *

PrestoFlame logs burn bright but they don't burn that long. As the ashes in the fireplace fold into nothingness, Arnie drives the two women home. First, he drops Kathleen at the hospice. "Tomorrow morning I'm sleeping late," she says as she gets out of the car. She knows that this is a hidden declaration of her new freedom.

"Good idea," Mary responds. "It's been a long and wonderful evening."

"And very draining," Arnie adds.

Arnie heads for Mrs. Callaghan's.

"Stop for a minute," Mary asks almost in a whisper.

He pulls to the side of the street. Mary reaches over and kisses him on the mouth. Her lips linger against his. "Thank you," she says as she finally pulls away.

"You're welcome." They hug for minutes. Finally, Arnie starts to put the car in drive and to pull away from the curb.

"Let's go back to your apartment," Mary suddenly suggests.

Arnie is flabbergasted. It takes a moment for him to respond. Finally: "If you're sure? I don't want you to have regrets afterwards."

"I'm sure. I don't think I've ever been surer of anything." The sparkle in her eyes reflecting the streetlight ahead of them tells him that she is indeed sure – more than sure, Mary is clearly happy – happy with her own excited wanting.

* * *

There is a moment's flicker of hesitation as she pulls her slip over her head. That is the only one. Mary Flanagan is just as hungry for the physical love between them as Arnie. Until that evening she has suppressed the awareness of that hunger. She has kept it locked inside – inside a vault that had accreted over years of self-denial – years of unthinking faith. But now it is aroused. It burns more brightly, more warmly than Mary could ever have imagined.

Perhaps Max, looking down from Heaven, might have been laughing at the two middle-aged lovers standing naked at the foot of Arnie's bed. This is not a moment of physical beauty or of sexual pyrotechnics. This is not the heedless force of suddenly released lust. It is simply a moment of love – love that requires expression – that demands consummation.

They stand hugging one another and saying nothing. Slowly, they stroke each other's body, feeling the nooks and crannies that have been hidden so long. Finally, with one coordinated movement – almost as if it has been choreographed – they lie on the bed. They lie and hold each other tightly as if terrified of ever being parted.

Neither the cold analytic purposefulness of Arnie's marriage nor the stolid wholesome, unbending love between Mary and Sean had prepared either of them for the intensity of this night. Their hands ply careful channels along each other's bodies. From time to time, one of them stops the ceaseless exploration to lean over and kiss the other.

Their kisses caress places that have too long been ignored. For the first time in her life Mary experiences the exciting pleasure of a man kissing her nipples; and she enjoys the strange saltiness of this loving man's body – not just his face and lips, but his arms, and chest, and buttocks. And Arnie, too, is experiencing the electricity of love. He feels his manhood swell and raise itself to new attention. His penis becomes tumescent and it challenges him with its eagerness. When he is sure that they are both ready, he carefully rolls himself on top of Mary. So very gently, using his hand to guide it lest he cause her pain, he inserts his penis into Mary's vagina.

"Ohhh," she moans with soft pleasure.

"Ahhhh," he responds.

More than those, words are not necessary.

When Mary awakens the next morning, her first thoughts are that Sean had never made love with her, that they had only had sex. Her second thoughts are of the Church. She will not be going to Saint Margaret's that morning – not for mass and not for confession. In fact, she doesn't think she will be going to confession for a quite a while; nor does she feel the need. She has no sense that she has sinned: there is nothing to confess – there is only love, its consummation, and its continued desire – such sweet, comfortable desire.

# Chapter Seven

"That's amazing!" Sean is sitting in the lounge. He is watching one of the institute's motivational videos. The center has visited a number of their alumni and filmed them living productive and, to some extent, independent lives. Men and women with less range of motion than he are driving specially designed vans, doing phone sales, even working in offices. Sean watches and can feel a renewed desire for independence.

The video ends with a sunrise and a song from The Sound of Music. Then one of the center's encouraging slogans is superimposed on the dawning day: "The difficulties of life should make us better, not bitter."

"Cool," Sean thinks to himself, "I like that one."

Sean doesn't spend much time watching television these days. He is too busy working. Physical therapy, occupational therapy, group therapy: these are the stuff of seven days a week. The only one in which he doesn't try to take an active part is the group therapy. Sean Flanagan hadn't been brought up to indulge himself in introspection or to do a lot of talking.

The recreational time that is available is spent either in some type of physical activity such as wheelchair soccer or in the community getting used to navigating through a world of unintentional barriers. Some barriers are physical, like a sidewalk without a curb cut. Many more are psychological, such as the stares of passersbys and the overly solicitous offers of help.

Before, when he was still at home with his mother, Sean had seen himself as totally limited. Now that he is trying to master his life, he is unwilling to accept his physical limitations. He is determined to take charge of the remainder of his life.

Before the accident, before Vietnam, Sean had never accepted limits, and he doesn't want to accept any now. But, obviously, there are many. Although physical therapy had improved the range of motion in his right arm and added some small amount of dexterity to his hand, his left arm remains useless. Eating is a chore that sometimes requires assistance – assistance that he must reluctantly accept. Deliberately the dietitian includes the difficult foods like steak and corn on the cob. When it is necessary, he is learning, you ask for help. He is learning that pride destroys freedom – that real independence must include accepting dependency.

It is easiest for Sean when Karen is on duty. They have developed a special camaraderie. On the plane from Boston, Karen had talked about her younger brother, who has cerebral palsy. An inexperienced doctor had used forceps during the delivery, and Johnny was left unable to walk without braces. Karen had been her brother's legs until she took a health course in high school and learned that there was a better way. That realization had inspired her to become a physical therapist. She has been working her way through school as an aide, which also means that she is getting the practicum credits she will need for a license. Her brother, who is now in high school, plans to become a lawyer. "No," she says, "he isn't interested in medical malpractice. He wants to practice criminal law – probably from watching too many Perry Masons."

Everybody likes Karen. She has an easy smile and a no nonsense approach to problems. The director has already made it known that she will have a job as a regular therapist as soon as she finishes her training. The residents also love her. It seems as if each month at least one of the male residents propositions her. She fends them off with a combination of straight forwardness and warmth.

"You're a great guy, just not my Mr. Right."

"You'll find your girl soon. I'm sure of it. It's just not me."

Since no one expects her to say yes, it is all in fun and leaves everyone with a good feeling. At least the men can tell themselves that they have flirted with a good-looking woman, which makes them feel considerably more normal.

Sean never tries to flirt with Karen. His feelings for her are more real, and much more powerful. At night, in his dreams, when he can still run and climb and build, Sean lives a life that he shares with her. Sometimes he dreams of sex and sometimes of sitting around with friends talking about the things people talk about when they're sitting around that way. In some of his dreams there are children climbing trees and chasing golden retrievers. The girls look like Karen, and the boys have his sandy hair and her brown eyes. His favorite dream is a barbecue with him flipping burgers and sipping beer. In that dream, after the neighbors have gone and the kids are in bed, he and Karen make love on the living room floor.

There is ecstasy in those dreams. There is excitement. There is life's meaning.

The aides never say anything when they come in the mornings and find his pajamas wet with cum. Sometimes, when they get together in the staff room for a break, the staff talk about the sexual needs of the residents. Most of them wish there were a way to at least hire prostitutes and gigolos. Sometimes they joke about one of them winning the lottery and using the money to set up a sexual therapy program.

The center's administration has struggled uncomfortably with the issue. One aide had been fired for masturbating a resident even though she had begged the aide to do it – even though everyone agreed that the aide had honestly been trying to help.

Sexual contact may be against center policy, but love isn't. Sean doesn't know it, but Karen spends a lot of her free time dreaming about him. She isn't sure why. There have been other good looking guys around, and most of them haven't been in wheelchairs. But, there has been something about Sean from the first day – something very special. She likes his determination, but more than that she likes the fire she feels is glowing inside him.

There is passion in Sean, passion which hasn't known release since Vietnam. It isn't simply sexual energy although she can also sense the intensity of his libido. There is another greater passion: it is the zest for life combined with the toughness that his father had worked so hard to instill in him. Karen knows enough about Sean's life to know that Sean Senior would be proud of his son – proud of the way that Sean digs into the hard work of the center – proud of his angry determination to beat his handicaps. And, in her heart of hearts, Karen is proud of him, too – far prouder than she has ever been of any other resident – far prouder than the limits of her professionalism should have allowed.

Karen's dreams are more realistic than Sean's. She doesn't think of him without the chair or the dependencies. Those are part of her dreams. But, so are the sex, the children, the neighbors, and the joy.

Karen isn't sure how to make Sean aware of her feelings. Part of her simply wants to come right out and tell him, to go up to him and kiss him. But she knows that would only lead to her being fired – the rules are very clear. He will have to make the first move, and she will have to respond in a way that he can understand while no one else realizes what is going on between them.

Physical therapy is difficult and painful. The group therapy sessions can be even more painful – not physically but psychologically. The residents are encouraged to talk about their anger and about their many frustrations. Sex is a constant topic, not because they are incapable of sexual arousal but because the rest of the world can not see their sexuality. Sean doesn't talk about those frustrations. He is afraid that his feelings for Karen will come out if he does. Sometimes, when she is one of the aides in the therapy room, it becomes particularly difficult for him. In a way he is glad that so much of his body is inert. It feels as if every bit of him wants to shake in sexual excitement.

"What about you, Sean?" the therapist is pushing on him to take part. "Don't you have some fantasies? I understand that before ... that you used to be quite the stud."

The rest of the group laughs. There is a shared sense of embarrassment – embarrassment for Sean and for themselves.

Sean wants to conceal his dreams – to make believe they don't exist, but he knows that the aides have already told the therapist about his wet dreams. He knows that quadriplegics don't have privacy.

"Sometimes at night. It's like I'm back in junior high. I hate to think about it so when I wake up I just force myself to forget the whole thing." He wonders if the therapist knows that he is lying. More importantly, he wonders if Karen, who is sitting along the back wall of the room where she can move quickly to assist anyone who needs her, knows what is really in his mind.

"If you could have one day of being whole again, is there some girl you'd want to go after?"

Sean tries to figure out what the therapist knows. He resents the nosiness of the question. He responds, "All of them!"

"Come off it, Sean," his roommate cuts in. It isn't that Sean has shared his dreams with Joe. Joe isn't sure whom Sean wants, but he knows Sean is just as human as the next guy. Just because he and Sean are in wheelchairs doesn't mean they aren't normal – that they didn't have desires.

"What are you talking about?" Sean's defensiveness is palpable.

"About you, man. You went to Vietnam a normal horny guy. Nothing happened there to change that part of you so own up to it."

"Fuck you, Joe." Sean has turned a self-revealing embarrassed red.

"Come on Sean," Sandra cuts in. "We all know. At night when you dream, you're not in the chair then. None of us are. Whom do you want then?"

"You." Everybody laughs. Sandra is the oldest resident. If her family didn't have friends on the board, the center would never have taken somebody so old. That would have been a mistake. Sandra is not only as determined and hard working as anybody, but she also has a no nonsense attitude that helps keep everybody honest when they would all prefer to live in denial and fantasy.

At this moment Karen is hurting for Sean. She is also hurting for herself. She wants him to say something about her, something she can use to build her hopes and possibly their relationship.

"Sean, there has to be someone in those dreams of yours." Joe's tone is conciliatory, but he isn't letting Sean off the hook either. He is determined to meet the responsibility that all the residents feel towards each other.

"You do have those dreams don't you? The ones when you're back to normal." The psychologist knows that Sandra had been right, that they all had dreams of being whole. "Your feelings are part of the rehabilitation process. You know that, Sean. Someday you're going to have to come clean in here, but for now we're out of time. We'll get together again tomorrow."

The psychologist remains in his spot and writes his session notes as the chairs roll out of the room and toward the physical and occupational therapy rooms. There is still time for some more work before dinner.

The other aides have left behind the residents, but Karen has stayed. "Yes, Karen?" The psychologist looks up.

"I was wondering if you think he'll ever open up. I met his mother. I was the one who went to get him. She isn't the kind of woman who would believe in therapy." She pauses to find the right words. "A dyed-in-the-wool Catholic. You know. I'm sure she didn't teach him to talk about his feelings, certainly not about dreams."

"I understand, but he has to learn. Otherwise I'm not sure how he'll really do – not once he's out of here. He works hard, but effort isn't everything. He has to be able to connect to the world or he'll leave here and sink backwards. He needs somebody. Everybody does, but with a quad … well you understand."

She looks uncomfortable as she nods and turns to leave.

"Karen." The psychologist almost whispers her name. The woman turns back. "Speaking of feelings, you have a lot for him, don't you?" he asks.

Except for a blush Karen doesn't respond.

He repeats his question "You have a lot of feelings for him, don't you?"

She hesitates for a moment unsure if she will be getting herself, or worse, Sean into trouble. "Does it show?"

"Not too badly. Certainly not in your words, but in your voice – that's another matter."

"Yeah, I do. Is that bad?" She hopes the psychologist has heard her real questions: "Will it get him in trouble?" "Will I hurt his rehab?" "Will I hurt myself?"

"That's up to you." The psychologist sets his own wheelchair into motion.

# Chapter Eight

After a lifetime of religiosity, a lifetime of candles and masses, of confessions and penance, Mary is not worrying about absolution – not any more. Her mind is on Arnie. Her worries are about their shared happiness and on how to improve what is already so truly grand. They have practically been living together. Amelia Callaghan has asked her a few times when she will be moving out. "I don't want to lose you as a boarder. For one thing, you're an easy keeper. You're never here. You're always at that professor's house." She always refers to Arnie as "that professor." He's a man, and as such she doesn't want to accept him as a real person. "But it seems silly to me your keeping these rooms and spending all your time at his place."

"I know, Amelia; but he hasn't asked me to move in yet."

"Why don't you push him a smidgen? Lord knows he's in love with you. There hasn't been a week gone by that he hasn't sent you some present or other."

"I'm really happy." Mary's happiness shows on her face. Most days it seems as if she is glowing.

"Now that's something everybody knows. Why even Mrs. Stevens...."

"Who?"

"That goes to show what I'm talking about. She's the new woman, the one who took Sally's room. Well even she mentioned how happy you always look. 'What's she on?' That's what she said. 'What's she on that she's always so happy?' So Jane pipes up, 'Love, Mrs. Stevens. Mary's in love with her professor.' Well, didn't that set the table to laughing? It was a good pot roast, too. I feel bad charging you for those meals and you never eating them."

Mary presses her friend's hand. "Don't you be worrying yourself about it. When he's ready I'll move in. Until then, I love having this place, and especially you. You know that you're my best friend – possibly the best I've ever had. There was Lois. I do miss her, but I could never have... She would never have understood. I mean her idea of fun was Canasta, Bingo, maybe going to a sale at Jordan's, not …" In her discomfort, Mary carefully wipes her glasses clean, gently sets them back on her nose, and fluffs the feathers of her hair.

"She wouldn't have understood the physical part?"

Mary nods in agreement.

Until Arnie, Mary Flanagan had never enjoyed her body. When she was a girl and after she had started menstruating, she had asked her mother what went on between a man and a woman. "Well," her mother had replied, "the woman lies on her back and closes her eyes, and the man shoves his thing in her. It doesn't hurt too much and it makes them happy. So, when it comes your time to get married, you be sure to make your man happy."

That was as close to sex education as Mary had ever come except for the nuns repeatedly telling her that the purpose of sex was to have children. "It isn't pleasant," Sister Andrew had told them. "Perhaps in Paradise it was, but after the Fall – now that's a different story altogether. Then God made it a pain for women. It was Eve's sin, and now it's our curse."

Mary's mother had shown her how to use old sheets to make padded rags to catch the monthly flow of blood. She told her daughter that the bloodstained rags were to be washed carefully and separately from any clothing. Between uses they were to be stored in a special box at the back of the closet. Her mother had told Mary that it was special blood put inside her womb by the Holy Mother to cleanse it so it would be ready for a new soul. "That's why when it's that time of the month, you must not. No matter how he begs. Husbands have to understand. It would be a sin, a mortal sin. Now you remember that Mary." Her mother had stood firm and uncomfortable as she said this, and Mary had known it was as true and right as the words of God.

Before she and Sean had married, they had met with the priest. He had told her that a good wife met her husband's needs, kept the house, and raised the children. If you were a good Catholic, you tried to have children, as many as you could. There was no other reason for sex. He had been quite clear about that. There was no divorce, he had added; marriage was for life. "Therefore, before you come to church, kneel yourselves down and take an honest look at your love. Ask yourselves if it will pass the test of time because it's time that tests a marriage and tests it well."

Sean had been no more prepared to be a lover than Mary. The first night he had groped at her as if they were wrestling. When she had cried out in pain, he had exclaimed with satisfaction. Somewhere in his adolescence he had been told that the proof of a man's potency was his ability to make the woman scream. That night he had felt affirmed.

Except when she was bleeding or very pregnant, Mary had never turned him away. Neither had she ever had an orgasm or even a moment of physical joy. Now, seeing the pleasure that Arnie finds in their lovemaking, Mary wonders if Sean had enjoyed their sexual grappling any more than she.

It is the pleasure of her physical relationship with Arnie more than anything that leads Mary to question the Church. One day she wonders if Jesus and Mary Magdalene had had a sexual relationship. The thought terrifies her. At first she decides that she should stop seeing Arnie – that what is going on must be evil. Then she thinks that perhaps love and sexuality are part of being truly human. "If Christ was human and God, he shouldn't have missed out on the good human parts," she reasons. Secretly she hopes that He and Mary had as wonderful love as she is now sharing with Arnie. She wonders what Father Frank would have to say about this, but she knows it is a question which she will never ever raise.

She still occasionally goes back to Saint Margaret's – drawn there by habit and a need to remember from whence she had come, but she doesn't go for confession and never goes to the rail to receive the sacraments. At the end of the mass she leaves by a side door and avoids the priest's questions and those she might like to ask him.

Sometimes she goes to the church around the corner from Amelia's. She has learned it is Presbyterian. Once in a while Kathleen has gone to the Presbyterian Church with her. There Mary does take communion, and it seems to her that the transubstantiation of the bread and wine of the Protestants is just as real, or not, as that at a Catholic mass. "'Tis my faith that makes the difference," she tells herself. This is a Host that she can accept, for it is not tied to following the Church's rules. It is a gift – a gift from Christ – a gift from His love.

Sometimes Arnie has gone to church with her. It doesn't matter to him which one they attend. He never kneels, and he never receives the Host. After the service, he talks about the sermon. At first it had seemed strange to Mary and Kathleen to think about the sermons. They had both grown up believing that the purpose of church was the sacrament. People were supposed to leave the mass thinking about Christ's sacrifice. It had seemed that sermons were only for the purpose of restating the rules. Now they find themselves discussing and questioning ideas.

At times there are clear differences between the sermons at the two churches. At first Mary had wanted Arnie to explain away the differences or to tell her which was the right version. As she has become a freer thinker, Mary has given up looking for simple answers. Instead, she rereads the passages from The Bible that have been used and tries to reach her own conclusions. She is still taking adult education classes. American History and English Literature are her latest courses. Some of those readings and discussions also made her uncomfortable, but that, she knows, is one price of a real education. Arnie tells her, "New ideas take a lot of work, and the old ones fight like hell to keep their place."

The physical love that Mary and Arnie are sharing opens the door to a new world. She remembers a dream which she relates to Arnie while they are sitting in his living room.

"I was carrying this heavy object – I'm not quite sure what it was – up these steep stairs. They were real narrow, too. I kept telling myself that I had to reach the top of the stairs even though I was so very tired. Then I came to a landing. The stairs kept going up, but I stopped to rest. There was a set of doors, like the sliding doors of an elevator. I couldn't open them, but I wanted to. I put down whatever it was I was carrying, and the doors opened. There was a beautiful field filled with wild flowers and smelling like lilacs. As I went into the field, the doors closed behind me, and then I started to dance." She gets up and tries as best she could to imitate a ballet.

Arnie smiles and also gets up. They dance about the room in a music-less parody of ballet. Then they reach for each other and swaying softly in time to music, which they alone can hear, the two lovers embrace. Arnie gently nibbles at her left ear, and Mary sighs with contentment. They kiss deep and long, their tongues touching in tender greeting. Then they start to laugh.

"What are you laughing at?"

"I feel like we're in a movie. We're at that magic point when you should sweep me up into your arms and carry me into the bedroom."

"I had the same image. But, if I tried, my back would go. I'd end up in bed for a month."

"It's a shame that we didn't meet years ago when you might have...."

"Might-have-beens don't count. Let's be thankful for today."

"And tomorrow," Mary adds.

"And many more tomorrows."

They hold hands, and he leads her into the bedroom. They do not fumble with each others clothing but quickly take off their own like an old married couple excited by the closeness of years rather than the adrenaline of the moment.

They lie naked on the covers listening to the steam hiss in the radiators. Then they roll toward one another and couple lying on their sides. The energy of their passion slowly rolls them over until Mary is on top of Arnie. He reaches his head up from the pillows and kisses her lightly on the nose. It is a tender, affectionate kiss telling her that his love is much, much more than sexual.

"Oh, Arnie. I love you." She pauses. "You know what?"

"What's that?"

"I love loving you. I never understood that when they were saying it on soap operas, but now I do. I do love loving you!" She giggles like a schoolgirl.

The phone rings. They try to ignore it. "It's probably some sales pitch," Mary suggests.

"I wonder if they know when the worst times are. When Robert was a baby, he always started to cry when his mother and I were going to make love. These computers are probably programmed to do the same thing."

He realizes that Mary had grown very still. "What's the matter?"

"I don't like to think about it – about you and her. It hurts me."

"I'm sorry, but she was part of my life just as you were married to Sean. We can't make our pasts go away. We can only make our present beautiful and try to make our future even better than that."

"I know you're right." She sits up and reaches for her glasses. The phone is still ringing. "Maybe you had better answer it."

He reaches over and picks up the receiver. "Hello." He listens for a moment.

"What?" he asks in disbelief.

There is a pause as he listens again. Then Arnie asks, "Kathleen, are you sure?"

"He did?" Mary fears for the worst at these words. What, she wonders, could have happened to make her daughter call them so late. She thinks of her son, and wonders if something awful had happened to him.

"I didn't have any idea. When did he call?"

Mary searches Arnie's face for clues. As he talks, she frantically tries to get his attention. She feels as if she will burst at any moment.

Finally Arnie says, "Here, tell your mother." He hands Mary the phone. As he does so, he mutters, "Well, I'll be damned!"

Kathleen is telling Mary the news. Sean, not reaching Mary at the boarding house, had called his sister. He will soon be returning to Boston to start planning his future. Karen would be coming with him to assist, and he had a great surprise for them.

Once she has hung up the phone, Mary sits in silence – half stunned and half elated. She has not yet told Sean the extent of her relationship with Arnie, and she wonders how he will react. When speech finally returns to her, she asks Arnie what he thinks.

"He'll be happy for us both," is Arnie's answer.

"Will he?" muses Mary. "I doubt it." She is sure her son will condemn them not simply because of his religious upbringing – in truth he had never really been much of a Catholic, but because he can never hope to have the intimacy which they share with such great happiness.

"It must be so hard on him," Mary observes.

"What?"

"Not having a relationship."

"Then who is this Karen?"

"Just one of the aides. She was the one who came to get him. I guess she gets to return him, too." For a moment Mary flashes back to Sean's head through the back window of the ambulette. It was the last time that she had seen him. She wonders if he has changed. She wonders how much he has changed.

There is a sudden twinge of fear – fear that he has not changed, fear that he will need her, fear of what she will have to give up. With that fear comes guilt – painful guilt.

"Just one of the aides?" Arnie questions.

She nods.

He hugs her tightly.

* * *

They were on a trip to the mall. The occupational therapy department had given each of the residents a list of items to buy, or at least to pretend to buy. The items were individualized, based on the emotional significance and the inherent difficulty of the objects as well as the length of time in the program of the resident. Sean had come a long way in the many months he had been in Minnesota. This day his task was to buy clothing: a shirt, pants, shoes and, most embarrassingly, underwear. It required his instructing salespeople as they try to help him. It meant publicly acknowledging his dependency on that help and at the same time maintaining his sense of control and his right to make decisions.

Karen had been assigned to follow him at a distance in case of difficulties, but Sean had handled the tasks far more quickly and easily than either he or the center's staff had expected.

"How'd I do?" he asked as he rolled up beside Karen outside the mall's ice cream shop.

"You were terrific."

"Her voice is so sweet," he thought. "I can hear angels singing in it." Out loud he asked, "Good enough for one more thing?"

"What's that?"

"To buy you a soda."

"Sure." Karen wondered if her excitement showed. Over the months her love for Sean had grown, but nothing had been said between them. Some times she had felt that he had been watching her. But, whenever she had turned to look back, his eyes had been averted and he had always seemed engrossed in whatever task he was supposed to be doing.

They ordered two sodas. Karen helped him place his soda in his drink holder and to insert his straw. They sat without drinking or talking. Finally, Sean broke the ice. "It seems like we haven't had a minute together since you came to Boston to get me."

"We've worked together lots of times." Karen knew that her answer sounded disingenuous, but she hadn't been able to think of anything else to say.

"I don't mean that. I mean time together, you know, just us."

"I guess that's true. Did you want to?"

"Yeah." Sean was – at that moment – almost glad that he was paralyzed. He was terrified by the power of his wants – his desire to leap across the table and grab this woman.

"So did I." Karen felt the blood suffusing her face. Still, she fought the urge to look away.

"You did?" Beads of perspiration were working their way down his forehead. He felt the force of his excitement in his genitals. It still seemed so strange to him that he could sense that arousal and not be able to feel other things like the neurologist's poking or the occasional spontaneous jerking movement of a leg or even the need to urinate. When he had first experienced the sensation of an erection, Sean had wondered if it was only fantasy. Then he had seen the impression of his erect penis under his pants and had known that was one sensation that was truly his.

"Sure." Karen felt like she was on fire. She had always blushed so easily. It had been a great source of embarrassment and of teasing as an adolescent. It had always seemed silly to her that she would blush because she was embarrassed and then be embarrassed because she had blushed. "Am I as red as I feel?" she wondered. "Does Sean see how embarrassed I am?"

"You're sweating," she commented. "Let me wipe it off."

She reached over with a napkin hoping that she was obscuring Sean's view of her face.

"No, don't. I'll do it myself."

"I'm sorry. That was really dumb of me," She blushed even more, but she had, what seemed, a more acceptable reason.

Meanwhile, Sean was thankful that she had given him a moment to regain his composure – a moment during which his arousal might diminish.

It took a few moments for Sean to accomplish what for most people would have been the simplest of tasks, wiping his own face.

When he had finished, he stammered: "I thought... No, I hoped..." Sean could not get himself to complete the sentence.

"What? Sean, what do you hope?" Karen's tone was confused but demanding. In her heart, she was also caught up with hope.

"That you like me," Sean was finally able to stammer out.

"Of course I do," was her immediate reply.

"No, I mean that you really like me." Sean wasn't sure that Karen understood.

"I do." Tears had formed in Karen's eyes. "More than I should. More than that. There's something special about you, about my feelings for you. I..."

"For you, too?" Sean interrupted. He wished that he could do something, anything to show how strongly he felt for her. Except for the re-arousal of his genitals, he had to settle for words. "Wow. I've been hoping and praying, but I've always been too afraid to say anything."

"Anything about what?" Sandra rolled up behind him.

"Nothing," Sean muttered.

"I'll bet I know," Sandra teased. "I'll bet you finally told Karen how you feel about her."

It was Sean's turn to blush. He now turned a bright red. "You don't know what you're talking about."

"The hell I don't. Do you think you've been fooling people? What do you say Karen?"

Karen had to think for a minute. She knew that her answer would be all over the center by supper. She said it anyway. "I say that I love Sean." She said it so emphatically that she surprised herself.

"You do?" If he had been capable of doing so, Sean would have leapt over the table and grabbed Karen in his arms. It was moments like these that being paralyzed really hit home. It took what seemed like hours to maneuver his chair around to Karen's side of the table. She leaned towards him, and they kissed on the lips – a long, lingering, delicate, and loving kiss.

To Sean it seemed like he had never kissed a girl before. He closed his eyes, and the intensity of the sensation raced though his brain. He felt as if he were on fire – but it was a fire of warmth and joy. It had been so long since he had felt such excitement and desire. Indeed, he had never really felt this way before. He felt so very alive that he would not have traded the moment for anything – not even for his spine to be suddenly healed.

When he opened his eyes, he realized how many people had been watching. He wondered what they were thinking, how they felt about an invalid kissing a pretty girl. He realized that he didn't care – that none of that mattered. He started to laugh. "At least I'll have something to say at the next group."

Sandra laughed, too. "I guess it's all over between us, lover boy."

"I guess so."

"Well, I won't say the better woman won just the luckier one."

Karen reached over and kissed him again. "Just in case you're wondering if I knew what I was doing," she whispered so that only Sean could hear.

"I was wondering if either of us knows what we're getting into," Sean responded more loudly.

"It's called love," Sandra answered for them both.

\* \* \*

Deliberately Sean did not tell Kathleen the day and hour of his flight. Karen and he had decided that they would get themselves set up in a hotel before letting Mary or Kathleen know they were actually in Boston.

A national and even international communication network exists for every identifiable group. This is equally true among the handicapped. A specially equipped van will be waiting for them at Logan Airport. A room with wheelchair accessible bathroom is reserved at a decent, but not overly expensive motel. Sean has phone numbers they can call for additional assistance if it is needed. Their bags are packed. They are ready to leave the next day. It is then that he has called, first trying his mother's boarding house and then his sister at the hospice staff residence.

Not only do Kathleen and Mary have no knowledge of how immediate Sean and Karen's arrival is or of the nature of their relationship, but also they have no idea that he is coming to Boston for job interviews. The invalid who had gone to Minnesota is returning ready to begin a new career – ready to take on life on its own terms.

There are three job interviews scheduled. One is with the state government monitoring compliance with regulations covering the rights of access for the handicapped. The second, with a pharmaceutical firm, is informational phone work. The third, which seems the most exciting, is helping newly handicapped people find resources and equipment they will need to make their lives work. Funded by a nonprofit agency, that job seems to Sean to offer the most meaning for his life.

The other thing that offers meaning for Sean at this moment is his wife's pregnancy. He and Karen were married six weeks ago. The service had been at the center. Karen's family had attended, but Sean had decided to not invite his. He wasn't sure they would accept a wedding performed by a Justice of the Peace. Sean had no way of knowing the changes that have been going on within them.

It had been a simple wedding. His roommate, Joe, had been Sean's best man. Karen had asked a delighted Sandra to be her matron of honor. Karen's brother had come back to Minnesota from college for the wedding, and he had thrown his arms around Sean expressing the family's delight that Karen had found a man whom she could truly love. "We may be on wheels," he had said, "but we're still men. Have a good life and many children."

The honeymoon had been a long weekend in a Minneapolis hotel. Despite his fantasies, it had surprised Sean how much sexual excitation lay within him. To his pleasure Karen had provided enough physicality for them both. It had been during that weekend that she had conceived.

A month later, when Karen's guesses had been confirmed by a gynecologist, Sean couldn't believe it.

Once he got passed the disbelief, once he realized that Karen was carrying his baby, it was as if Sean had been transported to a world beyond happiness. After years of thinking that he had lost his manhood in Vietnam, he was overjoyed to know that he had truly and completely found it again. Suddenly, the dam burst. He sobbed for some time. Then his sobs alternated with laughter until it seemed that he could hardly breathe. Finally, his tears and laughs had subsided into hoarse gasps and his face had broken into a shining smile.

For the last six weeks of his stay at the center, Sean and Karen shared what was called the honeymoon suite. This was a small apartment used as a last part of rehabilitation. There a resident, and spouse – if there was one, could practice living without the various supports of the center. Shopping, cooking, cleaning, and all the other bits which make up day to day life could be practiced, and the success of the center's rehabilitation work could be seen in the outcome. For Sean and Karen it had been a great success even though Sean, like so many of his predecessors in the suite, had to remind his bride that he could do many things himself and at times had to admit to himself that there were things that were beyond him.

It was during that time that phone calls had been made and resumes had been sent. At first, Karen had also been making job contacts. But four weeks into this last segment of Sean's rehabilitation, her pregnancy became more apparent. Indeed, the last two weeks had been spent with Sean holding her hand as she suffered morning sickness.

"I guess our roles have reversed a bit," he had observed.

"It just goes to show the wonders of the human spirit," she had replied.

The occupational therapy department – rising to the occasion – helped Sean learn skills for helping with the baby. They used a doll for practice. At first it had been a soft stuffed doll. Many times it had fallen to the floor. Later, when Sean became more adept, they switched to a more fragile, porcelain doll – one that would truly be injured if Sean were to let it drop.

It was at once a terrifying and exhilarating thought for him: fatherhood. He wondered how his mother would feel about being a grandmother, and he worried about Kathleen's reactions. How would she deal with his fatherhood when her own hopes for children had been so cruelly cut short?

The newlyweds had thought of staying in Minnesota, but Sean and Karen had decided that as bad as Boston's weather could be it was preferable to the long cold winters of the Midwest. And, perhaps most importantly, they realized that there were far fewer services for the handicapped in the East. They were determined to make a difference: to be a model for other couples facing similar difficulties. In a sense, their love had intensified and strengthened their idealism.

The center's van brought them, their luggage, Joe, Sandra, and a few other people to the airport. One of the well-wishers was the staff psychologist. He took Karen by the hand and gently pulled her away from the knot of people. "I just want to tell you that I wish you well."

"I know that. I wish you well, too." She turned back to the group still gathered around Sean and then, hesitating, turned back to the psychologist. "I know how you feel about me, Steve," she said. "I've always known. In fact, we may even have ended up together if Sean hadn't come along."

"But he did, and now you're going."

She bent down to kiss him and turned to walk back to her husband, the waiting plane, and their new life.

# Chapter Nine

"Mr. and Mrs. Flanagan, Yes Ma'am. I'll call them. Who should I say is here?"

Mary looks at the desk clerk. He seems a polite young man dressed in a clean white shirt and a tie that is slightly stained but properly held in place by a clip, not one of those tie tacks that remind her of shoe salesmen and insurance agents. "No, just Mr. Flanagan, Sean Flanagan."

"Yes, Ma'am. The gentleman in the wheelchair. He and Mrs. Flanagan, real nice people. Really in love, too. I hope my girl and I look half as happy when we get married."

"I don't understand. My son isn't married."

"I don't know, Ma'am; but I sure do hope so – for the baby's sake."

Mary blanches. "What baby?"

"The Missus. She sure seems pregnant to me. If he's your son, you're going to be a grandma – no question about that." He smiles at her, which only increases Mary's confusion.

Her mind is a whirligig of feelings. Concern and fear, anger and resentment, love and tenderness, anticipation and anxiety: they all spin within her; but the confusion is the strongest of all. Not knowing what else to do, she stands rooted and stares at the clerk.

"Do you want me to call them?" he asks.

All Mary can think is that she wishes Arnie were here with her, he would know what to do. "Wwwhat?" she stammers.

"Would you like me to call their room, to let them know that you're here?

"Oh..." She stands mute.

"Ma'am?"

"Yes. Yes. I suppose you'd better."

He calls a room and speaks into the phone. "They'll be right down. Why don't you sit over there? You might be more comfortable." He points to a grouping of leather covered furniture.

Mary continues to stare. She is still standing in that spot when Sean and Karen come out of the elevator.

"Mom," Sean calls. The sound of his voice pulls her from her trance, and Mary turns to greet her son and her new daughter.

Confused as she may be, mixed as her emotions may have suddenly become, at the moment of seeing Sean, Mary feels a wave of happiness. She is happy to have her son back. Much more, her heart is gladdened by the look in his face, the smile in his eyes, and the happiness in his voice.

Sean and Karen reach out to each other and exchange a tender touch. Then they continue forward to embrace her. As simply as that, Mary understands that this is a relationship of love, that theirs is a marriage of joy. She takes in Karen's already swelling belly, and the realization hits – she is going to be a grandmother.

Mary moves toward them. The three come together in the center of the lobby. It is as if a cone of love has come down and surrounded them.

They talk at once. It is a babel filled with laughter and delight.

It is only at night, when he and Karen are again alone, that Sean reflects on the changes in his mother.

Meanwhile, she, riding on the bus, traveling to Amelia's boarding house, is looking forward to the next day when they will be joined by Arnie. "I'm sure they'll get along great. I think Arnie will really enjoy having a grandchild. I know I will."

\* \* \*

The events swirling around her have changed Kathleen Flanagan. Although she still devotes herself to her work at the hospice and is still well loved by the dying patients, she no longer compulsively attends the religious services of the nuns. The need to punish her mother and God by proving her own worth has been replaced by an acceptance – a reluctant acceptance – but, nevertheless, an acceptance of the vicissitudes of life.

Also, Kathleen has become increasingly aware of a small voice that keeps urging her to take back her life – to find the joy to which she is entitled. In her mind there is that voice, and it sounds a lot like Max.

Kathleen often thinks of Max. Of all the people for whom she has cared at the hospice, he alone had given her a new perspective on life's meaning.

This day she and her mother are discussing one of Mary's courses. "Einstein said he couldn't believe God played dice with the universe," Mary quotes her professor.

"Dice, maybe not – jokes, definitely," Kathleen responds.

"Sometimes cruel jokes," adds Arnie who has been quietly reading in the corner.

Sean and Karen's marriage is not, however, a cruel joke in Kathleen's mind. She had unexpectedly been elated by Karen's pregnancy. "If I can't be a mother, at least I can be a good aunt," she had cooed as she held Karen in a close embrace.

"I don't exactly see you as Auntie Mame," Mary had commented. Both she and Kathleen had read the book at Arnie's urging. Both had offered their copies to Karen, who had surprised them by having already read it. "Life is a banquet," she had quoted.

"And most poor suckers are starving to death," they had finished in unison laughing in their shared pleasure.

This night they are once again discussing the impending baby, who has become so much a center of attention for them all. Kathleen, who has bought yet another new-born outfit, one covered in circus scenes, is talking about her expectations for the child. Her voice is pitched high in excitement and her arms are moving in sweeping anticipation. "You never can tell. Maybe a baby will loosen me up. Perhaps a trip to India or a safari to Africa to watch the great wildebeest migrations. We'll climb the Matterhorn. And of course, ice cream cones and circuses and lots and lots of spoiling."

Sean and Karen look puzzled. "Don't worry." Arnie having seen the quizzical look reassures. "Auntie Mames are good for kids."

"At least in the right dosage," adds Mary.

"Of course," Kathleen starts to reassure her brother and sister-in-law.

They are gathered in Amelia Callaghan's living room. Arnie's apartment is not at all accessible, and Amelia has a ramp to her back door. It had been installed years before for the wife of a previous owner – at a time when invalids were truly invalidated, when they were sent – like deliverymen, salesmen, beggars, and other undesirables – to back doors – away from the judging eyes of neighbors. Amelia is happy to have them. She likes feeling a part of

Mary's family even if her part is limited to making the tea and providing a meeting place.

"Amelia," Mary frequently says, "Why don't you join us?"

"I don't think so, dear. You have so much to work out for yourselves. I can give up a little space and a pot of tea for such a good friend."

Sean had been confused at first by the changes in his mother and sister. Their acceptance of his marriage has been strangely upsetting to him. Even though he does not believe in the church, he feels as if the scaffolding that had always held the structure of the family's life in place has suddenly collapsed.

One evening Sean shares this sense of loss with Karen. "It's weird. You know, if tomorrow I woke up and could walk, part of me would still miss this damn chair. I'd feel liberated – sure, it would be great. But, I'd still feel that a part of my life – a part of my self – would be missing. That's how I feel about how they've changed."

"They certainly are different from the way you described them – from the way your mother seemed when I first met her."

"From the way they were."

"But so are you." Karen reaches over and runs her fingers through his hair. "Just promise me you won't go bald."

He laughs. "Well, my father didn't, they always said I favored him."

"I wonder if our son will look like you."

"Why are you so sure we'll have a son?" Karen has made a number of similar comments over the weeks since they had learned of her pregnancy.

"A mother knows those things."

"Does she indeed?" To the best of his ability Sean reaches out to hug her, and Karen sits in his lap. "It's a good thing I have a wheelchair built for three."

"More I hope. I'm not planning to stop with one."

Sean has been offered all three jobs for which he had applied, and they are now looking for a suitable apartment. "Give me a chance to catch up first."

"At least umm, let me see, seventeen months."

"Are you sure you're not the Catholic here?"

"OK, will you settle for two years?"

They were both giggling like kids. "Let's go to bed."

"Only if you agree."

"To what?" Sean asks.

"To more kids."

"If you still want another one when this one is two, I'll be game. Just remember I don't do diapers too well." He steers his chair into the bathroom, and Karen hops off. Despite Sean's limitations, the quality of their physical life, their sexual relationship, exceeds any of her adolescent imaginings.

"I love you!" she calls after him.

"I don't blame you," he calls back.

"I really mean it," she calls to the closing door.

"So do I," Sean calls back. Then he opens the door and adds, "And, I love you."

* * *

Kathleen is happy for her brother and Karen and for her mother and Arnie. The only one for whom she is not happy is herself. "There has to be someone for me," she thinks. "I've done enough penance for a failed marriage. I've suffered enough for a lost womb. My life doesn't have to be a wasteland, too."

Kathleen isn't sure if the changes in Mary's views will extend to accepting divorce, to accepting remarriage. Much as she wants to, she is afraid to ask; but she is quite sure that she, too, has a right to happiness. She knows that the problem will be finding the right person. Her marriage with John had been a disaster and had ended in misery. Mary has obviously been lucky. So has Sean. If she meets someone, will she be as fortunate? There is no way to know. There is only acceptance – acceptance of the endless joke that is life.

Kathleen has from time to time looked through the personal ads in the newspapers, and she wonders if they ever work. Her pessimistic side thinks that it must just be a bunch of perverted and stupid fools who are involved. There is no one to ask – no friends who are dealing with same type of problem.

At times she sees what appear to be eligible men at the Presbyterian Church, which she now sometimes attends; but she isn't sure how to approach them. She decides to talk with the minister, Patricia Michaels.

"Why don't you come to our single adults meetings?" The minister suggests.

"I guess I'm not sure I'll fit in, Pat."

"Isn't that the real reason you haven't done anything? You're afraid you won't fit in anywhere. I believe that everyone fits in somewhere. Everyone has a place in God's plan. Don't worry about where you'll fit in. Try everything! Just don't put yourself in danger. Try everything and you'll find the right spot."

"Even personal ads?"

"Why not? Just use good judgment. You know, meet someplace public the first time. Don't give out your personal ... You know what I mean.

"Kathleen, your mother was very lucky. She just happened to go up to the right stranger. Your brother, too. He was incredibly lucky that Karen came into his life. They could have sent anyone, but thankfully ... Most people have to do a lot of searching to find that someone who seems right. It's time for you to start searching."

"I know."

"Usually you just have to kiss a lot of frogs before you find a prince."

"I don't think I mind the frogs, but the toads are another matter." They both chuckle. Kathleen turns suddenly serious. "How do I tell? How do I know if a guy loves me or if he's ...?"

"There's an old saying, one I grew up with." The minister smiles in reassurance. "'The goal of love is to give; the goal of lust is to get.' Make sure he wants to give."

"That sounds too ... I don't know ..."

"Dramatic?"

"Yes, dramatic."

"It is." She smiles again. "Do you like opera?"

"I don't know. I've never gone to one."

"Well, how about soap operas."

"I watch them some."

"Well, life is a comic soap opera. Everything seems so dramatic; but if you take a broader perspective, look at it from outside, then it's all kind of silly just because it is so dramatic. You just have to keep your perspective, your sense of humor."

"Did you know a man named Max?" Kathleen asks.

"I've known a few Maxes. Why?"

"He was a patient at the hospice. He always tried to see the humor in life."

"A wise man."

"When does that adult club meet?"

"Wednesdays from seven thirty till ten."

"Thanks, Pat. I'll see you then."

Kathleen leaves the manse feeling reassured. At some level she had expected Pat Michaels to discourage her, to tell her it wasn't worth trying. She also feels scared. Kathleen has never felt like she fit in. Her ex-husband had always joked that he had chosen her because she was such a wallflower. "I'll never have to worry about you," he'd say, "You'll be hidden away behind something whenever a guy comes along." It had made him feel secure, but Kathleen had hated the fact that he was right.

She realizes that part of her love of hospice work is the guaranteed acceptance. She knows the dying patients would grab hold of anyone who cares enough to come along. If they need her to conduct them across the river of death, she needs them to give her a sense of life.

"I'll make myself go," she promises herself. "I'll make myself go even if it kills me." With her determination firmly in place, Kathleen boards the bus that will take her back for her shift at the hospice.

It is a chilly day, but there is a hint of the coming spring in the air. "You can smell the spring," says the stranger who sits down next to her.

"Yes," agrees Kathleen.

"It always makes me feel younger, like there's more promise in the world." He is an elderly man, somewhat shabbily dressed. With her years of experience at the hospice, Kathleen can tell that he is also unwell.

"I hope you're right."

"You can count on it, Miss. There's always promise in the springtime." He rises and shuffles holding on to the seat backs for support to the front of the bus. As he gets off at the next stop, the man turns and waves to Kathleen. As she waves back, Kathleen feels a surge of reassurance. She can feel her back straighten. "Angels take on many appearances," she tells herself.

"If he can have hope, then I can, too," she thinks. It seems like the flowers will be blossoming any day now as she walks through the gates of The Sisters of Mercy.

\* \* \*

Mary and Arnie are taking a drive north along the coast. Mary loves to take long rambling rides – something that Sean had never been willing to do. "I drive all the time," he would say. "Why would I be wanting to drive in my free time?" And, Mary had never learned to drive. Indeed, the thought of learning had never entered her mind.

Mary had been forced to agree with her husband's logic – or at least to accept it. So their old black Ford was only used for necessities. After Sean's death it had been given to charity – a Catholic charity of course.

Arnie follows old Route One as it leaves the highway at Danvers and wends its way toward Newburyport. Once in that old port city, they drive along High Street and admire the historic houses with their widows' walks. The houses are at once beautiful and well maintained and at the same time forlorn in their commemoration of a long past and difficult way of life.

"I wonder if I'd have liked a seafaring life." Arnie muses.

"I can't imagine you cooped up on one of those old whaling boats, and I certainly don't want to think of myself standing up there," Mary gestures toward the widow's walk on the top of one of the largest houses, "waiting for you to return or for you…" She pauses for a painful moment. "Or for you to not return." A shudder runs through her body. "How awful that must have been – to see your husband's ship coming in to port, to run down to the docks with children in tow, and then to learn that he was not on board, that he was never coming back to you. Or, even worse, to hear of its foundering – all souls lost at sea. Those poor women." Her voice breaks as she moans, "Oh, those poor, unfortunate women."

Arnie tries to change the heavy mood. "But wouldn't I have some grand tales to tell you of places you'd never been, people you'd never seen, whales big enough to stave in a boat?"

"About getting seasick?" Mary winks at him. "I don't think there were many Jewish whalers, and I don't think you'd have been the exception."

They both laugh. The truth is that Arnie had been violently ill the one time he had ever gone deep-sea fishing. "I stayed green for a week," he retells whenever the subject comes up. It has become something of a family joke. Sean and Karen love to go out on a fishing boat whenever they have the chance. Sean has always loved the sea and boats. And Karen, despite her Minnesota roots, has learned to share his enthusiasm. Once they had even coaxed Mary and Kathleen into going out with them, but Arnie had demurred saying that he was determined to never step foot in a boat again.

"I guess I'd be better at wailing at that wall in Jerusalem. That kind of wailing is something that Jews have lots of chances to practice."

Mary can see the dark clouds crossing behind his eyes. "He thinks of those camps so often," she says to herself. "Everybody has their demons haunting them. I guess Arnie's no different. He may be intelligent and well read, but the demons are still there. We think they've been exorcised, but they come back – the demons just keep coming back, and we … we get to fight them over and over and …"

Just now, they are crossing the bridge into New Hampshire. "I wonder if they'll prosecute me," Arnie comments.

"What?"

"The government: will they prosecute me?"

"Why would they be prosecuting you?"

"It's called the Mann Act – it forbids taking someone across state lines for carnal purposes."

"Is that what you're doing?"

"Absolutely – if I can get away with it."

"That sounds good to me. I'll just have to bake you the proverbial cake"

Arnie laughs and adds. "Let Amelia bake it. She's a better cook than you."

Even though a bit hurt by his joke, Mary admits to herself that her friend and landlady is the far more accomplished cook. "And what kind of cake would you want?"

"Devil's Food obviously. Why else would I be sinning?"

"And is this trip a sin then?"

"Only if we don't make love."

Mary smiles, and nods her head in agreement.

They continue their northern progress. Their objective is the outlet stores in Freeport, Maine. Arnie has always wanted to visit L. L. Bean. He has been buying clothes from their catalog for years. Even though, except for his army experience – as a clerk in a reserve unit – he has never spent any time in the woods, he has always fancied himself the outdoors type – whatever that might be. So he has bought flannel shirts and hiking boots, chino pants and parkas – and he has made his own fashion statement as he has wandered the bookstores and coffeehouses of Boston.

Occasionally a student will ask him about his love of the outdoors and his favorite activities. Arnie is always honest and self-deprecating in his responses. He talks about his PrestoFlame log fires and the books that he likes to read while sitting beside them.

The couple hasn't thought to make reservations so early in spring so they have to continue on to Old Orchard Beach before they find an empty motel room. "If you're here for the shopping," the clerk offers, "the best time is around two or three."

"So, we're too late?" May asks.

"Nope, too early. Two or three in the morning."

"Why's that?" Arnie asks.

"'Cause that's when most of folks are in bed. You can get into the stores. Most times you can't even get a parking spot. AAy-yup, Try the middle of the night. That'll be best. Aay-yup!" His broad a accent makes this all seem normal and reasonable.

It hasn't occurred to them that they will be among the thousands of people from along the east coast who will have flocked to Freeport on this lovely early spring weekend.

They follow the clerk's suggestion for a place to eat an early supper. It's busy but friendly, and the fried clams and potatoes are excellent. Better, it seems to have more locals than tourists which pleases Arnie. After supper they take a walk along the boardwalk. It is still too cold for the attractions to be opened, but they're able to buy a box of saltwater taffy. Each of them tries a piece and almost simultaneously take the pieces of candy out of their mouths.

"God, that's awful," Arnie observes.

"I'll bet dentists love it," Mary adds. "It could pull every filling out of my head."

They go back to the motel. Having set the alarm clock for two and finding nothing of interest on the television, they turn out the lights and try to sleep. The last of the day's sunlight is poking its way though the gaps in the curtains and around their edges. Bands of light fall across the head of the queen-size bed and others reflect from the full-length mirror to play on the fading floral print of the wallpaper. "We're not going to go to sleep," Mary observes.

"I guess not." Arnie kisses her ear and fondles her breasts. She reaches down and caresses his genitals.

"You're so beautiful," he whispers.

She never tires of hearing his compliments. Still she feels compelled, as she always has, to demur. "Oh, you just say those things."

Arnie rolls away from her and stares at the ceiling. He turns back and looks directly into Mary's eyes. She is startled by the seriousness in his eyes. "Mary, I swear to you that in my eyes you are more beautiful than any woman in the world." He waits for her to say something, but she doesn't – she has no idea what to say. Arnie continues, "There's something I've been meaning to ask you."

"What?" Mary isn't sure what's happening but knows that it's important. There is a thin gasp of nervousness in her mind.

Arnie gets up from the bed and fumbles in his jacket pockets until he finds a small box. He kneels on the bed and thrusts it at her and gasps, "Will you marry me?"

"Yes, oh yes," she responds. Taken by surprise, Mary feels as if she is spinning – spinning and simultaneously soaring in joy.

Arnie takes the ring from its box. Mary holds out her left hand, and he slips the ring on to her finger. "It's beautiful," she croons. "It's so beautiful." She kisses him, gently with the sense that he is precious and fragile.

"Oh, Arnie, I'm so happy." Her voice is full of joy and excitement. She feels her heart beating with happiness. She hugs him and showers his face with kisses.

"Believe me, I am, too!" Arnie manages to say in between her embraces. He wants to dance around the room, to shout with joy, to fly to the moon. Not knowing what to do with his excitement, he pulls Mary from the bed and hugs her tightly. Gently, he lays her back on the mattress. "I love you so much," he says.

"Oh, I love you. I love you. I truly love you," Mary responds with all her heart.

Arnie kneels next to her on the mattress and kisses her body in a hundred places. She giggles at the intensity of his kissing. "I want to kiss you forever, make love to you forever, be with you forever."

Mary wraps her arms around his neck and pulls him on top of her. "Make love to me now," she moans. "Make love to me now – now and forever." Their hands, their mouths, their souls touch and caress. Mary can feel the rough softness of his penis as it gently pushes inside her. She can feel the thrusting of his pelvis as one with her own. She can feel the sudden excitation of their shared fulfillment. She can feel the total togetherness that makes them as the first couple in the Garden of All Love.

When they have finished, Arnie and Mary lay, in mutual exhaustion – two spoons nestled on the bed – Mary behind Arnie, Arnie closer to the window.

The only sound in the room is the buzz of the heating unit. Through the window and the cracks around the door, they can feel the cold air coming off the ocean. The last shreds of sunlight make their way through the curtained window. Mary watches Arnie's back slowly rising and falling with his breathing. She runs her index finger along his spine. Arnie shivers slightly at the sensation – it is the shiver of delight. "I love you Mary Flanagan."

"And I love you, Arnie Berger."

That is the last thing either of them hear until the buzzer wakes them in the middle of the night.

* * *

Kathleen has always enjoyed walking. Now it has become a major source of – if not pleasure – at least release. She walks regularly. It is one of her very few self-indulgences. Although the grounds are well-manicured and beautiful, she much prefers leaving the hospice, the patients, and especially the sisters behind and walking through the neighborhood. On lovely days like this particular early spring Sunday, she often walks for hours, passing unnoticed along the sidewalks – observing and often envying the suburban life that flourishes around her. Although she is not a nun and although the sisters have some time ago given up their habits, there is something about Kathleen that usually makes the people whose paths she crosses assume that she is a religious, someone more ethereal than real and, as such, someone who can easily be ignored. So she floats like an unnoticed butterfly passing from blossom to blossom in search of some rare nectar.

Today Danny O'Brien is busy washing his Saab when Kathleen walks by. She has noticed him other times when she has taken this particular route. But, with her new attitude, this time she takes an extra look.

People like Danny O'Brien don't just wash their cars – they bathe them with deliberation. First they get ready, which starts with the right clothes. Danny always changes into his cutoff jeans, the last pair he has left from college. He has to suck in his stomach to snap them shut, and they have long ago stopped feeling comfortable, but they represent his youth so he won't throw them out. He doesn't tuck his Grateful Dead T-shirt in. He probably wouldn't have anyway, but with it hanging out no one can see if the snap on his shorts has opened. His old tennis shoes go on his bare feet, and he feels like he is ready to go back in time and play Frisbee in Hollis Quad.

His equipment, too, is laid out carefully. Sponges, clean rags, a plastic pail, the garden hose, Turtle Wash and Wax, a Dust Buster, and finally cleaners for the glass, the vinyl, the leather upholstery, the chrome, and especially the tires – the car will not be to his liking until the tires gleam – not like new, but shining beyond newness. Even the placement of the car is – to his mind – just right. It is carefully parked in a specific spot so that he can get maximum efficiency from the hose.

His neighbor, Harry Brown, is tending flowerbeds. Not particularly a lover of nature, Danny leaves that task to the gardener. "Hey, Harry, how's it going?" he calls to the neighbor, who is busily weeding around the azaleas.

"Damn weeds just keep growing." It is a ritual exchange. The two men aren't close, but they have as many rituals as any fraternity. That is one of Danny's special qualities; his every relationship has rituals built in: little sayings or a special piece of body language that makes the other person feel that theirs is a unique relationship

Danny is aware of a change in the light. He looks up and sees Kathleen watching him. He smiles. "Hi."

She half smiles in response. Embarrassed by his notice, she starts slightly as if to move away.

"Do you like cars?" He isn't sure where, but he knows that he has seen her before. "She's cute enough," he thinks. "Might as well chat her up."

Kathleen, not having really taken a step, feels she has to respond. She smiles shyly – not flirtatious but friendly. "Actually, I don't know much about them. I've never even learned how to drive."

"Seriously?" Even while he is saying this, Danny is wondering if he shouldn't perhaps take a more serious tone, one more appropriate to the classy young woman he perceives her to be.

"Why? Is there something wrong?" She can feel herself tensing, pulling back, becoming defensive. "I always wanted to learn, but I never had the chance."

He takes another look at Kathleen and decides that she might be worth his time. "I tell you what. You help me wash, and I'll give you a driving lesson."

"I don't even know you," Kathleen responds with hesitancy.

"Harry here will vouch for me. Won't you Harry?"

"Lady, I'd stay far away from that crazy Irishman. You should never trust a man who doesn't garden."

"I don't really think I should," her voice conveys doubt and a hidden wish.

"Suit yourself. If you ever change your mind, stop by any weekend. If I'm not home, my mother almost always is. I'll tell her if a beautiful woman named ..." He pauses.

At first Kathleen doesn't understand why he is waiting. Then she wonders if it's ok for her to answer. Finally she stammers, "My name is Kathleen, Kathleen Flanagan."

"Pleased to meet you, Kathleen Flanagan. Danny O'Brien at your service." Danny winks at her, and Kathleen feels a rush of confusion – her face flushes. "We Irish folks have to stick together especially around a Brit like Harry." Danny's sweeping gesture toward his neighbor sprays her with soapy water from the sponge he's holding.

The cold tingle of the water makes her laugh lightly.

"Good. A sense of humor is the thing to have, but I am sorry." He offers her a clean rag.

"That's all right! I'm sure I'll dry before I get back."

"Back where?"

"Subtle, boy," Harry comments.

"I live at the hospice, the one near the Star Market, in the staff housing."

Danny smiles broadly. "The freckles on his forehead seem to dance when he smiles," Kathleen observes to herself.

"Would the nuns be upset if I were to drop by some day?"

"That would depend on your intentions."

"Better than they were when I went to Saint Edward's."

He grins again, and Kathleen is struck by the sparkle in his eyes. She waves as she walks away.

"That's a nice girl, Danny." Harry remarks as Kathleen leaves. "Not a bad looker either."

"That's for sure." Danny turns back to the car, but his mind is following Kathleen down the street.

* * *

Danny's mother has been watching from behind the dining room curtains. The curtains had come from Galway as had the O'Brien and the Hennessy families. The Hennessys had been among the gentry. The O'Briens had not. The marriage of Elizabeth Hennessey and Patrick O'Brien had not been celebrated by the bride's family. Instead, they had offered the couple their fare to Boston – the American home of displaced Irish. Distance could, they hoped, reduce the embarrassment of their daughter's marriage and free them from responsibility for her after its inevitable failure. The curtains had been part of Elizabeth's dowry along with a variety of house wares. Over the years she had added carefully chosen items to that dowry.

Her home and her only child have been the lodestars of Elizabeth's life ever since the day that she had first discovered Patrick's infidelities. There had been many, too many for him to recount clearly. They had started in the old country, continued on board the Queen that had carried them from Liverpool, and then increased in frequency – if that was possible – in their new home. She hated to admit it, but her parents had been right.

Materially, at least, Patrick had prospered over the years. He had risen through the ranks of the police and was now one of the department's highest ranking officers. He had also invested in a tavern, euphoniously named Patrick's, which was prospering – due in part to its almost magnetic powers in attracting police, firefighters, and city workers. It was rumored that Patrick sold favors and that his barkeeps took bets. However, no one was ever going to investigate those rumors – at least no one in Boston's administration nor, most likely, in the state's.

Patrick and Elizabeth have never divorced. "That way she and Danny keep their benefits and their rights to my estate," Patrick had explained to a friend while they shared a pint. "It's the least I can do for her – faithful as she is."

The friend had laughed and added, "And as unfaithful as you."

"I have made a sorry husband, that I'll admit. I'm sorry for it, but sorry doesn't make it right." With that he took a deep draught of ale and wiped the foam from his mouth with the back of his hand.

Elizabeth would never have agreed to a divorce. Even if the Cardinal had been willing to grant an annulment – and given Patrick's many assistances to His Grace that was a foregone conclusion – she would have been scandalized by the very word. She had made her position more than clear. "No, I'll have no other man in my bed. Someday, perhaps, himself will return. Then we shall see. For now I'm content enough with the raising of my boy. There's no way that he'll be like his father, not if I can do ought about it."

Danny had been taught at an early age that his father was not to be trusted and certainly not to be emulated. When Patrick had on a few occasions tried to be a father, he found his son already turned against him. "I can't blame her," Patrick had confided to his partner on the force. "She got no bargain in me. The least I can do is let her have her little boy."

Danny had been in grade school when Patrick had made that decision. Afterwards there would be presents for birthdays and

Christmas and mandatory attendance at major events like confirmation and graduation from St. Edwards and later from St. Julian's and Notre Dame; but Patrick never again tried to be a father to his son or a model to the boy.

From Elizabeth's perspective that had been all to the good. She had kept her son close to her and to God. No matter what his surname, he had been raised a Hennessy.

Allowing Danny to go away to college, even a Catholic college, had been difficult for Elizabeth. She had tried to convince him not to go, but – for once – he had fought her. His friends were all going away, he argued. How could he be different? They compromised. He could go away if he promised to return home for all vacations and to avoid loose women and non-Catholics.

"Which is worse?" Danny had asked.

"A Catholic woman who has lost her faith," Elizabeth had answered strongly.

"Be careful of those urges," she counseled. "The Devil's in temptation, and he'll lead you to Hell as soon as you can say the word."

"And, what word is that?" Danny had asked. He was a good boy and a good son, but he couldn't completely ignore the adolescent impulse to get a rise out of his mother.

"S–E–X," Elizabeth had spelled the word rather than saying it. "That is the Devil's tool. Do you understand?"

Danny had nodded his head. He knew that his friends thought otherwise, but he also knew how strongly his mother felt and how badly she had been hurt by his own father. It wasn't that he necessarily planned to abide by her precepts only that she should never know when he didn't. In the meantime, he may have been interested in them, but he distrusted women and relationships.

It was no wonder that Danny had done so little dating – that he had only twice dated the same woman more than once. But that was not common knowledge so his friends, co-workers, and neighbors wondered why this eligible and friendly man had never married.

* * *

What attracts Danny to Kathleen are the subtle ways in which she is like his mother. She has the slightest hint of an accent – not unlike Mary's but tempered by being raised in America. Her eyes are, although weak, soft and warm like his mother's – somewhat darker, but very like hers in the comfort they suggest. Kathleen's hair has the same sense of life – perhaps the remnant of some untamed Irish spirit. But most of all, it is the gentle, unassuming manner that shows itself in her voice, her mannerisms, and even in the way she moves. Almost instinctively, he knows that she is a woman easily mastered.

Elizabeth O'Brien nee Hennessey is taken aback to see her son consorting so openly with the enemy. "Who is she?" she demands as soon as Danny comes into the house that early spring Sunday. "What was she wanting?"

"Who is who?" He asks too off guard to realize that his mother is talking about Kathleen.

"That hussy you were talking with before. That's exactly who."

"That girl? She's very lovely. She works at the hospice – lives with the nuns, too. A nice Irish girl! A good Catholic girl! Her name is Kathleen Flanagan, and she reminds me of you. I thought all the good girls were gone, but I think I may have found one."

"Indeed! And, have you now? Well, time will tell." Elizabeth doesn't know whether to be pleased that Danny has used her as the standard by which to judge a woman or horrified that her son may actually have found someone whom he might some day love. She goes up to her room, to her little shrine to The Blessed Heart, to pray.

# Chapter Ten

It is about five in the morning when Karen feels the first cramping pains that wrench her into wakefulness. She reaches over and touches Sean's face. His face twitches, but his eyes remain closed. "Sean," she whispers as if afraid that he might hear her. Then again, louder, "Sean – Sean Flanagan."

The urgency in her voice makes Sean sit bolt upright in his mind. Again, as he so often does, he curses to himself when he realizes how little movement he has. It is especially painful at times like this, when the woman he loves needs him. "What?"

"It's time, dear."

"Time for what?" Sean's head has not yet cleared.

"The baby."

"What? Really? Now? How do you know?"

"The labor ... Uh, ooh, the labor pains have started."

It takes some time for them to get ready. By the time the calls have been made, the dressing done, Sean gotten into his chair, and them arranged in their van heading for The Mount Auburn Hospital, the pains are only a few minutes apart. They use the car phone to call ahead, and there are two attendants from the emergency room waiting to help Karen onto a gurney and roll her into the hospital and up to the obstetrics suite.

They move so quickly that Sean is left behind. By the time he gets directions and waits for the elevator, they are moving Karen from the prep area into the delivery room. One of the nurses, who has been specifically detailed by the doctor, is waiting to help Sean get washed and gowned. He wheels into the room just as the baby's head is poking through Karen's vagina and into the waiting world.

"I never saw an easier birth," the doctor comments as he gently pulls the baby to ease it from the birth canal.

"Easy for you," Karen gasps between pains. "I felt it all."

"Just a little more," he reassures.

"I'm here, darling," Sean says softly – in the most reassuring voice he can manage under the circumstances. Meanwhile, he is thinking, "It's a good thing I'm in this chair. God, I hope I don't faint."

"Seannnn!" His name takes on the pain in her belly.

"Push again," commands the doctor.

"You're doing great, Mrs. Flanagan." The nurse wipes the beaded sweat from Karen's face.

"Here he comes." Karen pushes again. The pain stops. There is a moment and then a healthy cry. "He's perfect," announces the doctor.

One of the nurses whisks him away and brings him back a moment later. "Six pounds, eleven ounces. All his fingers and toes. And wanting his mother." She lays the little bundle she has been carrying down in Karen's arms. Sean rolls over and reaches out to touch first his son and then his wife. There are tears in his eyes.

"Have you given him a name yet?"

"Sean Patrick Flanagan, III," Karen announces.

"No way," says Sean. They have discussed this topic a number of times, but it is still to be resolved.

"Are you sure?"

"Absolutely, Karen. The relationship between my father and me wasn't something I'd want to reproduce. Sean will be his middle name. That's close enough." Turning to the nurse who had asked, Sean informs her, "He's Robert Sean Flanagan." The nurses look at each other and smile.

"Would you like to hold your son before he goes to the nursery?"

"I sure would." The nurse picks Robert Sean Flanagan up and nestles him carefully between his father's body and arm. "I've never been so happy." The tears are streaming down his cheeks. A drop hits the baby on the nose, and the little nose twitches. Sean and the one nurse who has seen it laugh.

"That really was one of the fastest and easiest births of my career."

"Thanks, Doc."

"You're more than welcome. But next time, could we try for a couple more hours sleep." He shakes Sean's hand, takes Karen's for a moment and squeezes gently, stops – a gentle smile on his face – to look at the life which he has just delivered, and leaves to wash up and then drive home to what remains of a night's sleep.

Mary, Kathleen, and Arnie have all assembled in the emergency room waiting area – the only place available at this hour – when Sean comes to tell them about his son. Everybody is grinning except for Arnie. At that moment he is thinking of his own son, of his dead Robert. "How many years ago was it that I was so happy to have a son?" he thinks to himself. "It seems like lifetimes ago."

Mary slips her hand into his, and they kiss. She can see the pain working its way through him, and she knows what he is thinking. Sean sees it, too. "At least now you have a grandson."

"Thanks, Sean. That means a lot." Arnie chokes. "You have no idea." He walks beside Sean's chair as they make their way to the nursery.

"I hope you don't mind," Sean says to Arnie in a voice that no one else can hear.

"Mind what?"

"We named our son Robert."

"That … I mean …" Tears are welling up in the older man's eyes. He tries again to speak. "I can't tell you …" He falls silent. For the moment there is no sound except for the sniffing back of his tears. Arnie gropes for his handkerchief and dabs at his eyes. Then, having failed to stop the flow of emotion, he bends down to hug Sean.

Sean has often wondered what his life would have been like if he had been raised by somebody like Arnie. "You're a wonderful man, Arnie. Thank you for being here for my mother and for us."

"You're welcome," Arnie mutters. "You're so very welcome."

Such are the moments of life's brightness.

Quietly they all make their way to the nursery to take a peek at little Robert who, exhausted by this great adventure, is fast asleep.

\* \* \*

It is only after she has left the hospital and is in a taxi heading back to the hospice that Kathleen gives in to her tears. She had hidden her pain better than Arnie, but it has been no less real.

"Somebody die, lady?" the driver asks, trying to make his voice sound caring.

"No. My sister-in-law had a baby." Kathleen chokes out the words through her sobs.

"Congratulations," he responds not knowing quite how to deal with his passenger's tears. "Boy or girl?"

Kathleen doesn't bother responding. She knows that it doesn't matter to the driver, and her soul is wrestling with far heavier matters.

Much later she will finally fall asleep. For the second time since she has come to work at the hospice, she will sleep late. She will miss the morning devotions. She will be late getting to the patients. It will not be a comfortable sleep. Her dreams will be pained. But, she will sleep in.

The people around her will try to understand what is bothering her, but none will. Only Mary, wrapped in the comfort of Arnie's arms, will comprehend. She will pray for her daughter even as she gives thanks for the new life that has entered hers. She will pray, and she will say the rosary as she does every morning. She will use the same beads that she had brought from Ireland so many years before. They are worn and well known to her fingers. Through all they have been consolation. Through all they have been love. Through all they have been courage. So it is that this woman of so many emotions prays this day.

# Chapter Eleven

"It's a good thing it was such an easy birth; he hasn't been easy since. I'll tell you that!" Karen is sharing the woes of parenting with Mary. "I'd do anything for a good night's sleep. He eats constantly. My breasts are sore from the sucking. At least his diapers don't smell."

"That is one advantage of breast feeding," Mary agrees. She has come, as she does every second day to visit her daughter-in-law and especially her grandson. She had reluctantly kept her distance while Karen's parents had been in town. "I don't want to overburden Karen," she had explained to Amelia and Arnie.

The Andersons had stayed a week helping Karen and Sean and at the same time taking enormous amounts of energy from them both. Mary and Arnie had stopped by once during that week, and another time they had invited Karen's parents to a pleasant restaurant for dinner. Now, however, the Andersons have returned to Minnesota, and Mary is busy being a very happily attentive grandmother.

Karen, on the other hand, is not quite so happy. "I know she means well," she complains occasionally to Sean, "But I feel as if she's watching over my shoulder. It's like she expects me to drop Robert on his head at any moment." Karen has become somewhat cranky from the stress of the baby. As much as she hates to admit it, she sometimes resents the fact that Sean simply can not be the ideal helpmate.

"The guys at work were teasing me today about not sleeping. I guess it comes with having a baby." Sean chuckles, but his laugh rings with insincerity.

"You're changing the subject." Karen's voice has become slightly strident.

"I know."

"I was talking about your mother."

"Do you want me to tell her to stay away?" Sean tries to keep his voice as calm as possible. He knows that they are on the edge of a swampy place – a place into which neither of them wants to venture.

"Of course not." The truth is that Karen doesn't have any idea what she really wants Sean to do or to say. "It's just that I'm feeling the strain."

"I know. I wish I could do more."

"So do I." It is the first time that Karen has voiced any discontent with Sean's physical limitations. She can feel her heart plunge. "I'm sorry," she says almost at once.

"Don't be. You're right! I'm not much use around here." The pain in Sean's voice is palpable. "We both wish I could do more. It isn't just to help you; he's my son, too. I want …"

Karen knows that she has to back away before they enter that uncharted and dangerous territory. "You may not be able to help in some ways – but you earn a good living, you're a good lover, and you're more supportive than most husbands. Don't go knocking yourself."

There is a long pause. Sean maneuvers himself to the refrigerator, opens it, and with great difficulty takes out an iced tea. "Do you want something?"

"No, thanks." She waits until he brings her the bottle, which she opens. She puts in the straw and hands it back to him. He takes a long sip.

The pause gives them both a chance to regain control. "Sean, I love you. You do know that, don't you?" she asks plaintively.

"Of course I know that, silly, and I love you. And," he pauses for emphasis, "we both love Robert even if he does keep us up half the night."

"Having a child is very special. It goes beyond words."

"I know what you mean."

"Sometimes when your sister is here, I feel so badly for her."

He repeats, "I know what you mean." Kathleen has visited at least once a week since Robert's birth. Each time she has held him, Sean and Karen have seen the wistful look in her eyes. She sings the lullabies that Sean too remembers – lullabies that Mary had sung to them when they had been very young. When Kathleen sings, the pain and loss in her voice bring tears to their eyes. "I wonder if she and Danny will get married."

"Do you think she's told him?"

"Told him?" Sean echoes.

"That she can't have ...."

"I don't know, but I don't think it would stop him. He's the kind who would adopt," Sean interrupts.

"I'm not so sure."

"You're not?"

"I think he has a lot less love for Kathleen than he has for himself."

* * *

It appears that Sean had been right. Danny's response when Kathleen tells him about her infertility is, "There's always adoption." He adds emphatically. "What counts is the love between two people."

They are taking a ride. Kathleen is at the wheel. She is not yet a comfortable driver, but she has been learning. Danny insists that she do most of the driving when they go out. There are moments he finds it necessary to pump imaginary brakes, but most of the time he is able to sit back and relax. If she doesn't yet feel quite ready for her road test, it is a more accurate measure of her insecurity than of her abilities behind the wheel.

Driving is not the only thing Danny has introduced into Kathleen's life. They have done more things together during their short relationship than she had done during her entire earlier marriage. Danny has an inexhaustible supply of energy and a good income from the electric company where he is a line repair supervisor.

Early on he had described his job to Kathleen. "During the winter it can be unpleasant, but most of the time it's a great job. I ride around in a company car checking on crews. When I started, I had to climb poles and freeze my butt off, but not now." He had not bothered to add that his father's contacts had reached beyond the civil service and into Boston Edison.

Mary, for one, has been glad to hear that Danny had such a good income. She has always feared Kathleen's job at the hospice. More than the reality of Kathleen's tiny paycheck and eventual impoverished old age, Mary has been concerned that Kathleen would become infected with the horrible AIDS virus. She clearly hopes that Danny will encourage her daughter to give up that job. In one discussion with Amelia she has made her feelings quite plain, "I think it's wonderful the way she helps others, but I worry about her. I always have. I think that's why she took the job, to make me feel guilty."

"I take it you approve of Danny," Amelia responds. They are sitting in Amelia's parlor drinking tea and catching up. The uncomfortable tone in her landlady's voice escapes Mary's notice.

"That's true enough, but more importantly I've changed my views. There's no good reason why she shouldn't remarry. To spend her life making believe that she's still married to John, it just doesn't make sense." Mary takes off her glasses and wipes them clean. Inside, beyond words, she still has trouble accepting the changes in her own positions on so many things. Occasionally she wonders if she truly believes these new views or if they are simply a way to allow herself the freedom that she wants, the freedom to be with Arnie.

"It would be easy, wouldn't it?" Amelia asks.

"What?"

"To go back, Mary, – to go back to your old beliefs. It would be easy." Amelia has a way of knowing Mary's heart. Sometimes Mary wonders if they had been sisters in a previous lifetime. Mary doesn't really believe in reincarnation, but still she wonders about Amelia and herself.

There is a Native American throw on the couch – a gift from a boarder who had moved to New Mexico. It depicts a tortoise carrying the world. From the center of that world there issues forth a variety of animals and the clans of a people. The diversity of colors and variety of animals elicits simultaneous feelings of harmony and dissonance. Mary plays with the orange and blue fringe as she talks to her friend. "I suppose it would be, but then I'd have to consider Arnie a sin." She pauses. "I wonder if real love can be a sin. I wish I knew God's mind."

"So do we all, dear. Would you like some more tea?" Amelia refills Mary's cup from the pot. She has brewed the tea in an old-fashioned way – loose leaves in the pot. Now, she pours the tea through a small silver strainer to remove those leaves. With each cup, she seems to scrutinize the soggy leaves before discarding them – it is a ritual of prognostication, a power wished but seldom attained.

Mary reaches over and adds one carefully measured spoonful of sugar and a dollop of heavy cream. Carefully, as if stirring the future, Mary moves the spoon in orderly figure eights. She lifts the rose covered white cup to her mouth and takes a sip. All the while she is ever so slightly shaking her head.

She puts the cup down and holds her left hand in the light. The small diamond sparkles. Behind it her wedding band, the one Sean had long ago given her, is snug in place. "Do you think that I'll be happy?" she asks her friend. "What do you see in the leaves?"

Amelia laughs. "I have no idea what they mean, but I hope that you find what your heart desires. Oh, my dear, I do hope it so."

* * *

The sun has set and twilight is gathering when Mary leaves to go to Arnie's apartment. They meet at the front door. He is coming back from a class. The fall semester has just started although there isn't any indication that summer has ended. The classroom has not been air-conditioned, and sweat is showing under his arms. He is tired and feeling just a bit cranky.

"I visited with Amelia, today," Mary comments as they work to prepare their supper of spaghetti and garlic bread.

"Uh-huh." He takes a sip of the red wine they have opened. "I expected that you would."

"We talked about Kathleen and Danny."

"And does your soul sister approve of him?" Arnie is well aware if somewhat skeptical of the special bond between the two women.

"I don't know. I think she approves of love and doubts all men – not you, of course, but Danny, well, he's another story."

"That's what I call a true philosopher."

"Arnie, what do you think?"

"I'm in favor of love, too."

"No, I mean about Kathleen and Danny."

"I don't know what there is to think. They go driving, to concerts, to amusement parks, to movies, bowling, and everything else you can name. They enjoy each other. That much is obvious.

Are they in love? I don't know. They're both so reticent. What happens between them when they're alone? I don't know that either."

"I hope he's not going to hurt her. John did enough damage." Mary worries more about her daughter than she usually is willing to admit. Now that Sean's life seems to be stable and happy, she has intensified that worry.

If someone were to have asked, Mary would have admitted that it had been easier when Kathleen and Sean had been children. There had been accidents and illnesses, bad teachers and schoolyard fights: all manner of things to concern her but she had entrusted them to God's care. If bad things happened, it was part of His plan, and she could ride through the storms secure in the vessel of her faith. Now, she no longer feels that security. She knows she cannot stop bad things from happening. It is too easy for beings to fall from the delicate balance of this world – to fall into an unknown abyss.

Mary has only to look at her children's lives to recognize her helplessness – and God's, which is, for her, the worst part.

\* \* \*

"I feel so helpless." Robert is suffering his first real cold. Or, perhaps more honestly, his parents are suffering through his first real cold. The congestion in his chest makes Karen labor with each of his breaths. "I wonder if our parents felt the same way."

"I'm sure they did. In fact, my guess is they still do. My guess is that we'll still be worrying about him when he's thirty. I guess that's what parents do." Sean's response is lighthearted; still it demonstrates how much he has matured.

Karen laughs, but the anxious look does not leave her face. "It's such a terrible responsibility. I wish I could just take him home to my mother and say 'Here you take him – Mommy, make it all right.'"

It is Sean's turn to laugh and to nod in agreement.

The sudden sound of the baby's sneeze freezes them both, and then they start to giggle. "This is ridiculous," Sean observes. "We're acting like a simple cold is the end of the world. What will we do if something really bad ever happens?"

"I think I'll die." She is standing looking down into Robert's crib. Over his head is a mobile of colorful animals arrayed in circus merriment. Straightening up, Karen hits the mobile with her head and sets it in motion. The gaily-colored plastic animals clicked together.

Sean puts his chair in motion so that he can take her hand. "Nobody is going to die."

"I know. I'm just an overprotective mother. Sometimes I wish he'd disappear! He's so much work. Right now I look down at his vulnerable little body, and all I can think about is protecting him. How do we keep him safe? How do we keep him well?"

"Remember these feelings. We'll need them when he's a holy terror charging through the house or, better yet, when he's a teenager and we never know where he is." He turns to leave the room.

Karen turns off the nursery light and quietly three-quarter closes the door.

They sit in the living room watching television. Sean no longer wants to watch old reruns. Now he loves mysteries. He tries to figure out who did it before the show's detectives – most of the time he is unsuccessful. "That doesn't make sense," he often declares when he has failed, "They didn't give us all the clues."

Karen knows that he had wanted to be a policeman – that had been before he had gone to Vietnam. When the subject comes up, and it often does, she tells him how glad she is that he isn't a cop. "I'd worry all the time," is her standard line.

"You wouldn't have to because we would never have met," is his equally standard response.

"Then I'm even happier that you aren't." It is one of the little rituals of their life together – one of those rituals that communicate mutual affection – that communicate caring – that communicate enduring love.

\* \* \*

Kathleen and Danny, also, have their little rituals. One of their favorites is the way they kiss each time they meet. First, Danny kisses Kathleen on the forehead. Then they kiss on the mouth – not so much in a sexually intense manner as one of familiarity. Next, he nibbles gently at the nape of her neck, reaching his head around to her back as she cooperatively leans forward. Finally, they again kiss on the mouth – this time with more intensity and tongues in intimate dance.

It is a minuet which only they know how to perform. Theirs is not as passionate a relationship as it is one of comfortable amity. They have a mutually enjoyed, but a non-sexual bond, an intense friendship. It is understood between them that someday they will have to face the issue of sexuality, but for now it seems that it is enough for them to both to enjoy the many hours they spend together.

It is perhaps a strange thing, but the young couple are far less passionate and far less demonstrative than Mary and Arnie.

On this fall Saturday, Danny suggests they go horseback riding. Kathleen had some time past mentioned that it has always been something that she wanted to try. Danny had stored that comment away in the list of things he might do to please her. Looking in the Yellow Pages, he has found a stable that offers trail rides in the Blue Hills.

Since neither of them has ridden before, the stable manager picks two old and gentle horses that are well used to the routine. They know exactly when and where they are supposed to walk, trot and canter and where to turn. It would not have mattered what Kathleen and Danny might try or what they might think they are doing, the two horses – long past feeling rein or kick – will simply follow the route of hundreds of previous trail rides.

Danny is frustrated. He wants to show off. He certainly doesn't want to be riding what is in effect a live carousel. He tries kicking and pulling on the reins to make his horse follow his cues, but to absolutely no avail. He shouts commands that are ignored – if the horse even knows what the words mean. Then, growing angry, he shouts invectives with no more effect.

By the time they have returned to the barn, Danny is in a horrific mood. "I wanted to ride a horse not a damned kiddy car," he complains to the manager. "I felt like he was riding me." It is the first time Kathleen has known him to show any real anger. She is uncomfortable with its intensity.

"You did say you had never ridden before. We have a policy of keeping our customers safe. I'm sure you can appreciate that."

"Well, I want to ride again. This time we want more spirited horses." The words seem to spit out.

Kathleen winces. She is already saddle-sore. If Danny were to ask her, she would embarrassedly admit that she really didn't want anything more spirited.

The manager is very conciliatory. "I tell you what, sir; I'll give you a credit so you folks can come back and ride free the next time. If I'm not here, you just tell whoever is that Ida said you should get good horses."

When Danny is in the men's room, Ida speaks to Kathleen. "I saw your face when he wanted to ride again. If I were you, I'd just let him come by himself. We'll give him a horse that will give him a different kind of a hard time, and he'll learn to appreciate the gentle ones."

She thanks Ida, but the manager's comments have made Kathleen uneasy. Danny's behavior worries Kathleen. He has always seemed so easy going. It isn't that he has irrationally lost his temper with the manager or behaved badly. It isn't that he has shouted and cursed at the indifferent horse. It is just that he doesn't seem to have cared how she might feel. She has never before thought about how stubborn and proud he might be.

"You're right," he answers when Kathleen remonstrates with him on the way home. "I should have asked you before I talked to her, but I got a little hot under the collar. I don't like being treated like a damn cripple." Danny realizes at once that he has stepped in it, but he can't think of anything to say – Sean now hangs like a pall in the car.

Kathleen drives home in silence, and Danny doesn't dare to interrupt her thoughts. There is nothing he can say to make the situation right. She pulls his Saab into Danny's driveway. "I think I'll walk today." There is iciness in her tone. He puts his arms around her, but Kathleen pulls away with a perfunctory kiss.

"You know I'm sorry about what I said. I wasn't thinking. You know I respect Sean. It's just that I don't ever want to feel so out of control, so helpless. It was infuriating the way those horses didn't respond to us. Anyway, I am sorry."

"I know that, Danny."

"I really am."

"I know. Just let it be."

"I love you," he tries.

"And, I love you. We'll talk later." Before he can say anything else, Kathleen starts to walk off.

Once more Danny feels like he has lost control of the situation. His first urge is to follow her, but he thinks better of it and goes into the house. As if punctuating his sense of rightness, he slams the door on his way in. "Those damn horses," he shouts to the empty foyer, "those God damn horses."

Kathleen walks slowly back to the hospice. "I know he's sorry," she thinks; "but sorry doesn't make it right."

\* \* \*

"Aren't you afraid?" Karen asks her sister-in-law. The two women are seated at Karen's small Formica kitchen table. In front of them are half empty coffee mugs and Dunkin Donuts – plain and chocolate frosted – that Kathleen has brought. The baby sits in his highchair and makes occasional burbling sounds each of which elicits a reaction from mother and aunt.

"In a way, but I'm careful. I mean there's always a chance of infection, but we're all at risk so we're all careful. Also, we do a lot less stuff with needles than they do in a hospital. It isn't like we need blood work to know the residents are dying. They all are. If they didn't have AIDS or something else terminal, they wouldn't be in the hospice."

"I know it's stupid of me; but every time you're here and handling the baby, I worry. I don't mean for you not to come. Sean and I like having you here. I just start worrying. I know that even if you had the virus, it would be hard for him to catch it. I know it, and I still worry."

"That's only natural. At the hospice we get some family members who won't go into the room. They stand in the hallway as if there was some kind of invisible barrier protecting them. It's really sad."

"How does Danny feel about your working there?"

"Mixed. He says I'm doing a wonderful thing, and then he tells me that he's scared the same as you guys, the same as mom and Arnie. It is a scary place, especially with HIV. There's more than enough suffering in the world, and that's one plague that isn't going away any time soon."

Karen gets up and busies herself with Robert's formula. She is still breast-feeding him, but his appetite now easily outruns her milk supply. She tests it on her forearm the way her mother had shown her. Assuring herself that it is the right temperature, she hands the bottle to Kathleen who now has Robert carefully cradled in her lap. "Goodness, he's growing! It's just amazing."

"The doctor says he's one of the healthiest babies she's ever seen."

"And Mom says he takes after Sean – right?"

"Of course."

Robert sucks at the nipple until he has emptied the bottle. Expertly, Kathleen holds him over her shoulder and massages his back until he rewards her with a little burp. Karen decides to brave dangerous waters. "It's a shame, Kath, that you can't have kids. You're such a natural mother."

Karen nods sadly. "Danny says we should adopt. I wonder if that's such good idea. With all the drugs people use these days, I wonder how healthy a kid is going to be."

"Healthy or not, you and Danny will love him." Karen tends to forget her own mixed feelings about Robert when Kathleen is around. Besides, it seems unkind to talk about the negatives when Kathleen feels so deprived. Over the months of her pregnancy and since Robert's birth, Karen has grown ever closer to Sean's sister. When Kathleen is around, Karen doesn't have the same feelings of being observed that she has with Mary. "Possibly," she thinks to herself, "it's because I feel superior knowing that I can have a baby and she can't." Thinking such things makes Karen feel guilty, but those thoughts run deep and they just won't go away.

Kathleen has never made a secret of her sorrow or her feelings that somehow there must be something wrong with her as a person – something for which she is to be forever punished. She has shared her feelings and her dreams with Karen. The saddest dream is one in which she can see inside herself and she sees that she is empty. "I feel like a desert," she has told Karen. "Nothing can grow inside me."

"But things do grow in the desert, and I can see the beauty that grows inside you." It is a statement of complete sincerity.

"If you see beauty, you can't see the envy, the jealousy toward you."

"Of course I understand that. It's only normal for you to feel that way. I'd be jealous if the roles were reversed. Still you've been here for me at every turn. From the day Sean and I came back to Boston, you've been there for us. Thanks! I really mean that, Thanks!"

Often the two women have talked about Danny. Even while she shares her sister-in-law's assumption, Kathleen isn't really sure that they will ever get to marriage. "I think he's still a virgin," she comments one day. "I'm not sure how he really feels about women, what he thinks about sex. He puts on a great show, says all the right things, but I'm just not sure."

"I can understand that," Karen says. She hopes that Kathleen will keep on talking.

"He's so tied to his mother." She reaches out her hand to Karen before continuing. "And, I'm not sure why, but I don't think she really likes me."

"She probably wouldn't like any girl he was seeing."

"That's probably true. It goes both ways. They seem so close. She worships him and indulges him. You know, he doesn't give her any money – not that she'd take it. How can I compete with free room and board?"

Kathleen stops to gaze into the distance. "But he talks about adopting kids so I guess he must have some ideas about getting married. I just wonder if he'll make the break."

Kathleen pauses again.

"Maybe, he'll want me to move in with them both. You know, his mother is always polite to me, but there's still that something. Sometimes I just know that she hates me – and probably fears me, too."

"Would you?" Sean interrupts from the doorway where he has silently appeared.

Kathleen and Karen speak simultaneously, Kathleen saying, "No, I couldn't," and Karen saying, "Hi, honey, you're home early."

# Chapter Twelve

They haven't discussed it before. They have each thought about it – thought about it and then avoided the topic. But Robert is getting older, and they really can't ignore the issue any longer. For one thing, Sean knows that in her heart his sister, for all her anger at the Church, would not be able to live with the thought that her nephew has not been baptized – not after her own child had died without that seemingly all important rite. He also knows that for all her new thinking Mary will be scandalized if Robert is not duly sprinkled.

For her part, Karen also wants the child baptized. It just seems like the right thing to do. But, she doesn't want a Catholic priest performing the ritual. Of good German Lutheran stock, Karen is not a great churchgoer, but she is steadfast in her anti-Roman attitudes – prejudices she had imbibed along with her first bottles and a strange appreciation for ice fishing. Even in liberal Minnesota, she had heard anti-papist attitudes restated over and over again during Kennedy's bid for the presidency. She knows, but never says, that her parents' anti-Catholic bias is one reason that they have never expressed any real acceptance of Sean. At times she has wondered if that hasn't been a bigger issue for them than his wheelchair. Like her marriage, she would prefer having no church to putting up with a Roman one. Still she does want their baby baptized.

It is Arnie who eventually solves the problem. As a religiously uninterested party, an agnostic Jew, Arnie doesn't care if the child is or is not baptized. And he certainly doesn't care about the differences among Christian denominations. To him all rituals are for the purpose of bringing people together. Therefore, he reasons, the person to officiate at a baptism is the person who does the least to divide the participants. In his mind it would be preferable if that person were to serve as a bridge to even closer ties.

Who would be better, he asks, than Pat Michaels. She has been there for Mary. She has been supportive of Kathleen. She is liked and respected by all. And, she is an ordained minister.

Nobody has anything negative to say. Presbyterian will certainly do. So, it is agreed. Pat Michaels will officiate. Even Amelia is happy because there will be a woman in charge. Whatever nagging doubts that might linger in Mary's mind have been swept away by the general tide of good feelings.

The plans are made. The baptism is to take place at Pat's beautiful old Presbyterian Church. Afterwards, there will be a small party at Amelia's. Karen would have preferred to do the party herself, but she has decided to let Mary and Amelia have their day in the sun.

Both the baptism and the party will involve a small group of people – that small group that has come to be "family" in all their minds. There is Robert, Sean, Karen, Mary, Arnie, and Kathleen. Danny will be there. His mother, if she will come, will be included for Kathleen's sake. And, of course, Aunt Amelia and Reverend Pat will be there. Jem Christobal, who had once helped Sean and with whom Mary has kept friendly contact and who was so important in all that has happened in Sean's life, has been invited, but no one will be too surprised if she doesn't come.

There really isn't anyone else to invite. The Flanagan family has long since written off Mary and her children. That had happened when Sean had come home from Vietnam. None of the family members had wanted to make the commitment to be there and to care so they had had drifted away – Christmas cards the last contact.

Karen's family was in far off Minnesota. They would receive announcements, and some might even send gifts. But, it is unlikely that any of them would come that long distance, and it seems unfair to ask them. "I don't want my parents coming out of guilt, and my brother can't afford to," Karen has made clear. Secretly, she wishes that her brother could be there but says nothing – afraid that Sean will insist on paying the fare, which they can't afford any more than her brother.

As for friends, there are some, but none who are really close. "Acquaintances," Arnie calls them as he and Mary discuss possible invitations.

"You're right," she agrees. "Everybody we might think of has already received birth announcements. They don't need or want to come."

"And we certainly don't need them adding their two cents about the whole religious thing," Arnie adds.

A date and time have been agreed. It is to be a Sunday afternoon at two o'clock.

\* \* \*

It is a beautiful day – a day of affirmation and renewal. The sunlight seems to sparkle in the air, which is fresh but with the slightest hint of ocean salt. What clouds there are, and they are few, seem to form happy figures playing in the sky as Mary and Arnie make the short drive to the church. It is so perfect a day that they even find a nearby parking place. "God must really approve," Arnie observes as he pulls his Buick into the spot.

"You shouldn't take God so lightly," Mary chides him. "I'm sure He has better things to do than to worry about our parking spaces."

"If He keeps his eye on the little things, He won't be able to get us into problems with the big ones."

Mary, despite herself, laughs. "Arnie, you're terrible," she says as she playfully hits his arm.

Mary has been to the Presbyterian Church many times since her first visit, but this is the first time that she really takes a good look at its interior. It is an imposing place – even more grand than St. Margaret's. The stained glass windows create patterns of light that are in their own way as miraculous as the scenes that are being portrayed. She pulls on Arnie's arm and whispers into his ear. "I wonder if the impressionists were inspired by going into churches like this."

He smiles, remembering their first trip to The Museum of Art and Mary's first wondrous reactions. "I have no idea," he whispers back, "but it is incredibly beautiful." Quietly he marvels at the scope of Mary's intellectual growth since he has known her.

As Pat had instructed, they have gathered in the front of the church. A sterling silver basin is sitting on a piece of lace, which protects the top of a simple rosewood table. Next to the basin is an equally well-crafted silver ewer filled with water. A carefully folded towel is also on the table.

Mary's eyes take in the elaborate pulpit and the simpler and perhaps more elegant lectern on which a copy of "The Holy Bible" rests. It is open, and Mary very much wants to see what verse the last person has read. Also, although she would have been embarrassed to admit it, she wants to see how the Protestants have altered and defiled The Holy Word. There is – still and always – that slight disapproval, that nagging discomfort.

There is an almost unnoticable noise as a door near the choir stall opens. Karen comes out first. She is wearing a simple blue dress and a smile that seems to light up the building. Behind her rolls Sean dressed in his best suit and carrying his son on his lap. Robert is wearing the christening dress that Mary had used for both her children, the one that her parents had sent when her Seany had been born. She had saved it all those years in case she would someday have a grandchild. Then – convinced that it would never be used – she had kept it as an act of contrition, to remind her that God is not bound by human plans and desires. Now, unexpectedly, her dream has come true – Robert Sean Flanagan is about to be baptized.

Standing beside Sean, talking to him and the baby, is Rev. Patricia Michaels. Mary has never before seen Pat dressed in her clerical best. For the occasion she is wearing a bright scarlet gown with white trim. Around her neck she wears a single strand of pearls. Her earrings are also simple and stunning. Her short hair has been freshly done and looks soft and wavy. Even her shoes, simple flat-heeled but bright red, are just right.

When they arrive at the rosewood table, Sean nods to Kathleen and Danny, who come forward. Kathleen takes Robert and holds him lovingly. "Who gives this child to be baptized?" asks the minister.

"We do," respond Karen and Sean in perfect synchronization.

"And who guarantees that he will be brought up to know God and to venerate His Holy Son?"

"We do," respond Danny and Kathleen. Their voices are ever so slightly out of synch. It seems as if Danny's voice is just behind and echoing Kathleen's.

It had been a foregone conclusion that Kathleen would be Robert's godmother. The choice of Danny had been somewhat more of an issue. If he had been able to have his way, Sean would have chosen Arnie. But Arnie had demurred saying that while he was incredibly flattered and wanted to agree, he would not be able to do justice to the responsibility of raising a Christian child. Being a teacher, Arnie has always taken such responsibilities very seriously. Sean and Karen knew and accepted that his was the honest doubt of a sincere man. There really being nobody else to consider, Danny has been chosen by default, and the choice does make Kathleen happy even if Elizabeth Hennessy disapproves of her son's participation in a Protestant rite.

Pat takes the baby from Kathleen's arms. Holding him expertly in her right arm, she puts her left fingers into the ewer, pulls them out dripping slightly, and sprinkles Robert's head while making the sign of the cross above it. "I baptize you Robert Sean Flanagan in the name of The Father, The Son, and The Holy Ghost."

Everybody answers with a murmured, "Amen." Even Arnie adds his voice to the muted but sincere response.

Pat hands Robert back to Kathleen. "I don't suppose you came expecting a sermon," she says. "I know there are only a few of us here and that we're all friends. Also, babies are notoriously uninterested in what ministers have to say."

Sitting to one side, Danny's mother stirs uncomfortably and frowns in anger. The rest of the group laughs a little, as much from a sense of discomfort as at Pat's joke.

The pastor continues, "Sacraments are very important in religion. They are the sacred acts, sacred acts that we use to remember and more importantly to reenact the most seminal events of faith. Baptism is a sacrament among Christians because through it we emulate Christ's being baptized by John, one of the truly seminal moments in Christ's earthly presence. It represents not simply a washing away of sin. Indeed, Christ was without sin. It also signifies the dawning of Christ's awareness of His Father's plan. It is at that moment that Christ's passion on earth truly began.

"But, there are other sacred acts of Jesus which came before that baptism. The first was being born. Because we have no way to reenact that moment, we tend not to recognize birth as a sacrament. But, if we stop to think about it, wasn't that a remarkable act – The Son coming into this world to dwell among us.

"Now, in Buddhism, there are myths of Siddhartha's early years, for instance that he was born able to walk and to talk and that where he stepped lotus flowers appeared. There are no such myths in Christianity. Jesus came into this world an infant much like you, Robert Sean." She takes a moment to smile at the little boy. "He came bringing the same need to trust the world to care for him that every child brings to the moment of birth.

"We do not know what would have happened to the world if Joseph and Mary had been less diligent in raising Jesus. We do know that he was born with enemies and into a world of real privations. Joseph and Mary rose to the challenge of keeping him safe – not just safe for themselves and their family but safe for us all, safe for all time.

"Clearly, we owe them thanks for their care just as we owe Him thanks for His coming among us. Today, let us thank Robert Sean for trusting the world enough to also come among us, and let us thank his parents and his God-parents for having the courage to make the commitment of keeping him safe and of nurturing him.

"Robert, this is your second sacrament. Your birth was first; now your baptism. You're far too young to remember either. Some day, however, you will learn about such things. I hope that on that day you will appreciate our joy that you are among us and, also, appreciate the wonderful love of your parents and the other people gathered around you today.

"May your life be full of wonder, joy, and love. In the name of The Father, The Son, and The Holy Ghost. Amen"

Once again they all answer, "Amen."

Thus it is that Robert Sean Flanagan enters the company of believers and the community of Christ.

* * *

Jem Christobal has come to the baptism. She has brought a plate of brownies – homemade by her husband – and a gift – a baby's suit, too expensive by half for her income and too fancy and ruffled for Sean and Kathleen's tastes, but still very appreciated.

"I wouldn't have missed it for the world," she assures Mary. "I'm only sorry that my husband can't be here, too. The restaurant … You know how it is. He did want to meet you-all."

Mary nods in agreement. "Hopefully some other time."

"I sure do hope so …"

Jem makes her way about the room. Her anxiety motivates her outgoingness. She and Kathleen seem to form an instant bond, a recognition of kindred spirits filled with care for others. They chat about hospice care and The Sisters of Mercy Home for the Incurable's need for more aides. "Are you recruiting me?" Jem asks.

"I'm sure the sisters would be happy if I did."

"I'm not sure that I could do death that well."

"That is a problem for a lot of ..."

Danny has been standing next to them. Having barely taken Jem's hand, he looks bored and uncomfortable. He tugs on Kathleen's arm. "We've got to talk with my mother. She looks really uncomfortable."

That is true. Elizabeth Hennessy is clearly not enjoying the little celebration. Standing to one side, she has been glaring at her son and periodically making gestures with her head – gestures of an impatient desire to leave.

"Now, is that lady your Momma?" Jem asks, flashing her warmest smile. "I've just got to give her one of Charlie's brownies.

She walks over to the table where the food has been laid out, takes a brownie and puts it on a small paper plate. She carries it over to Mrs. Hennessy and introduces herself. "I'm Jem. My husband made these here brownies. You just have to try one." She hands the plate to the older woman, who takes it with irritated reluctance.

"I don't really ..."

"Oh, you just try it! They are sooo good." Jem smiles a practiced innocence. She acts as if it has never occurred to her that the other lady wants nothing to do with her. Perhaps in another setting, but she refuses to accept that any of Mary and Sean's friends might object to the color of her skin.

Luckily, Amelia has sized up the situation and comes to the rescue. "Are you Jem?" she asks as she skillfully gets between the two women. "These brownies are really delicious. Your husband's a chef isn't he? Where does he work?" All the while she is leading Jem across the room.

When she looks back, Jem catches a glimpse as Danny and his mother are leaving. The uneaten brownie is left on a table. Kathleen is looking after them in obvious discomfort. She looks at Jem, smiles, and takes a big bite of the brownie in her own hand.

Jem, in appreciation, returns the smile and waves. Kathleen reflexively returns both gestures. Bits of brownie fall to the floor, and both women laugh. Kathleen stoops to pick up the crumbs, and Jem crosses the room to help.

# Chapter Thirteen

Mary – with her characteristic preoccupation about doing right – has been putting Arnie off. He wants to make their wedding plans, and she wants to wait until Kathleen and Danny's intentions are clear. "I don't want to have him feeling pressured," Mary explains to Arnie as she runs her right forefinger over the engagement ring. "If we announce a date, he might feel that he has to. I'm afraid that would make him run for cover." They are spending another comfortable evening lounging in his apartment.

Yet, as comfortable as the evening may be, Arnie is more than a bit impatient. He wants to be married. He isn't sure why – other than a few college functions and of course Mary's formal leave-taking from Amelia's boardinghouse, there would be no real change. Still, he wants that ceremony to take place. With all his heart he wants them to be married, to be transformed into a single, sacred unit.

Despite his annoyance, he tries to have a reasonable discussion. "Do you really think he's that skittish, or is it that you feel that Kathleen is that vulnerable?"

"I guess some of both." Mary does a lot of worrying about her daughter. In her heart she isn't quite convinced that Danny is going to be a good husband. Like Karen, Mary, also, sees Danny as too tied to his mother, too immature and unprepared to take on the responsibilities of married life. At the same time, she instinctively knows her daughter's pain. She wants Kathleen to be happy. Now, without the pressure of her old rigidly interpreted religiosity and especially with the pleasure that she is finding with Arnie, Mary can accept – perhaps too easily – Kathleen's remarrying as answer to the emptiness of her life.

"Is there some way we could maybe goose him along?" Arnie makes a pinching motion with his right hand. It is meant as a joke, but it also signals his edginess. The summer has passed without their making any formal wedding plans, and he is very aware of the question he can't avoid: will Mary ever feel free to follow through on the commitment they had made in Maine. He cannot resist iterating his position, "I don't want to pressure you, but I do want to set a date. We don't have to have a big wedding or anything like that, but it does have to take place."

"I know how you feel, but I'm not sure why? I'm the one who should be citing scripture here and pushing you. What's your great moral imperative?"

"Those philosophy courses are beginning to rub off. There's no moral imperative. I'm just getting older, and I want to be married and live comfortably. Look at Sean and Karen. Hell, I'm jealous of them! I know we're as close, that our love life is just as good, that we have more freedom to come and go; but I'm still jealous. They have the security of a piece of paper that makes them one. I guess underneath all my intellectual crap I'm simply old-fashioned."

"I promise. If Danny hasn't asked Kathleen by Thanksgiving, we'll announce the date."

"What date?"

"If you want to invite people, let's go for June. If that isn't an issue, then January."

"What do you want?" Arnie asks.

"You." Mary grabs him around the neck and kisses him, thrusting her tongue into his mouth in a way that would have once been inconceivable to her. "Now! I want you right now! Right here and right now!"

Arnie gently pushes her away. "January or June, which do you want, people or not?"

Mary starts to cry. "You've never pushed me away before."

"I'm sorry." He reaches out to her. "It's just I want to set the date already."

"Don't you think I do?"

"I'm not sure. Sometimes I feel like you're really afraid."

Mary hates to admit it even to herself, but Arnie is right. There is a part of her that is afraid of the commitment he has been asking. At some level of her being she doesn't want to give up the freedom that had never been hers before. At another level, and even more uncomfortable, is her fear that the word "married" might somehow change their relationship – superimpose a load of expectations and moral judgments that had sat so heavily – and so unconsciously – on her life with Sean. "Maybe a little."

She moves nervously about the room, picks up a book from the coffee table, flips some pages, and puts it back. Finally, she speaks again. "June. Let's set a date in June and invite people."

"You're sure?"

"I'm sure." She crosses the room and again grabs him – perhaps a little less strongly – by the neck and kisses him passionately. This time Arnie doesn't push her away.

They half walk and half drag each other into the bedroom. Mary reaches over and undoes the buttons of Arnie's shirt. At the same time, he is working on the zipper of her dress and then on the clasp of her bra. In bits and pieces, with almost adolescent fumbling and laughter, they undress and tumble onto the waiting bed. The spread is from Africa; it is bright with flora and fauna. "That lion must be envious," Mary says.

"Why?"

"Because he can't make love as well as you," she responds and throws herself on him.

Clearly, the storm has passed. The tension has, at least for the moment, been averted. It is going to be another idyllic evening.

* * *

Amelia has appointed herself an honorary aunt and has come to relish the role. "Of course I'll stay with him," she responds to Karen's request. If she wanted to be entirely honest, Amelia would have added, "It will be the best part of my week."

Amelia's is a limited life. She has come to love Mary and also to envy her. Yet, despite her belief that Arnie is a wonderful man, Amelia is not about to change her own life style and start looking for someone or even to make an effort to engage the world. She had been terribly hurt and has long since resolved to keep herself out of harm's way no matter how lonely her life might be. The occasional trip to Sean and Karen's house in Cambridge is one of the few outings she allows herself to enjoy – otherwise preferring to hide in her overly genteel if fading parlor, where she can hold forth to the young women boarders who find their ways into her home as if she is a sadly experienced and mysterious woman of the world – a mysterious figure for those who come and then move on in steady progression.

Sitting with a copy of "The Boston Herald" as a shield, she takes the forty-five minute transit commute as an obstacle to be overcome. "At least," she thinks, "Mary and Arnie will be able to give me a ride home."

The Flanagans are going out to dinner. They are celebrating Robert's first steps – or more correctly his first clown-like attempts at steps. It seems to Amelia that they are always celebrating. Over tea earlier that afternoon she had commented, "Mary, I've never seen so much joy in one family."

"I have to admit that we're going out more to give Karen a break than to celebrate. The poor girl is feeling overwhelmed. I don't think she realized how much work she was going to face, and a toddler is even harder than an infant."

"Maybe they should get some help. Wasn't there that woman who used to help with Sean?"

"Jem. Yes, she was at the baptism. I've thought about suggesting they call her, but I don't think Sean would accept the idea. You know how proud he is. He doesn't like to admit that he's handicapped. It's really unfair to Karen, but that's how he is. Even when Karen was in the hospital, Kathleen and I were the only ones he'd let help. And as soon as she got home, Karen took over like she hadn't been through anything. Her mother was helping with Robert, but there was no way Sean could have tolerated his mother-in-law's caring for him. When you think of what she has to do, I swear I don't know where she gets the energy and determination."

"So you and Arnie are taking them out to give her a break. That's a good idea."

"I just wish you'd come with us."

"Then who'd watch the baby? Besides which, you know I hate going out."

"You will come to our wedding, won't you?"

"For that I'll make an exception. Have you set a date?"

"Not officially, but we're talking about June."

"That's fine. My calendar is open that month."

"Don't mention it to the kids."

"Oh?"

"We're hoping that Danny asks Kathleen before we have to say anything." Mary notices her friend wince. "You have a problem with Danny, don't you?"

"I'm not sure." Amelia shifts in her recliner. "I'm just not sure."

"Well, they seem happy to me." Mary's tone is less sure than her words. "I just want Kathleen to get out of that hospice before she gets the virus. I understand that one of the nun's blood tests came back positive the other day."

"Did Kathleen tell you that?"

"No, I figured it out. Suddenly one of the best nursing sisters is given light administrative duties. It's happened before."

"That doesn't mean its AIDS." Amelia's voice shakes.

"No, I suppose not." Clearly, Mary doesn't believe this.

Both women sit in silence for a few minutes thinking about the horribleness of the plague that is sweeping America and the reality of the risk to Kathleen and by extension to the rest of the family. "I keep thinking about the baby," Amelia finally adds.

"I know. I hope they find a cure before he grows up."

"That's not …"

"I know," Mary interrupts. "Let's not go there. I can't… I couldn't."

Amelia nods in understanding agreement. It is a sobering thought on which to leave, but Mary has promised to do some errands before meeting Arnie at his apartment. She puts on her lightweight blue coat and then exchanges it for a heavier one, a dark red one that Arnie had insisted on buying through the L.L. Bean catalogue. "I can feel winter coming," she says to herself. "It feels like there are knives in the air."

# Chapter Fourteen

The winter air feels like daggers as they breathe. When they exhale, a cloud of white announces itself. They half expect it to condense into ice and shatter as it hits the ground. It has snowed recently, and there are patches of ice and crunchy snow on the sidewalks and streets. Still, at Arnie's urging, they choose to go to the harbor for dinner. The restaurant is quiet, and the maitre d' tries to steer them to a table near the bar – near the other diners. But, somewhat to his consternation, Arnie asks for a table overlooking the icy water.

He seats them and goes off to find among his shorthanded staff the unhappy waitress and busboy who will have to take on this outlying table. He can only hope that the tip will be worth it, or he'll have to somehow make it up to them. "Perhaps Michelle," he thinks, "and Sergio. They're always the easiest."

The harbor is choppy this evening, and the few small boats that have been left at mooring are bouncing up and down. Having asked to eat by the water, Arnie chooses to sit with his back to the windows. "As the host, I should give up the view," he says sitting down.

"It's either the view or your dinner," cracks Sean. To Danny, he comments, "The great sea captain, Arnie'd get sick in the bathtub."

"That, too." Arnie smiles as he motions to the two seats to each side of him inviting Kathleen and Danny to join him.

Sean maneuvers his wheelchair into the spot opposite Arnie where Karen has pulled away the chair to make room. Mary sits next to her son, and Karen takes the sixth place.

A few minutes pass. Finally, trying to put on a friendly face despite her irritation, Michelle comes over and introduces herself while Sergio fills water glasses and puts bread and butter in place.

"Would everybody like wine?" Arnie asks. There is no objection so he orders a bottle of domestic Chardonnay. He describes his wishes, "nothing fancy or expensive, just a good wine for decent people".

Michelle makes a suggestion, and he agrees. She heads off somewhat happier to know that the bill will include a bottle of wine. That usually means a bigger tip, and it always means an extra two bucks from the restaurant – incentive pay they called it.

Meanwhile, Sergio has left and has come back with a tray of celery, carrot sticks, radishes, and large black olives, which he carefully centers.

"The healthy part of the meal," Karen jokes.

"If you're a rabbit." Eating vegetables is an ongoing if good-hearted issue between Karen and Sean.

"The lobster here is terrific," Arnie advises.

"I like clams," Danny responds.

"I've never had them here, but I'm sure they're good, too. What about you, Kath?"

"I'll try the lobster."

"I thought you liked clams, too," Danny whines at her.

"I do, but I think I'd like to try the lobster. It's something I don't eat very often."

"Well, if you want to take a chance," Danny offers. "I mean you know that you like clams. You may not ..."

"I'm sure I'll like it. It's a real treat to try something different." Kathleen's tone has grown as sharp and icy as the wind.

"I get the feeling there's something bothering you two," Mary says as inoffensively as she can.

"Just the usual issues." Kathleen shrugs her shoulders as she speaks.

"Would you care to share," Arnie asks. He has no idea what the "usual issues" might be.

"No, we'll work it out," Danny answers with an abrupt manner that makes everyone even more uncomfortable.

"OK," Arnie responds wishing that he had never mentioned crustaceans. "Does everybody know what they want?" he asks to lead the discussion away from tension.

By this time Michelle has returned with the wine. She makes a fancy – tip inducing – ritual opening, offering the cork, a taste. Arnie hands the glass to Danny, "What do you think?"

Danny gulps it down. "Fine."

Arnie nods to the waitress who pours for them. "Are you ready to order?" she asks.

They murmur assent.

After going around the table, Michelle summarizes. "Let me make sure I have this right: Two baked stuffed lobsters, one steamed lobster, one lobster Newburg, one fried clams and one flounder. Right?"

They all nod in agreement.

"Any appetizers?"

Arnie looks around the table. "Anybody?"

"Do you have some clam chowder?" asks Danny. He has meanwhile emptied his wine glass and reaches for the bottle.

"New England or Manhattan?"

"You've got to be kidding? Do you really serve that New York junk here?" Danny's voice has an edge.

"Yes, we do, sir," the waitress answers in a placating tone. "You know we get a lot of tourists here, and they eat it. But the New England is very good – more of a house specialty."

"I'll pass." After the young woman has left them, Danny comments, "I don't see why they can't just serve good old New England chowder."

Nobody responds. His comment hangs like a heavy fog over the table.

After a moment's uncomfortable silence, Danny asks, "Am I the only New England patriot here?"

Mary notes the tension in his body as he speaks. She wonders what is really the matter. "This is the worst ..." she thinks, but she says nothing.

"No," Arnie, trying to lighten things, answers, "I must admit I resent the way we've become homogenized. I like regional differences. I like being from New England. I think its television that's destroying our sense of place." He's glad to play the professor for a moment and steer the conversation away from Danny's distemper.

"I missed Boston when I was in Minnesota. Not that it wasn't beautiful there," Sean adds quickly.

"And, I miss Minnesota," Karen comments. "I suppose it's whatever you grew up with."

Mary sighs with relief as Danny seems to relax. "I wish I'd seen more of this country. Actually, if you leave out my trip from Ireland, the farthest I've ever traveled is to Maine with Arnie."

"That was a good trip," Arnie puts in. "Of course, the company was the best part." Mary blushes slightly even as she smiles in assent.

"I've always wanted to see Ireland."

"Did you, Kathleen? So did I."

"But, Mom, you were born there."

"I know, but I never saw it. I lived in a little village until the day I sailed for America. Looking back I can't imagine how I got the courage to make that trip."

"Mary Flanagan, you are a courageous woman. We all know that," Arnie declares.

"I'll drink to that," says Sean managing to get the straw from his wine glass into his mouth.

* * *

"What do you think?" Arnie lies staring at the ceiling. He holds Mary's hand. Gently, almost unconsciously he caresses her knuckles with his forefinger. He pulls her hand to his mouth and kisses it.

"I don't know."

"It must be very hard for you."

"Ambivalent, isn't that the word you used the other day? That's what I feel."

In her other hand Mary holds a book. It is opened. Next to her head is her rosary.

"So you're reading The Bible?" Arnie tries to make this a neutral question. He carefully moderates his tone to show no feeling or attitude.

"And praying."

"And praying," he echoes. "I hope it helps."

"It makes me feel better." She squeezes his hand. "It's all I can do."

"I know," he murmurs with empathy. "I only wish …"

"That you could pour salt on the waters and heal them."

"What?"

"Elisha, one of the prophets. The waters of the city, in the river, was bad. He threw salt on them and healed the waters."

"I wish we had that power."

"So I pray."

"I understand. Darling, I do understand. I only hope that whatever happens ..." He has no idea how to continue.

"Whatever happens, I love you." She puts the book down and roles over to kiss him twice – not on the mouth but on the eyes.

He pulls her tight. "God knows that I love you, too."

"But, Arnie, I'm scared – I'm terrible scared for my daughter. I want her to be happy."

"We all do, we all do."

They lie in silence.

Mary awakens in the early morning. Her Bible rests on the blanket next to her. During the night she has taken hold of her rosary. It is still tightly clutched in her hand. Arnie is still asleep. He is lying on his back and breathing slowly. She rests her head on his chest.

# Chapter Fifteen

The paths along the banks of the reservoir are uneven. It takes all a jogger's concentration to keep from tripping and tumbling into Boston's water supply. That is probably why so many joggers have passed her prone body without noticing. It is only when one, glancing up at the sound of a scurrying animal, starts back in shock and lands on his seat that she is seen. "Oh, my God!" he exclaims as he scrambles back to his feet. "Oh, my God," he repeats so taken aback that he doesn't even notice the pain from his fall, "somebody get help. Somebody, anybody, for Christ's sake, get help!"

Gingerly, as if he is approaching a dangerous animal, he inches his way towards her. "Miss, Miss. Are you OK?" His voice is at first a whisper, which grows louder and more tremulous.

Kathleen doesn't stir.

"Miss!" He is shouting now. His wide eyes take in the scene. Her panty hose have been ripped off. They and her shoes are in a small tangled pile a few feet away. Next to them are her well-worn green parka, scarf, and dark green gloves with leather palms. The sheepskin hat with ear flaps that Karen had given her is tossed farther from her body. Kathleen's plaid skirt has been ripped. It still clings to her waist but has been pulled up and now covers her torso rather than her legs and buttocks. Her head is turned sideways, and the jogger can see that there is a thin stream of blood still coming from her mouth and soaking into the ground next to her broken glasses.

He bends over her, afraid to touch. "Get help," he shouts into the frosty air – still to no one. They are alone. "For God's sake, get help," he repeats once more. He isn't sure, but he thinks he sees her body moving ever so slightly. "Is she still alive, or is she dead?" he asks aloud in the frigid empty air. "Help!" he screams.

There is a handbag nearby. Instinctively he reaches for it. He can not bring himself to touch her body, but the inanimate handbag is less threatening. Its contents seem untouched. "Mrs. Dougan," he whispers to her. If yelling hasn't worked, something in his brain tells him that softness might. "Mrs. Dougan," he tries again.

He is looking at an identification card that Kathleen carries in her wallet. Ironically, it is the one piece of identification on which she still uses her married name. It is her library card, something that she had stopped using once she had decided that her life would never move forward. At one time Kathleen had been an avid reader, but that had been when she thought it would still matter if she were to learn – that had been before it had seemed that her life had stopped.

Knowing Kathleen's name makes her seem more alive. The jogger focuses himself enough to pull off the top of his jogging suit and use it to cover her upper body. Still he can't bring himself to actually touch her, not even to adjust her clothing.

Kathleen makes no response. "Oh, my God," he exclaims again.

He hears the sound of another runner. Even though the trees are bare, the jumble of bushes makes it difficult to see. Jumping up from his crouched position near Kathleen's head, the jogger waves his arms and yells, "Over here. I need help. Over here." He can hear the pace of the other runner quicken.

A young woman breaks her way into view.

"Over here!" he yells again as if she would somehow pass him by. "Help!" His voice has taken a more desperate tone. It occurs to him that the police might blame him. They will certainly question him. He will definitely be late for work. He wonders if someone else had already found this Kathleen Dougan and had left her lying there rather than face such inconveniences. For a moment he wishes he had done the same, but he is a basically decent human being. He knows that he could not have left her there.

The woman jogger is someone he has noticed before, but they have never met. Indeed, they have never even nodded to each other when passing along the labyrinth of paths that crisscross the reservation. She is a striking blonde in a silver jogging suit. He figures that it must have cost a hundred dollars or more and admires how well it shows off her body. He has wondered, when he has seen her previously, how to introduce himself; now in this strangest and most ghoulish of ways a method is presenting itself. He feels guilty to think of such things while there is a victim lying inert near him.

"This woman needs help. I think she's alive, but she doesn't respond. Do you know first aid?" It occurs to him that he must sound like an idiot. The words are spilling out of his mouth without time to censor them. There is no time for social amenities or to think about manners. The woman pushes him aside and takes in the scene.

She kneels down next to Kathleen's head and puts her ear to Kathleen's bleeding mouth. "She's alive. She's breathing. I'll stay with her. You run back to the concession stand and call 911. There's a payphone; it's ..."

"I know," he cuts her off in mid-sentence. He is relieved to have her take charge. He is thankful that he no longer has to think about what to do – that he has been given a specific job. "I'll be right back." He sprints away. Part of him wants to turn around, to go back and introduce himself. The chance might not present itself again. Then he realizes that she, like he, will be spending the morning with the police. Suddenly, the probability of police interrogation seems less daunting. "I'll be right back," he calls again over his shoulder and almost trips.

The woman in the silver jogging suit gently pulls the remains of Kathleen's dress down over her buttocks and legs. She takes off her silver jacket and cushions it under Kathleen's head. "You must be cold lying there," she mutters. She rummages through Kathleen's bag and finds a white handkerchief fringed with lace. She uses it to dab at the blood. Somebody has knocked out two of Kathleen's front teeth; the blood is still oozing from the sockets. There is, she realizes, dried blood crusted under Kathleen's nose, and one of her eyes has been blackened. "Who did this to you?" she asks the inert figure. "What son of a bitch would beat up on you like this?"

Usually, she thinks of herself as a sophisticated woman of the world not easily shocked by the daily news stories of mankind's bestiality. But this isn't a story on the six o'clock news, it is a reality in which she finds herself rocking back and forth on her haunches and emotionally very and terribly involved.

Somewhere in the back of her mind she recollects stories of dying elephants. The other elephants would gather around their dying comrade trying to urge it back to its feet and then, having failed, they would give a forlorn trumpet before leaving their dead comrade to the jungle – the jungle which would reclaim the carcass and continue the cycle of life and death. She wonders, rocking back and forth by Kathleen's head, if she were not experiencing a similar instinctive need to raise her fallen comrade. "Get up, damn you," she hollers in outrage. She isn't sure from where in her unconscious the rage springs, but it is taking over her mind. "Don't let the bastards do this to you," she screams. "You have to fight back. You have to get up!"

In the distance she hears the wail of a police siren accompanied by the keening moan of an ambulance. The imminence of help brings her back to reality. "Help is coming," she reassures Kathleen's prostrate form. She repeats it, "Help is coming." This time it is to reassure herself.

For the first time she is aware how long she has been crouched next to this stranger. Her haunches hurt. Her body is cold. And, most of all, she is angry – furious at some unknown perpetrator, some nameless evil.

She can hear the heavy footfalls of the approaching help. It sounds like an army charging down the path. She prays that it will be an army that can do some good.

"Damn," one of the army exclaims. Presumably he has slipped or tripped on the uneven ground. They come into view. The jogger who had found Kathleen is in the lead. He is followed by a policeman and a policewoman, who in turn are followed by two emergency medical service workers struggling to keep up while carrying their gear.

"Help!" the woman jogger yells as if they can't see her and aren't coming to her. "Help!" she screams from somewhere in her collective unconscious.

A few minutes later the two joggers stand next to each other talking with the policeman. The man, Joe Gatano, is admiring the lady, who has identified herself as Susan Cohen. In his head he keeps hoping there will be a more suitable opportunity to ask her – to ask her what he wonders – to ask her for a date, for coffee. He knows that he won't, that somehow the opportunity will never come, that he will always be too hesitant that she would surely say no anyway. Is it, he wonders, that he is too shy or that he knows she could never trust him having met under these horrible circumstances? He isn't sure. It doesn't really matter. "That," he says to himself, "is just the way life works or maybe, more so, really doesn't work."

Under the silver jacket, which has now been tossed to one side by the E.M.S. workers, Susan Cohen is wearing a white camisole. Joe admires the tightness of her shivering body and her small breasts poking at the white cotton. She can feel his eyes on her. One part of her responds with anger and another part with a reciprocal energy. "He's cute," she thinks. Then, "What the hell am I thinking about? There's a woman dying – a woman who some bastard man attacked. Men are such shits – such God-damned shits!"

The policeman is meticulously questioning and re-questioning the two joggers as if they have some secret evidence which would immediately solve the heinous crime at which all three of them were trying to avoid looking. For the fourth time he asks Joe to estimate the time at which he had first seen Kathleen, or the victim, as the police officer refers to her trying to dehumanize and objectify her. He keeps writing notes in a small spiral bound notebook as if Joe has said something incriminating. "And how much later did Miss Cohen arrive on the scene?" the officer asks – also for the fourth time.

As Joe is about to answer, the policewoman, who has been overseeing the medical team to make sure that as little evidence is compromised as possible, turns to her colleague, "They're taking her to City. She's obviously been raped and sodomized and beaten up, but they think the worst is the psychological trauma. She's regained consciousness, but she appears catatonic."

"Or in shock," adds one of the E.M.S. workers.

"God damn," mutters the male officer.

"Can you guys give us a hand getting her out of here?" the other member of the ambulance team asks the cops.

"One of us has to stay here with the evidence," the woman officer responds, but my partner can give you a hand.

There is a momentary pause. "I'll help, too," Joe offers.

They each grab one of the four handles of the stretcher. "Careful," one of the EMTs says. Susan can tell from his voice that he had been the one who had nearly fallen on their way down the path. They make their way with slow deliberation.

Susan and the policewoman stand staring at each other over the small patch where Kathleen's blood has soaked into the ground. Nothing is said between them. Nothing needs to be said. They both realize that they live in a world in which it could just as easily have been one of them who had been lying there that morning. The policewoman in silent recognition of that reality reaches down and touches her gun. Susan winces. In the distance they can here the ambulance screaming their protest into the quiet Boston morning.

* * *

It had been a pleasant night – a light supper followed by a romantic movie, a cup of tea that had lasted for hours as they shared ever more of their lives. Then nestled in each others arms, they had slept – an innocent and loving sleep. No wonder that Mary and Arnie are still in bed – awake, making love, smiling at one another, happy in the moment – when Amelia calls this cold morning.

After looking more carefully through Kathleen's bag, the police have found her address at the hospice, but somehow they have neglected to correct her name on their records. She is still listed as Kathleen Dougan.

Sister Angelica has been sitting by the phone since early morning. The mother superior had assigned her to the task as soon as she had realized that Kathleen had not returned the night before. "Something must be wrong," she had reasoned, "it just isn't like Kathleen."

Sister Angelica is so sure that any call would have to be about Kathleen that she doesn't even listen to the family name the detective uses. Without a moment's hesitation, she provides Mary's name and address as next of kin.

Amelia is busy in the kitchen when the phone rings. She answers with an impatient, "What?"

"I need to speak with Mrs. Dougan's mother," the policeman responds. "This is the Boston police department. Is she there?"

Amelia is startled and taken aback. "Mrs. Dougan? I don't know who that might be. Are you sure you have the right number?"

"This is the number the sister gave me."

It takes a moment for Amelia to realize that he must be talking about Kathleen. Then, nervously, she asks, "Are you calling about Kathleen? Kathleen Flanagan?"

"Yes, Kathleen. Kathleen Dougan. Is her mother there?" The officer sounds impatient – as if people have deliberately been trying to confuse him.

"That must have been her married name. She uses Flanagan now."

"Fine, fine," the officer responds impatiently. "But is her mother there?"

"No, I'm afraid she's not here right now." Not knowing what else to say she adds, "I expect her momentarily. Can I have her call you?"

He gives the number and his name.

"Can you tell me what this is about? Mary will be terribly upset if I just tell her to call you. Is Kathleen all right? I mean she's not..." Amelia leaves the question hanging.

"No, she's not dead. But she has been hurt."

"Oh, my God, where is she?"

"Just have her mother call me, Detective Flynn." He repeats the number.

"But, where's Kathleen? I'll have to tell her or she'll get frantic."

"She's at Boston City, but make sure her mother calls me before she goes over there."

"Was she raped?" It is the first thought that comes to Amelia.

"Just have her mother call." He hangs up preemptively.

"An automobile accident?" Amelia continues into the dead phone.

It takes a moment for her to compose herself well enough to remember Arnie's number – moments of heart-pounding terror.

The phone rings a few times before Arnie answers. "Hello," he barks. He resents the intrusion into this moment of idyllic love. Almost winded and spent with passion when the phone has burst in on their moment of climax, he is in no mood to talk.

"Arnie, it's Amelia. Put Mary on!" Amelia's voice makes the urgency of her call apparent. There is mumbling as Arnie talks to Mary and then a fumbling sound as he hands her the phone.

"Amelia?" Mary's voice comes on the line. "What is it? Are you OK?"

"It isn't me, dear." There's a pause, and Mary can hear her friend drawing a deep breath. "The police just called. Kathleen's in the hospital."

"What?"

"It's Kathleen. She's been hurt. She's in the hospital."

"Where?" Mary cries out in a trembling voice. "My God, Amelia, where is she?"

"She's at Boston City Hospital. That's all I know," Amelia is fighting to keep her own voice as level as possible. "The police officer didn't give me any details. I tried, but he… I barely got him to tell me where she is. He left his name and number. He said it's urgent that you call him before you go to the hospital."

"I've got to go to her," Mary wails.

"First, call the cop. He said it was very important that you …"

"Who?"

"The cop, call him." Amelia gives Mary the name and number and then repeats it.

"I'll meet you at the hospital, Mary. Call Detective Flynn, and I'll meet you at the hospital."

Amelia hears Mary repeating her words to Arnie and his voice in the background. She can't hear what Arnie is saying, but from his tone she can tell he is alternating between some kind of masculine protesting outrage and concern.

Arnie takes the phone. "We'll meet you at the hospital," he orders.

Amelia starts to respond. Before any words have come to her mouth, Arnie has slammed the phone back into its cradle. The last thing she can hear is Mary's wailing in the background. The sound lingers in her brain even after she returns the hand piece to its receiver and begins to gather her own outer clothing for the painful trip to the hospital.

On the bus she will rock back and forth, and she will keep asking herself, "What happened to her? How did this happen? Why? Oh, why?"

* * *

Detective Jack Flynn tries to stay very matter of fact on the phone. "Mrs. Dougan is your daughter, is that correct?"

"Yes, but she doesn't …" Mary lets the rest of her correction hang. "Is she OK?" Mary tries to make her voice demand an answer, but she knows that it is quavering with terror. If it had not been for Arnie she would have already been on her way to the hospital, but he has insisted that she follow instructions.

It has always been his belief that when reason and order fail, there is little else to do but follow orders and hope. Now, he insists that Mary follow orders while he is hoping for all of them.

"The doctors seem to think that she'll recover," Flynn responds in his most professional tone. "They'll be able to tell you more at the hospital." He clears his throat before continuing. "What I need to know, Mrs. Flanagan is, well, was your daughter out on a date last night?"

"Why? What happened? Did somebody hurt her?"

"That's what we're trying to piece together. Do you know if she went out last night?"

"Yes. I think they were going to a movie."

"They? Was she with someone in particular?"

"Her boyfriend." Mary gives Flynn Danny's name, address, and phone number.

"Do you know if they've been fighting?"

"No, I don't think so," Mary responds. "But ..." She doesn't complete the sentence.

"But what?" Flynn's tone is demanding.

"Well, nothing you can put your finger on, just an edginess."

"Between them?"

"Not so much between them, just that Danny, he seemed to ... Why don't you talk to my friend? Maybe he can explain it better." She starts to hand Arnie the phone.

The officer shouts into his end of the conversation, "Wait, Mrs. Flanagan."

She pulls the receiver back. "Yes." Her voice seems hollow.

The policeman keeps her on the phone for a couple more minutes getting details. Finally, she protests. "I have to go. My daughter!"

"I understand," Officer Flynn answers – not understanding at all. "There is one last question if I may. Where are you now? I don't get the feeling you are at Mrs. Callaghan's house."

"No, I spent the night at my boyfriend's, my fiancé's." Feeling vaguely embarrassed, as if she had been found out, Mary gives the officer Arnie's name and address.

While Mary is on the phone, Arnie has gotten dressed. He hands her a quickly written note: "I'll get the car and meet you in front. I'm sure she's all right." As he hands her the note, Arnie takes Mary's right hand in his and gently kisses it. She tries to smile at him, but can not. Instead her face reflects the pain that is shooting through her heart and soul.

When she gets off the phone, Mary wishes that Arnie hadn't left. It is chilling to be alone even within the safety of his apartment. She picks up the phone thinking to call Sean and Karen but realizes that she would only upset them and that there is no way they can help. Mary tries to never think of Sean as an invalid, but there are times such as this when she wishes her son were whole so that she could lean on him.

She puts the receiver back in its cradle. For a moment, she wanders aimlessly about the room – fingering familiar objects as if they could give her a sense of security. Then she remembers that Arnie is coming back with the car – that she has to get to the hospital. She starts grabbing clothing.

The Buick's horn honks just as Mary is finishing her hurried dressing. As she starts out of the apartment door, she stops just a moment to adjust her glasses and to fluff the feathers of her hair. "Oh, my God, Oh, my God. Christ hae mercy," she moans as she walks to the car.

Arnie has just pulled the red Buick to the front of the building. Before he can get out to help her, Mary opens the passenger door and gets in. She closes the door without looking and catches her coat in it. A small piece of fabric hangs out. Mary is unaware.

On the way to the hospital Mary sits hunched forward with her face in her hands. Arnie keeps his right hand on her shoulder except when he needs it for the wheel. They say nothing. Words would only intensify the sense of helplessness and worry.

As he pulls into the emergency area, Arnie says, "You go in. I'll park and meet you inside." He looks sideways at her and iterates, "I'll be right in." He moves to give her a hug, but Mary pulls away.

"Inside," she echoes aimlessly.

"I'll meet you inside," he iterates.

Mary throws open the door and almost leaps out. As she does, she notices that her coat has been hanging out the entire ride. This irritates her. Then she realizes that she and Arnie have not showered. Now she is upset. She wonders if the doctors will notice. She had always insisted that Sean and Kathleen wear clean underwear in case they had to go to the hospital. It had been one of those silly things that parents say and that kids make fun of. Now it hits her with some unconscious force. She wonders if her unshowered state will somehow affect what will happen to her daughter. Then she realizes that she is thinking nonsense. "Christ, oh Christ, hae mercy."

All this goes on in Mary's head as Arnie reaches over and closes the passenger door. Mary hears it slam behind her as she bolts through the automatic doors of the hospital. "Dear God, let her be all right. Please, let her be all right," she prays.

"God, I hope they'll both be ok," Arnie thinks as he parks. There is a patch of ice on the pavement. Not seeing it as he rushes back towards the emergency room door, Arnie slips and almost falls. "Will we make it?" he asks himself. "Can we do this?" Then he realizes, "I have to be strong. I have to be strong for Mary.

* * *

Danny isn't at home. His mother says that she hasn't seen him since he left to pick Kathleen up the night before. "I think he said something about dancing afterwards if they had the enrgy." This is all ascertained between Mrs. O'Brien's tears and questions. "He's never been in trouble before," she keeps repeating.

"We don't know that he is now," Jack Flynn mutters through clenched teeth. He doesn't like this woman. He doesn't like the fact that she hasn't so much as inquired about Kathleen's condition; she is too preoccupied with her son – with her obviously too precious son. This leaves the detective feeling somewhat uneasy if not downright disgusted.

He explains to the weeping woman that officers will be sent to interview the bartenders and bouncers at all the clubs in town, especially those near the reservoir. "Can we have a recent photograph?"

She gives him the most recent photograph she has. She had taken it herself. Danny and Kathleen are sitting on the chaise lounge in the backyard. Kathleen is wearing a modest one-piece bathing suit. Danny has on his prized cutoff jeans with the snap at his waist opened. One of the other detectives, a woman, looks carefully at the photograph. "He was comfortable around her," she observes.

"Yes," Mrs. O'Brien answers. "I thought they would soon be getting married." She pauses. "Soon, I thought they would – married soon."

"Is she pregnant?" asks the female detective.

"No. Soon – because they thought they were in love." There is a defensive edge in the mother's voice. "Don't tell anybody I told you this. I'm not sure Kathleen's mother would want you to know," she speaks in a near whisper.

"Go on," the detective's voice is eager. He is sure that a clue is coming.

"She couldn't have children," Mrs. O'Brien whispers "The poor dear."

"Oh," his voice sounds like a deflating balloon. "I'm sorry. You understand we have to consider everything."

To himself, he reflects, "Maybe that's why she sounds so, so what? Indifferent to this woman's condition? I wonder how she feels about the idea of their marrying."

Elizabeth O'Brien has continued. "My husband is the deputy to the commissioner. Of course I understand, but my boy has been raised right. He's good and God fearing. He was an altar boy. Did you know that?"

"No, ma'am," Jack Flynn responds as he writes that irrelevant fact in his book. Now that he knows who Elizabeth's husband is, he is planning on being as deferential as possible.

"Find my son. He must have been hurt, too." There is a painful pause. "Or killed." Mrs. O'Brien starts to wail at this sudden realization.

Flynn wants to do something that the woman's husband will appreciate. He starts to put his arm around her heaving shoulders, but he stops himself. "She could misinterpret," he thinks.

"We'll do our best." It is the best reassurance he can offer. "You can depend on that. The Boston police take care of our own."

\* \* \*

On the way back to the precinct, Flynn's partner radios a description of Danny's Saab. The description is broadcast, first on the local police radio and then throughout the state. Eventually, when the car hasn't been found, the net is widened. New York, New Jersey and the rest of New England is notified and then the entire country.

The photograph is also sent out on the wires. Police cars as far away as Chicago will have copies of the photograph sitting on their dashboards.

"She's a nice looking woman," one officer in Indianapolis comments.

"Why would a boyfriend do that?" his partner asks – making an obvious assumption, but still an assumption.

"Why does anyone? I'm not a shrink."

"Do you think they know?"

"Shrinks? Hell, no. They think every bastard is a victim of his background. To listen to them, every perp's mother should be locked up."

"Maybe he didn't do it. Maybe he's a victim, too."

"Maybe. Who knows?"

"His father's on the job."

"The old man must be frantic."

"You'd think so."

"Yeah, or maybe not. Who knows?"

The dragnet widens, but there is still no Danny.

There is also nothing from Kathleen. She lies catatonically – slowly physically healing but not emotionally – staring at the ceiling and not speaking. With time she will respond to simple commands, "Lift your left index finger, scratch you right ear, turn over." But, when asked questions, there is nothing. "If it's light in here, lift your right hand." Nothing. "If you remember what happened last night, nod your head." Nothing. "Did Danny hurt you? If he did, make a fist." Nothing.

It has becomes one of those cases – an outrage un-avenged, a crime unsolved, a victim un-recovered.

* * *

From the first day, Mary has been constantly by her daughter's side – day after day, evening after evening. Arnie stays with her as much as he can. He arrives in the morning unless he has to teach a class. As soon as the class is over, he is there. Mary is glad for his concern but somehow oblivious to his companionship and indifferent to the love behind it. Her own passion has been repressed – replaced by overwhelming maternal concern.

Amelia, also, is there almost constantly. Mary feels somehow more connected to Amelia. They share an unspoken anger, a bond that ties them not only to Kathleen but also to all abused women – not only against some unknown, or perhaps not unknown aggressor but also against all men.

Sean comes and holds his sister's hand. He comes whenever he can. He feels a tenderness that they had never shared as children, a joint purpose such as they had not known as teenagers. He doesn't know what to say, as if anyone does, so he repeats and repeats, "Hang in, Kath, just hang in." He does not share the images that are conjured sitting next to her – the images of Vietnam, the images of the wounded, the images of the shell-shocked, the images of horror. He doesn't mention them to Mary. He certainly does not share them with Karen. Instead, when he is alone, he sits staring inward.

Some days Amelia goes to stay with Robert, and Karen comes to the hospital. She, too, doesn't know what to do. She pats Kathleen's arm. She reads to her. She tries to make small jokes at which no one can laugh. Then she goes home and cries. She holds Robert close.

It is a continuous circle of concern. It is a continuous circle of pain.

Everybody tries to talk with Kathleen, to reassure her. Having talked with a psychiatrist, they try to talk about her feelings – to engage her emotions.

"You must have been terrified," says Arnie.

There is no response.

"It must have been so awful," tries Mary.

No reaction.

"You must be so angry," offer Amelia.

Nothing.

"If you'd like a drink, just blink twice," tries Karen.

No response to that either.

"God, I hate men," says Amelia.

"Oh, my daughter, my darling daughter," croons Mary.

The days pass and pass again.

* * *

"That no good son of a bitch; I wish I could kill him," Sean says when he and Arnie are taking a break in the corridor outside Kathleen's room. They have shared their suspicions: both sure that Danny is the one who has hurt Kathleen so terribly. Why? That they can not say. That they can not understand. Neither of them would ever attack a woman, especially not a woman for whom they had feelings.

"I know!" Arnie pauses. "I knew he could be irritable. He was terribly uptight that night at the restaurant. But, who would have thought? He just didn't seem the type. To lose control that way. I never ..."

"Maybe he's been doing drugs. Steroids, coke, who knows?" Sean pauses and then continues. "Maybe he just snapped, went off the end." He remembers Stan. He doesn't want to, but he remembers. "That's the way with Nam," he had once told Karen, "it just keeps coming back."

Stan Boynton, an average guy from an average town someplace in Arkansas, a guy just like him just from somewhere else. Just another grunt – loading helicopters, riding to nowhere landing zones, unloading, once in a while, a horrible while, bringing back wounded or evacuating a patrol that had gotten in too damn deep. Not something that was a routine you could ever get used to, but not like being on the ground.

Then suddenly Stan had snapped. A letter from home, a bad tab of acid, a whore who didn't satisfy: who knew? Did it matter? Anyway you figured it, the grenade had been tossed, the lieutenant had been killed, and Stan had been led off in all kinds of restraints. Just a different kind of casualty.

He pushes the memory down. He wants to gag on it, but he pushes it deep. "We may never know," he says – trying desperately to keep his voice matter-of-fact. "I just wonder when they'll find him the son of a bitch?"

"Given his father's connections I wonder if they're really looking." The thought causes Arnie to tense. His hands begin to curl into fists. "Relax," he says to himself. For the moment it works, but he knows that he and Sean are both seething.

Two weeks have passed. So far the authorities have not found Danny O'Brien. He has not been back to work and he has never called in. No one has heard from him – at least no one admits to it.

The police have done some investigating. A bouncer at a club in South Boston remembered Danny and Kathleen leaving around eleven thirty. The best the police have been able to do without Kathleen's help has been to place the attack sometime in the middle of the night.

\* \* \*

The parade of well-wishers continues in its solemn sense of obligation. The sisters of Mercy take turns visiting. So do the lay staff from the hospice. Family members whose loved ones have died in Kathleen's care come. They bring flowers, prayers and gratitude. Kathleen lies impassive.

Then there is a response – only once, when Pat Michaels comes to visit and to pray. Tears trickle down Kathleen's cheeks as her friend and minister kneels beside her. Otherwise there are no reactions: not to the needles the nurses use to take her blood nor to the kisses showered on her by her family.

The flow of visitors and caregivers is impressive – all the more so because Kathleen's life has been so cloistered. Amelia's boarders – present and past – come. They speak loudly as if to the deaf and then murmur a few formulaic words of encouragement. Her two rescuers come separately. They stand mutely wondering about the fragility of life. They have made no connection, which is probably just as well. They have only jogging in common – that and the horror of that morning. Neither of them has continued to jog around the reservoir. Without thinking about it they have found other places, other times of day, and – most telling – jogging partners.

Still the flow continues.

Only the O'Briens have been absent. Patrick – or more correctly, his secretary – did send flowers that wilted in a semi-hidden corner of the room. Elizabeth did nothing. And Danny – Danny's whereabouts are still unknown.

Eventually, the police will find the Saab, wrecked in a deep ditch in the mountains of western Pennsylvania. No sign of Danny and no evidence that anyone else has been in the car. The crime lab will find some hairs from Kathleen on the headrest, but that will hardly be a clue or a surprise.

The tow truck will pull the car from the ditch, and it will be impounded as evidence. But nobody will be sure what it is evidence of. The only things that will be sure are that whoever had been driving at the time of the crash is long gone and that the car is not worth repairing. Perhaps someday it will be scrapped – its metal turned to other uses. For the time, it sits in impound.

The police will from time to time reassure Mary that they are still looking for Danny – that he is still their primary suspect. But, Patrick O'Brien has made many friends and has many more people who are beholden to him. His only acknowledged son is not likely to be found by the Boston police department or, for that matter, by any other department in the country. The blue line will hold no matter how uncomfortable it may make Jack Flynn, his partner, or any number of other officers – officers who cannot go too far without risking their futures.

* * *

Although his name is still on the deed, Patrick has not been to the O'Brien home in years. Neither he nor Elizabeth has had any desire to set the neighbors' tongues wagging, and they have found that their own relationship – such as it has been – to have best been managed from a distance.

Nevertheless, he does go to see his wife late one night. It is a long conversation held in privacy. Nobody will ever learn what has been said between them, and no one will dare to ask. The next day Elizabeth seems greatly relieved – still sad, still lonely, but somehow quieter.

Over time Elizabeth's postman will notice that she has become quite eager to get her mail each day – that she will be particularly excited when that mail might include a letter from Ireland, a letter sent by Daniel Hennessey of Galway. "A relative?" he inquires. She nods once in quick agreement and ducks back into the house – simultaneously slamming the door and ripping at the envelope.

On those days, later in the afternoons, she might even feel well enough to walk about the yard, to nod to her neighbor, Harry Brown, to respond with a wave to his greeting. And he will wonder – but without speaking it – what she might have heard from her son.

* * *

Gradually Kathleen has been responding to simple commands. She takes no action without being told. Her movements have the fluidity of a rusted robot. Still, it is improvement, and that gladdens Mary's heart.

She is released from the hospital – there is no reason to keep her – no further treatment to be offered – no additional care to be delivered.

So Mary takes her home to Amelia's boarding house. Of course, there are bottles of medications that go with her. Kathleen takes the pills as she is told and still says nothing. It is hard to tell if they are helping, but nobody wants to experiment by stopping them. The persistent worry for all is that Kathleen might get worse.

Mary moves her daughter's belongings from the staff residence at the hospice and puts them in the room next to hers at Amelia's boarding house. The boarder whose room it has been tries to object, but Amelia bluntly tells her that she can take the one vacant room at the other side of the house or leave. The woman takes the empty room and glares at Mary over dinner. Mary is oblivious to the looks.

For the first week, Amelia brings Kathleen meals in her room. Eventually, Kathleen starts coming downstairs and eating with the other boarders. She sits at the dark mahogany table and picks at her food while staring at the bisque statues, which Amelia keeps in the breakfront. Periodically, Mary or Amelia urges her to take a forkful of this or a spoonful of that. Otherwise, she picks or ignores. Food is of no interest.

Kathleen sits between Amelia and Mary. They fill her plate and they urge her to eat. At first the other boarders had tried to make conversation with her. Then they had given up and ignored her. It is like dining with the Sphinx – or – perhaps more exactly – a black hole that seems to suck the life out of the room by its presence. After a while, even the conversation that ignores Kathleen is depleted. The boarders grumble among themselves, but nobody dares say anything to Amelia or to Mary.

The two older women talk from time to time – they talk of pain and loneliness. They speak of their heartbreak over Kathleen. They do not discuss what is happening to their own lives.

Days go past. Weeks groan on. Months stretch towards a non-existent horizon.

# Chapter Sixteen

Mary's preoccupation with Kathleen means that she has withdrawn from Arnie. Despite his frustration, despite the return to sexual deprivation, Arnie tries to be as supportive and as loving as he knows how. He does not pressure Mary – not to come to his apartment, not to go out for a date, not even to spend time with him while Kathleen naps in her room. "Stay with Kathleen as much as she needs – as much as you need. When you want a break, come to my apartment. If you and Amelia need to go out, call me. I'll come and stay with her." These are his words. He means them.

Mary's response is, "Thanks for understanding." But her words are said without emotion. She cannot help wondering how long Arnie will or can continue to understand. In fact, she isn't sure that she fully understands. She, does, however, know that she feels responsibility – the responsibility of motherhood but also the responsibility that comes from unknown, unspoken, unacknowledged guilt.

Sean quickly shows signs that he is losing his empathy. "I know she's hurting, but she has to try," he says to Mary and to Karen. He has long since repressed the years he had spent staring helplessly at the television – at the meaningless flicker of reruns. He doesn't say it, but he thinks, "If I can fight my pain, she can fight hers."

Somehow sensing his thoughts, Karen observes, "Different wars make different victims." Then she picks up their son and holds him close to her breast as if by doing so she might protect him forever.

Most of the time, none of them know what to say – not to Kathleen and especially not to each other.

Kathleen increasingly responds to their simple instructions, but there is still no real communication. Even answering straightforward questions like "Are you thirsty? If you are, lift your hand." results in no response, just a vacant stare into some unknown space – some unfathomable place of unremitting pain. As it has been from the first morning, she says nothing.

At first, friends and well-wishers have asked, "Is there any change?" But, when months have passed and there has been none, people stop asking. Many call less frequently. Some have stopped calling at all. Instead they now send cards with scribbled messages: "We're praying for you." "Hope you're feeling better." "Thinking of you." These join the collection of Mass cards and get-well cards that had come to the hospital. Mary carefully keeps them in one drawer of the mahogany dresser that had stood opposite Kathleen's bed in their home, then in her room at the hospice, and now at Amelia's.

"When she recovers, she'll be wanting to see them," she explains to herself as she tucks another handful of cards onto that drawer. She doesn't really believe it. It is just one more way that she can reassure herself that some day, eventually, Kathleen will recover.

It goes unmentioned, but both Mary and Sean remember the slow cutting off of communication, the same slow removal from contact that had followed after his return from the V.A. hospitals. They remember and they resent.

There is one exception, one person who keeps visiting, who keeps caring.

When she had read about the attack in the newspaper, Jem had called to offer her help. It has become her habit to visit on Tuesday evenings. Sitting beside Kathleen she talks about the week's events as if she were taking part in a conversation. She does not falter, she does not give up, she does not quit.

"What do you think about that, Kathleen?" she asks. Then, waiting a moment for the response that never comes, she comments, "I agree with you it certainly is outrageous."

Mary has offered Jem money. "I'm not doing this for money, Mary. I'm doing it out of friendship, no I guess for guilt."

"Guilt about what?"

"I know I started it all in motion. If I'd kept my nose clean and my mouth shut, none of this would have happened. It's all my fault."

Mary absentmindedly wipes her glasses and fixes her hair as she tries to frame her response. "Jem, without you Sean wouldn't have a life, little Robert wouldn't have been born, I wouldn't have had Arnie." Her voice chokes off. She reaches out both hands to Jem, who takes them in hers. The two women hug.

While they embrace, Mary thinks about Arnie. She thinks about his kindness and his concern. She thinks about his quirks and idiosyncrasies. She thinks about PrestoFlame logs and L.L.Bean clothes. She thinks about Newbury Street. She thinks, she remembers, and she smiles wanly. But, she does not allow herself to remember the love or its physical consummation.

Jem will return the next Tuesday and the next and the next.

* * *

"It's difficult living with a ghost," observes one of the boarders. She has met another boarder on the front steps. Both are just coming home from work. Tired from slipping and sliding on the frozen walks and dodging the slush splashed up by passing cars – a last late gasp of a cruel winter, they have taken a moment to breathe before going inside.

"A zombie is more like it," the other responds.

"You're right. She is the living dead." They both shudder at the thought.

"Do you ever think...?"

"If it could be me?" the second woman interjects. "Of course. We all do. That's just one more reason why it's so damn difficult living with her."

"They've never found him. It's been months, and they've never found him."

"The boyfriend?"

"Uh-huh. They've never found him."

"Do you think he did it?"

"We may never know. Maybe he did it. Maybe he's dead. You have to wonder."

"Maybe he's a zombie someplace else."

"Amnesia?"

"Something like that."

"Possibly. We may never know."

"Poor Mrs. Flanagan. She's a nice lady and so much pain."

"I think she handles it better than Amelia." The other woman nods.

"I don't think I've ever met a woman who hated men more."

"God, it's gruesome." They go in carefully opening and closing the door and tiptoeing past the living room door so that Amelia, Mary, and Kathleen, who are sitting inside, won't hear.

As they pass the door, the two women can hear Amelia saying, "They never stop, do they?" There is a pause and the clink of a teacup and saucer. "Did you ever read 'The Bible'? What a stupid question. Of course you did. You're a minister." The two women stop in their tracks wondering to whom Amelia is talking. "Men wrote it. It's sexist propaganda."

"Why do you say that?" Pat Michaels asks. She has come to visit. She is another of the small group who have not given up on Kathleen, or perhaps on her own responsibilities. She never speaks about it; but at some level she, too, feels responsible.

"Everyone fits into God's plan. Don't worry about where you'll fit in. Try everything." That had been her advice to Kathleen. Now she wonders if her advice had in some part caused this tragedy. It is hard for Reverend Michaels to visit, but she does. Each time she leaves still questioning her own responsibility still feeling her own guilt.

"Amelia, why do you say that?" she asks again. "Why do you think The Bible is sexist propaganda?"

"Specifically I had the Garden of Eden in mind. Look at Kathleen. Does she look like she tempted Adam? If I were writing the story, I'd say the serpent was between Adam's legs and he wanted a bite of the apple."

"Mmmmm." The sound is coming from Kathleen. Pat Michaels, Amelia, Mary: all three stare at her. The two boarders in the hallway stare at each other in disbelief. "Mmmmm," Kathleen makes the strangled sound again.

"What are you trying to say?" Mary asks. "Are you trying to tell us something?"

"Mmmmm."

"Kathleen, can you write it down?" Amelia suggests getting up to get a pad and pencil.

"Mmmmm."

Amelia brings the pencil and paper over to Kathleen's chair. The younger woman ignores. She stares straight ahead. Other than the street noises filtering through the walls, there is no sound.

Then, somewhere in the basement, the oil burner growls into life. Still, no one speaks.

"Mmmmm," Kathleen eventually tries again. Suddenly, her voice grows shrill. She screams in terror. "MAX." It is a plea for help – a gut-wrenching scream of terror. Yet, at the same time, it carries a deeper, more powerful meaning – one that speaks to the soul, to the human spirit. The two eavesdropping women feel goose bumps rise on their arms and shivers pass through their bodies. It is as if Kathleen has called God by his unknown and forbidden name. Again she screams. "MAX!"

The power of Kathleen's voice impels the two boarders up the stairs to their rooms. There is no longer an attempt at silence, but the women in the parlor are uninterested in their footsteps. They hear only the name which is reverberating in their hearts.

Kathleen again falls silent. Her silence fills the room and seemingly echoes through the house, out onto the streets – drowning out the sounds of normal life. It fills their hearts and their minds with its icy emptiness. It is the scream of holocausts. It is the cry of those who have seen in their souls the death of God.

* * *

Robert has another cold. He is not a sickly child, rather he takes after his parents and their robust childhoods, but he seems to have many of these nuisance illnesses. "That climate is terrible," Karen's mother had commented with little consolation and much condemnation.

The boy's little nose is running, and his breathing is uneven and wracked with coughing. The pediatrician has reassured them that it is nothing, but Sean and Karen worry. They want to call Mary, to fall back on her years of experience, or – perhaps – to momentarily refocus her onto them. Meanwhile, they take turns going into their baby's room every fifteen minutes and listening to his breathing.

Karen touches his forehead and comes back to Sean saying, "He feels warm, but I think he's OK." Then they sit staring, unseeing, at the television for another fifteen minutes, when they repeat their little dance of concern.

It isn't really the cold that scares them; it is the unspoken terror that underlies all of their lives. The assault on Kathleen has made them feel violated and fearful. It is as if life has lost its predictability to be replaced with danger. The solidity of day-to-day existence has given way to unspoken insecurity. Menace lurks in the very breeze. Peril is around every corner.

Sean and Karen avoid talking about Kathleen. Even when they plan to visit, they talk about visiting Mary or seeing Amelia. Kathleen's is a name unspoken.

When they do visit, they come in and kiss Kathleen on the cheek as if they are genuflecting and making the sign of the cross when they enter a church. Then they sit, eyes averted, and talk about other things: Robert, work, current events, television shows: anything that can distract – anything that makes life seem again normal.

Sometimes, but not often, they bring Robert with them. Usually, it is in response to a request from Mary. She keeps hoping that something – anything – will bring Kathleen out of her cataleptic stupor. Somehow she assumes that a baby's innocence will be the most likely stimulus. He crawls and toddles around the living room trying to grab things while Amelia, Mary, and Karen all work to stay ahead of him. With their help, he scatters toys. He builds block towers that collapses to the floor while he laughs. With relief the adults, except for Kathleen, join his momentary merriment. It is a mime, a short-lived imitation of normal family life.

Karen is always uneasy when they bring Robert to Amelia's house. She is unable to explain her feelings, but she is sure that it is somehow bad for him. She fears that they will see those negative effects in the future, but she cannot say such things to her husband or to Mary.

At the same time it bothers Karen to not bring him because she knows how important he is to Amelia and especially to Mary. Mary always has a smile for Robert. No matter how hopeless she feels about her daughter, Robert reassures her that life is continuing – that life is worthwhile.

When Robert is ill, as he is now, his parents hate to call Mary even when they want her advice and the comfort of hearing her say, "Don't worry! All babies do that," or "Babies run high temperatures. Just give him a Baby Tylenol." They know that she, too, feels the underlying vulnerability that Kathleen represents – that it gnaws at her being.

God and faith have seen Mary through so much. Now everyone wonders if Mary still prays, if she still believes in God. She no longer goes to church – not even the friendly Presbyterian Church. She no longer takes the host. She no longer reads The Bible. She no longer speaks of faith. That part of her life has seemingly disappeared.

But, then, she has also stopped reading other books and discussing other ideas. Since that horrible morning, it is as if her mind has shut down leaving an automaton – a robot that goes through the day's motions without feelings or thoughts. She cares for Kathleen, smiles at Robert, makes appropriate greetings to others, sits with Amelia; but the fire that was once her soul has died.

In her way, Mary, too, has become catatonic.

# Chapter Seventeen

Spring is trying to break forth. Yet, to Arnie the view from his window seems horribly bleak – for there is bleakness in Arnie Berger's heart. The weeks since Kathleen was so brutally attacked have been hard on him and harder still on his relationship with Mary. "I still love you," she tries to reassure him mechanically as she runs out the door after only the briefest of visits. "I miss you," she whispers almost conspiratorially as she hangs up the phone to attend to her daughter's needs. But the words do not lead to actions.

Thanksgiving has long since passed without an announcement of wedding plans. "I can't do anything until Kathleen is back on her feet," had been Mary's response when Arnie reminded her of the promise they had made to each other in Maine.

"I know," he had responded. He tried to be empathic, but inside he could not help wondering if Kathleen would ever recover.

"I understand," he had answered at Christmastime – his sympathy much challenged – while the world celebrated and glowed and he mourned for his love.

"Maternal instinct?" he queries with frustration and pain during their third discussion. He feels the tears of his heart. He feels the loss in his soul.

Each time, including this last, the robot that Mary has become has kissed him on the cheek and thanked him for his understanding. Each time his understanding has become all the more gloomy.

During this third discussion – or more exactly non-discussion – he asks, "Why don't we get married, and Kathleen can live with us?"

Mary does not pause, nor does she consider. "I can't do that."

"And why not?"

"Because I can't burden you that way. It would be wrong." There are tears in her eyes as she says it. "Don't you think that I've thought about it?"

"But, you've never talked with me ..."

"I can't do that to you."

"But you can burden me this way instead – you can burden me with the loneliness, with this pain? Don't you think I have the right to choose my own burden? Don't you think I should make my choice? Am I less," he takes a deep and painful breath before continuing, "less than Karen?" The frost in his voice betrays the growing anger, impatience and hurt within. "She can take on Sean, take on his care; but I … It would be too much? You think it would be too much. " His words stop. He is at a loss.

Mary's tears flow more freely. "I know it's not fair, Arnie. I know. What can I do? What can any of us do? It is who I am, who we are."

He wants to take her to him, to hold her, but some part of him will not allow that show of tenderness. Instead he hands her his handkerchief. She dabs at her eyes. Then Arnie responds to her question. "What do we do? We live together as best we can. We take care of our little patch of life and get on. At least that way I'll be able to hold you, to help you, to help you take care of Kathleen."

"I want to say 'yes,' but..." There are no more words.

He interrupts the silence. "But nothing, just say it." He holds out his hands to take hers. He kisses the back of her left hand and then her right. Now, he draws her toward him and holds her tightly against his body. They are both in tears. "I love you so much."

"You don't understand. I can't. I have to be there for Kathleen. Amelia thinks...”

Suddenly Arnie is nearly shouting at her, "I don't give a damn what Amelia thinks. I've grown to hate her. She's using Kathleen! Don't you see that? She doesn't want you marrying me. She wants you there. She wants the two of you, no, the three of you to grow old together – trapped in that house, in her anger." He lets go of Mary. His hands have fisted with resentment; he puts them to his eyes and rubs to keep the tears of pain and frustration under control.

Mary is shocked and totally surprised. "Arnie, how can you say that? Amelia is like family."

"I don't want her in my family; I want you. I'm sure she means well, but." He stops there afraid that he has already said too much. In his own thoughts he isn't so sure that Amelia does mean well. It seems to him that she had her own special agenda and that the only male who is any part of it is little Robert. He wonders at what age the child will suddenly be transformed into a hated "man."

More and more of Arnie's time is now spent looking through the blinds of his living room windows and watching the world pass in horizontal stripes. His students have started to notice the change, and they no longer greet him as he walks – head down and downhearted – about the campus.

The dean has called him in for a little talk. "Is there something the matter?" he asks already knowing the answer.

"It's Mary's daughter."

"Isn't she doing any better?"

"No, but it's more than that." Arnie stops and then goes on. "Mary can't get on with her life, with our life. It's ... I've got to ... It's that ... I'm getting just so awfully depressed."

It is the first time that Arnie has ever used that word about himself. His natural buoyancy had always been one of his greatest strengths. Now, it seems like he is slowly drowning, and he no longer has the will or strength to kick his way to the surface – to struggle for air.

Karen and Sean have noticed the change, too. They have tried to talk with Arnie, but he can only look sad and sigh in response.

They have tried to talk with Mary, but she has shut them out. "You don't understand. There are some responsibilities you can't walk away from."

"Mom, Arnie doesn't want you to walk away from Kath. He wants to share the responsibility. He wants to help..."

"She isn't his burden. She isn't his responsibility. I'm the one..."

"You're the one who what?" demands Sean.

"I'm the one who has to be there." Mary doesn't want to share what she is really thinking – that she is responsible, that she has to carry the guilt – the unremitting guilt – the unforgivable guilt, the guilt which cannot be confessed because there has been no sin unless wanting for your child is a sin, unless encouraging your daughter to live is a sin.

"Is she Amelia's responsibility, too?" Karen asks to change the tense direction of the conversation.

"That's different. Amelia is, I don't know, she's different. It's like she's Kathleen's mother, too. Or, maybe, it's that she feels like we're sisters – that we're all sisters." Then she has a thought.

Mary has never before been able to put her finger on the special nature of Amelia's involvement. Somehow, she feels that whatever was happening to her and Kathleen is also happening to her friend. "By taking care of Kathleen she's also taking care of herself. I think that's it – she's making up – to herself – for herself never having received the care she deserved. If there's one thing good coming out of this, it's that Amelia is better – unhappy, of course unhappy, but better."

"Then lean on Amelia, but don't push Arnie away. If you do, you may never have another chance." Karen is holding Sean's hand and cradling Robert with her other arm. "Believe me, loving and being loved by someone special, that's what it's all about." She squeezes her husband's hand. There are tears rolling down both of their cheeks.

Mary, too, is crying. "I know you're right, but I can't. God would never forgive me."

"Mom, that's what you used to say when I was still living at home, God would never forgive you if you turned your back on me. Don't you see how much better things could be? Do you really think that God wants us to be miserable?"

After her son and daughter-in-law leave, Mary thinks about Pat Michaels. The pastor's favorite Bible verse is "Make a joyful noise unto the Lord your God." She is always preaching that God wants people to be happy, that He has given them the earth to be a paradise not a punishment. Mary has worshipped with Pat, has believed her message, has shared her joy. Now, Pat comes to visit Kathleen, who once also believed and who now sits mute staring inwards. "Where is God's joy in that?" Mary has no answers to the question she is asking herself, and she knows that Pat doesn't have any either.

\* \* \*

It is another visit. It is yet another of the painful discussions. Mary is trying to find her way. She is expressing her sense of being helpless and lost to her son and daughter-in-law, "I don't know what God wants. I don't know that God does want. I used to think that the answers were easy. Now I just don't know." She has been sitting at one end of the sofa. Absently she fingers the fringe of the Native American throw.

"Maybe it's all a joke, a horrible, cruel joke. Arnie's son died in Vietnam, and my son is a cripple." The words hang in silence.

"Kathleen thought that she had love. Now where is Danny?" She chokes back her tears.

She gets up and starts to pace the parlor. "Arnie and I were … Oh, I wish. I wish I knew."

She stops in front of Karen. "Maybe God is testing me. Maybe He is just enjoying my torment."

The rage in her heart has allowed hurtful words to come out. Suddenly realizing, she gasps at her own declaration and turns to her son. "I'm sorry. Sean, I'm so..." She takes off her glasses and wipes them, pushes them back on her nose and, in her unconscious way, fluffs her hair.

"It's not your fault. It's the truth. I'm a cripple and Robert's dead. Kathleen is in, what did the doctors call it, a catatonic stupor. Danny, just where the hell is Danny? Arnie is miserable. So are you. None of it makes sense. It's like some kind of clown act – it's so damn cruel we have to laugh or …" He doesn't know how to finish the sentence. It hangs over their heads until little Robert starts to cry.

Karen picks up her son and kisses him. "Maybe, there is no 'or,'" she observes. "Maybe, we just have to laugh." She holds Robert up over her head and tosses him just slightly into the air and catches him again. The excitement of her actions changes his cries into squeals.

The three adults laugh. They do not know what else to do.

\* \* \*

"It seems so long ago," the Mother Superior of The Sisters of Mercy is talking. "I was just a novice then, and we still wore habits. There was a priest who heard our confessions, and he - I hate to say this, but he wasn't celibate. And there was another novice, just a little older than I. Louisa, a kind and caring soul, a loving person, from way north in Maine, French Canadian. Very simple. Very humble. Filled with faith. She was special. Even within the convent she stood out as one who had been called. He seduced her – right in the convent, in one of the linen closets. He seduced her. After that, she never spoke – that is except to say The Rosary. Every day she said her beads, ten, twelve, maybe twenty times a day. But that was all. The Mother Superior then, Sister Agatha-Ignatius, she decided there was something wrong with this girl. She called in a psychiatrist, and the psychiatrist finally got her to talk. She started to talk about that priest. She started talking about that priest and what the two of them had done, and the psychiatrist told Sister Agatha-Ignatius.

"The Mother Superior went to the novice's cell, not to condemn, but to comfort her and to tell her that she understood. By the time she got there, the young sister was dead. She had hanged herself right there in the convent. The priest, of course, denied it all so nothing happened to him. But Louisa, poor, faithful, called-to-serve-God Louisa – she was refused burial in sacred ground. We had the undertaker ship her body back to her family as if she had never been here. I suppose there was nothing else to do. We cried. We all wept as the hearse pulled away.

"I couldn't understand. It seemed so wrong. I went to Sister Agatha-Ignatius, and I remonstrated with her. 'How,' I asked her, 'can the Church condemn the victim and let the abuser go as if he were innocent?' She reminded me that God has His own wisdom and will deal out justice when He comes again."

She pauses for the message to sink in and waits until the nuns gathered around the table are all once again looking at her. "That's the best we can do, to have faith in his final judgment. Our lives bear witness to that faith! That and that alone is our lives' work!"

"Amen," says Sister Mathew Theresa in her lilting soprano voice.

"Amen," choruses the other nuns.

"Amen," adds the Mother Superior.

* * *

It seems to Amelia that the hours the three of them spend together in her parlor are among the happiest and the saddest of her life. At times, she sits behind Kathleen brushing her hair and humming contentedly to herself. Even though Kathleen makes no response, Amelia believes in her heart that the young woman is aware of her love and concern. This makes Amelia not simply happy, but something more akin to content – a contentment which she has not known in many years.

Mary has taken to staring blankly at the television. She doesn't bother with the volume. She isn't paying attention – she isn't paying attention to anything. She has locked herself out of the world and inhabits a private cell of grief. This is her self-assigned penance, the one she has demanded of herself – to remove herself from life – to sink into the tar-pit of her own voiceless agony.

At times she allows herself to think of the hours she had once spent with Arnie – the sweet hours that now seem so long ago. Now, they so seldom have times together – and that only the times when Arnie comes to sit here with her. Worse, when they are together, they almost always end with an argument – the argument – about the future, about the marriage they will not have, about the years of growing old together, about the happiness that will be foregone.

He had offered so many times to marry her and to have Kathleen live with them, but Mary had always demurred. Eventually, he had tried to stop offering, but he couldn't. He could not let go. He could not stop hoping.

He begged her, and his pleas went unrequited. And, still he could not resist – so great was his desire.

Mary is visualizing the last time they had been together. Arnie had insisted that they go out. To do so, he had begged Amelia to give them the opportunity, and she had agreed.

He had taken Mary back to the coffee shop where they had talked that first afternoon. "Mary," he had pleaded once again, "don't turn me away. Let me be part of your life. Let me be there for you … and for Kathleen, for you both."

"It isn't a life anymore," she had replied. "It can't be."

"Please, we...."

"Let me go Arnie! I can't. I was wrong. I was wrong to get involved, to turn my back on God, to," she had paused and taken a deep breath, "sin."

She got up, and he started to follow. "No, sit. I'll take the T."

Stung, he had sat back down and watched through tear-filled eyes as she had left the coffee shop. "I'll phone you," he had called after her.

From the rear he could see her nod her head, but she had said nothing.

Arnie Berger knew that he would not make that call, not again – that enough pain was enough.

He had sat for a long time. A student came by and said hello, but Arnie didn't look up. Thus began a new season of mourning.

# Chapter Eighteen

It is in the middle of the night that Mary dies – suddenly, without illness, but, at some unconscious level, not entirely unexpectedly. She does not appear for breakfast. She does not bring Kathleen down to sit in the parlor. Concerned, Amelia goes to find out what is wrong. She finds her friend slumped in the big leather chair, the one that had been her husband's. For the first time Amelia notices that Mary has pulled it away from the window. Over the window there is a curtain of Irish lace, one that Mary had kept tucked away. Behind it the blind is closed. The room is darkened and seems sealed from the world.

On the table next to her Mary had placed her Bible, her beads, and the ring that Artie had given her. She had once – during one of those arguments about getting on – tried to give it back.

He – in tears – had refused. "Whatever happens, keep it. I love you so much," he had gasped through the sobs.

So she had kept it as a treasure – carefully wrapped in linen and stowed in safety. But now it was there on the table bearing witness.

There is no obvious reason for Mary's death. As far as everyone knows she has been physically healthy. The medical examiner insists on an autopsy but he can find nothing. "Cause of death unknown," he writes on the official forms. "I don't understand it," he tells his assistant.

Jem shakes her head when she hears the coroner's findings. "I guess he don't know much about souls," she observes. "There's pains of the body, and there's pains of the soul. This poor lady died of the pains in her soul. They say that God don't give no one more than they can carry, but He sure done give her too much ... way, way too much." And, her husband holds her as she cries for Mary, for this woman who had once seemed so strong.

\* \* \*

There aren't many mourners. Mary's life has not really touched that many people. During the wake, Sean and Karen sit quietly waiting for the occasional well-wisher who will give them a moment of meaningless conversation: an old neighbor, one of the other boarders, the dean from Northeastern, a couple of Arnie's colleagues, some of Sean's coworkers – these are the people who for whatever reason feel called upon to visit the funeral home.

And, of course, there are The Sisters of Mercy. Each takes Kathleen by the hand and murmurs, "She's with God now." To each, Kathleen gives the same unspeaking nod of apparent agreement. Then they shake hands with Amelia, who is sitting next to Kathleen, watching over her. Amelia's face is caught between tears and a smile.

Mary's old friend Lois comes. She flies up from Florida to mourn the friend whom she had never really known. She comes to mourn for Mary but also to assuage her fear that life is always too short.

After the mass, they drive to the Cemetery of the Holy Presence. Mary is to lie next to her dead husband, near to Kathleen's buried infant. It is supposed to be spring, but the weather has grown cold – too cold to think let alone to pray, and light snow is falling. The mourners stomp the ground like cattle trying to warm themselves. Sean sits huddled in blankets. Little Robert is bundled with his father – only his little nose and eyes poke into the snow-lit brightness of the day.

The priest goes through the rite as quickly as he feels he can without giving offense. "Dirt to dirt and ashes to ashes," he thinks, "but no mention of this damn cold and snow. It's supposed to be spring."

Finally, he signs the cross and bends to say a word of care to Kathleen and Sean. They nod in acknowledgement even as they realize that he did not know their mother, that he does not know them. Without sharing the words, they both wish that Pat Michaels could have been officiating or at least that they had been able to arrange for Father Frank. It seems wrong that this uncaring stranger should be officiating at this, Mary's last sacrament.

Behind the caretaker's office, four gravediggers pass a bottle of cheap whiskey and curse the cold and the dead. "I'm for cremation," says one, "at least that way I'll be warm."

Two of the others nod in agreement. The fourth says with a laugh, "The hell you will. You're not cheating me out of a day's pay." The others chuckle, and the sound bites through the cold and reaches Arnie's ears. He looks in the direction of the four men and swears to himself that he will never laugh again.

They straggle back to the cars. Kathleen is being led by Amelia, but she pulls free and goes to the small grave nearby, the one where her child had long before been buried. She stands there until Karen comes and hugs her. They stand together for a few moments. Then the two women, arm in arm, make their way back to the waiting cars.

Nobody has felt the need for a limousine. Arnie's red Buick is the first car in the line – just behind the hearse, which is already pulling away. Behind the Buick is Sean and Karen's van. Amelia has ridden with Sean because Arnie hasn't wanted her with him. So, Kathleen is sitting beside him as the Buick pulls away. Behind Kathleen, Jem sits rigidly erect and staring straight ahead. Lois focuses her attention out the window. She is trying to remember the years she lived in Boston – she is remembering without purpose.

Kathleen sits with her head bowed. She, as always, has said nothing. Turning so that she is looking out the back window of the Buick, she can still see Mary's grave. Unconsciously, she pushes her glasses back on her nose. Then she slips her hands under her hair at the ears and fluffs it out. "Christ hae mercy," she says. Then, she takes off her glasses and carefully, very carefully, wipes them clean.

## AUTHOR'S NOTE

*I have no interest in dedicating this work. The people in my life deserving of my gratitude know that it is theirs in full measure. I would however like to thank those who have contributed directly and indirectly to this novel.*

*The indirect contributors have been many. They include long-ago colleagues on the faculty of Northeastern University and clients whose lives and personalities have contributed bits and pieces to plot and characters.*

*The direct contributors have included a number of early readers who have suggested ways to make the story and writing stronger. While fiction writing is a lonely and individual occupation, it – like most art – is improved by the observations and criticisms of friends.*

*My deepest thanks must go to two people without whose editorial help this would have been a messy effort at best:*

*My wife Roz has read and reread the manuscript of Widow's Walk many times. She has corrected grammar, spelling, and punctuation. She has provided a sounding board for ideas and a willing discussant for plot. I thank her deeply.*

*Cha Tori has provided great service as an editor. He has caught so many small errors that I have long since lost count. More importantly, he has helped me to avoid the error of being "the omniscient narrator," which has forced me to allow the story to unfold and for you, the reader, to reach your own decisions.*

*In the end, and after all those helping hands, I must take the responsibility for this book. I hope that you have enjoyed reading it and that it has caused you to think and to feel.*

# About the Author

A New Englander by upbringing and inclination, Kenneth Weene's career – primarily in New York – included teaching, pastoral care, and psychology. Throughout his career Kenneth has also been devoted to writing. His poetry has appeared in a number of publications – both print and web. He authored a number of professional publications. His short stories and essays have also been published. One of his short plays was recently workshopped. An anthology of Kenneth's work, Songs For My Father, was published 2002.

Kenneth and his wife, Roz, now live in greater Phoenix where he spends much of his time writing.

**ALL THINGS THAT MATTER PRESS** ™


FOR MORE INFORMATION ON TITLES AVAILABLE FROM
ALL THINGS THAT MATTER PRESS, GO TO
http://allthingsthatmatterpress.com
or contact us at
allthingsthatmatterpress@gmail.com

CPSIA information can be obtained at www.ICGtesting.com
Printed in the USA
BVOW011026240112

281271BV00001B/47/P